THE

HOOSIER

HOTBOX

The Hoosier Hotbox

A novel

By Daron Pearce

Published in the United States by Panel-thief.
www.daronpearce.com

ISBN 978-0-9863475-1-1
eBook 978-0-9863475-0-4

Edited by Lester Jacobson

COVER DESIGN BY HEATHER SEKSINSKY
www.seksinsky.com

For Savanna,

For waiting

Chapter 1

It all started the morning I woke up naked in Ellie's bed. Aww beautiful, amazing Ellie. I think I woke myself up, I was smiling so hard in my sleep. Even squinting at the glare coming in the tall window across the room couldn't bend my smile. And if you've ever tried smiling and squinting at the same time, you know how happy I must have been, lying there, blinking back the brightness, watching her slight shoulder rise and fall, hinting at the sweet rest of her I now knew just out of sight. My mouth started watering so bad I had to roll over to keep a puddle from forming, thinking about the night before.

She had one of those big, tall "Princess and the Pea" type beds that all pretty girls seem to have, mattresses piled high and far above the dirty floor, topped, appropriately, with a light, fluffy, down comforter like meringue on a pie. It was like we were floating on the same puffy white cloud, her head buoyant over the pillowy softness, her left arm curved comfortably out, reaching for the mane of some unicorn, I imagine, as she dreamed on. It felt, at that moment, like I had "arrived," whatever that means, like I was some kind of grubby farm hand that had been plucked from the field on the whim of a passing Goddess.

Yes, I was feeling pretty darn good and I was damn proud of myself, but there was just this one thing. I *really* had to pee.

The whiteness of her bright, immaculate sheets was electrified to almost blinding by a slanting streak of sunlight glaring in off the glass building across the street, bathing us in a beam of heavenly light like a picture of Jesus. The sharpness of it clenched and tickled that familiar tightness I'd woken up with just below my stomach. I mean, I *seriously* had to pee. But Ellie was lying across my arm, my hand full of bare skin.

I'd been trying to get myself into this exact spot for a few weeks and there was no way I was going to ruin it, or cut it short, just for some stupid pee break. So I laid there, ignoring my bladder, blinking and squinting into my pillow, breathing in the faint floral smell of Ellie's mussed, curly hair. Smiling. I was definitely having one of those few and far between, luckiest-guy-in-the-world moments.

Ellie slowly came awake, yawning with a long ballerina stretch. For a flash of a second, her eyes were crushingly blank when she turned to me, waking up with someone new for the first time. Then recognition came in and she smiled a thin good morning. I kissed her. She sat up, dropped her legs over the side of the bed and slid, toes reaching, all the way down to the floor.

Oh man, that was a good sight in the morning. She sauntered slowly to the bedroom door. I shielded my eyes from the glare with my hand, still tingling where she'd been laying on it, and watched her beautiful ass jiggle lightly as she reached up to take the short, blue silk robe from the hook on the back of the door. Her hips just wide enough to open that little V between her thighs. She tossed her hair back at me and smiled over her shoulder as she left the room.

Yep, I was feeling pretty good about myself. I had only been in Chicago for about three months at that point and, even though it had taken a little longer than I'd expected, I was finally getting somewhere. I mean, there I was lying naked in Ellie's bed, the *exact* type of girl I had fantasized about coming up here to meet.

Well, I hadn't moved to Chicago to meet girls, of course. I had moved up here to get a job. At least that was the official line, anyway, given to family and friends, and girls at bars, and whoever was asking. But let's be honest, I came up here for the women. The rest of it, like most of life, was simply logistics.

And what a pain in the ass those logistics can be too. I had already come to the city with far less money than I'd needed *and*, of course, I'd decided to rent an apartment there was no way I could afford. It was so easy to let your eyes get bigger than your wallet up here, especially when you've come from small-town Indiana with a large suitcase full of ambition. I had arrived big-eyed and flat-footed in a wonderful new metropolis, The City, and promptly started going broke.

But I could worry about that later. Right now, it was time to forget about my troubles and bask in the lovely softness of a beautiful lady and her lofty boudoir.

I laid back and smiled greatly. Ah, yes. I crossed my arms behind my head and was immediately sorry. The motion exaggerated the pressure against my bladder and I suddenly had to pee worse than I could believe.

It's only natural to have to pee first thing in the morning. We all have to and I had done the gentlemanly thing by letting Ellie go first. Yeah, that was good. It would only take her a couple more minutes, no problem. I put my arms back down.

But the ballooning of my bladder caused another kind of shift in my gut. My stomach was pinched and now my intestines wanted in on the action. I felt a rumbling start up like an outlying tremor on a distant fault line. Between the tacos I'd had for dinner and the beer we'd drunk together, there was some serious friction building up under the Earth's crust, if you know what I mean.

I moved to sit up, but the sudden shift in air pressure tried to relieve itself by pushing pee out. I rolled onto one elbow and grabbed my crotch. A gas bubble charged straight for the back door and I had to rise up and clench to keep it in. There was a veritable bullfight roaring up in my guts.

I breathed in through my nose, calmly exhaled through my mouth. She wouldn't be that long. No, she wouldn't. Just a few more minutes.

I laid back and relaxed a little when the pressure eased off a bit. The glare of the sun slid across the bed and took the edge off the brightness. Ellie had left the bedroom door open a crack and I tried to listen for the sound of the toilet flushing. I moved down to see if I could ease more off my bladder. The bull charged again and the gassy matador jumped at the other side to dodge him. I clenched harder and held on.

I wondered if maybe I could just let out a little air, just a little puff to ease the tension until Ellie came out. Maybe? No. If it smelled at all what would I do with it, fan it around? A bedroom already smells bad enough the morning after without adding extras on top of it. We hadn't known each other long enough for that level of intimacy. It took some real time before you could test a relationship like that. And I liked this girl too much. I had to keep her thinking I was a worthy man, capable of controlling every situation, even ref a grudge match in my own guts. I couldn't risk it.

But maybe just a little? Just a burp? No. No. She'd be out in two minutes. I clenched tighter. Mind over matter.

I concentrated my hearing like a super hero listening, willing the toilet to flush. I writhed sideways across the bed, beginning to lose my cool. What was she doing in there? I climbed down off the bed to my feet and jogged in place. You can't pee while you're running, right? It was worse. Gravity is not your friend. I squeezed, dancing in little circles. I bent over at the waist trying to keep the pressure off. It pushed against my bladder. I stood upright to ease my bladder and the bull charged again at the back gate. Bent back over.

I heard the toilet flush. The relief tightened my bladder and I couldn't hold it. I let go. NO. I couldn't. I heard the bathroom door open and jumped back on the bed pretending to just be climbing down as Ellie came in. Clenching and smiling, working to keep the tension out of my face, I slid down off the bed, all wooden and forced-casual. I slowly left the room, still naked, and bolted for the bathroom.

Awwww, I released a raging torrent of a river as soft trumpets played out behind me. It was the best feeling in the world. And just like that, the pain and torment was over and forgotten. It's amazing how something can hurt so much and so totally dominate all of your senses, then relief, the immediacy gone, and you completely forget it was ever there. Just like that, you're back to your old, smiling, happy self. Amazing, amazing.

In the medicine cabinet, Ellie had some sort of all natural toothpaste that tasted thin and the wrong kind of creamy. It was powdery too, gritty, like mayonnaise with sand in it, or drywall dust. Mint mayonnaise with drywall dust in it. After squeezing a clump onto my finger, I wrinkled my nose, brushed and gargled quickly with warm water. At least it smelled like mint, a definite improvement on my previous pasty, chapped, taco-beer breath.

An easy smile stretched out across my face as I looked excitedly into the mirror. I had finally spent the night at Ellie's. I could hardly believe it. I'd been chasing that girl around for weeks. And she'd been playing along too, giving me the run around, acting all chaste. I shook my head and the smile got bigger.

I ran my fingernails along my jaw, scratching at two-day-old stubble. It was a good face. I'd been doing pretty well with it over the years, even if the chin was a little soft. But the unshaved look helped, and smiling came easily to me. A broad, honest smile fit my face and complemented my eyes, so I wore it a lot. I liked to throw it around at people, see if it was contagious. Maybe it had something to do with my happy Midwestern upbringing, but even at 26, my eyes still had something of a baby-like glow, which a lot of girls seemed to respond to, and I wasn't too eager to lose.

I smiled at myself a second longer, then splashed a bit of cold water over my eyes to wake them up. I patted a little patty-pat on my cheeks like an aftershave commercial and turned to face the day. I skipped light-footed back toward the bedroom, relieved, refreshed and ready to start the day off on the right foot, wink, wink.

But Ellie was already in her jeans and pulling a t-shirt over her head as I got to the door. My smile flattened. Her arms were up, her face hidden by the shirt sliding down over her bare breasts. I shot a long arm out toward the disappearing skin and caught her around the middle. A small shudder of surprise rippled up her body as I came around behind her. Goosebumps rose and stood hard as I cupped my hands. Her delicate little ear was flush against my lips.

"Dressed already?" I said, in the huskiest whisper I'd ever used.

My hands played across her skin, spelling it out for the hearing impaired. Her body went lax for a moment, her weight against me. Her hands went to mine and traced their movements briefly. She sighed. Her neck bent back, her mouth reaching up. Then a different kind of shudder, more purposeful, went up, stiffened her back. She spun gently out of my arms to face me.

"I," she started to say with eyes still closed. Something like a wave went through her. I smiled knowingly. Then her eyes came open. "No, I," she said, "I have to go."

"Yeah?"

Her eyes went to the ceiling, down my body, to the bed, then back to the floor in front of her. "Yeah, I—I'm late already." Her hands automatically went up, started smoothing her long, curly, tangled hair where my face had been, pulling it around to cover the ear my lips had touched.

I threw my wry smile at her, challengingly. "You sure?" I said, stepping toward her. "I thought you didn't work today?"

"No, I don't—I have to—I promised I'd meet my friend Janelle downtown."

"What time? Surely you can spare a few more minutes..."

I reached for her hands, but she turned away looking for someplace else to put them.

"No, uh... No, I really do need to go. I, uh..."

She side stepped, and side stepped again completely out of reach. Then she snapped out of it and reached out for a floppy brown hand bag, started digging around it in.

"Oh...well... that's too bad." But I didn't want the scene to get solemn. So, I said more cheerfully, "You want to get some coffee first? I don't have anywhere to be. We could just go downstairs and..." Then, I suddenly felt really naked talking to her back like that and decided to stop there.

Ellie transferred things from the bag to a small black purse. I bent down and sifted through the pile of clothes, wrestling my underwear out of my crumpled jeans. She held her face in the mirror over the dresser and ran red lipstick around her beautiful small mouth. My lips puckered automatically, distracted so easily. My shirt was lying at her feet. As I stood to get it, she saw me in the mirror and turned, backing away like I was dangerous.

"Easy now," I smirked with hands out. "I'm just trying to buy you coffee."

She glanced at me quickly, then down and away. "I know," she said, smilingly awkwardly. "I would, but I can't. Really don't have time...I should've been on the train, like, twenty minutes ago." The smile gone.

"Oh, yeah, of course."

Things had gotten strangely distant. It felt like the morning after a one-night stand. But it wasn't. We'd been seeing each other for a couple of weeks. True, it was first time we had slept together, but that doesn't count. We'd already had the awkward first kiss, the stopping me at third base, the time I'd tried to kiss her in a bar and she slapped me, thinking I was someone else, then last night when I tried to put my finger in her b.... Point is, it wasn't a one-night stand, so why had it gotten weird.

But maybe it was something else. Maybe she just wasn't that into it. Maybe she wanted me to smack her ass and I hesitated. Or maybe...maybe I did let one slip! Maybe one had gotten away before I made it to the bathroom and she was disgusted, couldn't handle it. Shit. Feeling very self-conscious, I quietly finished getting dressed while Ellie moved things from the small black purse back to the brown bag, then to a different, bigger, black purse.

We were moving toward the front door together when her phone started vibrating loudly inside the third, and final, purse option. We both stopped at the front door as she dug it out and looked at it.

"Shit, I need to get this," she said, excusing me with a sorry questioning look.

"Yeah, of course," I said, smiling emptily. I leaned in to kiss her. She brought the phone up to her perfect little mouth and turned away saying "Hello?"

Ok. All right.

I let myself out, closing the door softly and quietly behind me.

I stood for a moment at the top of the oddly long, single flight of stairs facing downward. Her apartment was on the third floor at the back of the building, but the stairs stretched down two floors in one long reach to the front door. You could fall down those stairs and tumble head over heels for a solid minute uninterrupted. It was a staircase that belonged to one of those big slides at the state fair you slide down in potato sacks, The Super Slide, with the two humps in the middle and if you got enough speed you could catch some air going over each hump, or hop on your butt and pretend.

The stairs to Ellie's apartment were like those, except enclosed in narrow white walls and a low drywall ceiling, instead of corrugated, green plastic, with a brief landing in the middle for the second floor apartment. I stood with my back to her door, looking down the long flight of stairs at a little patch of bright light coming through the small window in the door at the bottom, wondering what had just happened.

Maybe it was nothing. Maybe I just being self-conscious and needed some coffee. After all, it had still been a pretty good night and I *had* woken up naked, next to a very beautiful girl. So I shook it off and trundled down the stairs, and stairs, and kept on trundling, until I pushed through the door at the bottom five minutes later into a wonderfully sunny morning, or mid-morning.

Chapter 2

The sun outside hit me like a bolt. I stumbled a few steps into the blinding light as if I'd been drinking for hours without standing up, surprised to find my legs wouldn't work right. Fortunately, I was able to steady myself by waving my hands around and managed not to run into anyone, or they managed not to run into me. I groped my way to the coffee shop on the corner under Ellie's apartment.

According to the chipped, wobbly, hand-painted letters on the window, they roasted their own coffee beans, which sounded amazing. When I pushed through the door, I realized they painted the words that poorly on purpose to match their overall DYI theme of raw plywood counter top, a little too high, and mismatched diner chairs with chunks torn out of the orange and yellow vinyl, the particleboard showing underneath. And strangely enough, you could hear the coffee roaster before you could smell it. Where normally one thinks of green, verdant South American hills when you think of coffee freshly roasting, here it was more broken-down-van-on-the-side-of-the-highway. The coffee, painfully screeching and screaming, cascaded repeatedly down the murky glass front of a bulky, squared, lime green hotbox contraption like an over-sized popcorn machine with a dent in it. A putrid yellow light from the super-high-watt heating bulb caught in thick wisps of smoke leaking out from under the machine and the strong smell of burnt motor oil pervaded, making me think less of guys with donkeys and more of my dad covered in grease and cursing. It was all a great effect, but I decided to skip the house roast and went with the Colombian.

The girl behind the counter gave me a cup so I could do-it-myself. I didn't know this, and she didn't say so. Instead, she just stared at me like I was some new kind of idiot until I looked self-consciously at my feet and decided to walk away. But I didn't figure it out that quickly, on account of not having had any coffee yet. I looked at her. She looked at me. I waited for her to put coffee in the cup. She looked at me some more, cocked an eyebrow. I looked at the empty cup and, without meaning to, noticed she wasn't wearing a bra. Honestly, I didn't mean to. Those two fine little points suddenly pointing at *me*, like a teacher whose class I'd just fallen asleep in. I don't know if this happens to everyone else, but when I've just gotten laid, like the night before, my animal urges kick in double-time. I walk around with my tongue out like a dog in heat, salivating at everything I see. It's probably embarrassing, and I'm not sure if it was obvious, but my eyes must have bulged in their sockets unknowingly.

So, it took me a second longer to realize I was supposed to walk away and get the coffee myself out of the pump thing on the end of the counter. I slinked away directly, not meeting her eyes again on my way out.

It was a perfect Chicago morning: eighty degrees and sunny with enough of a breeze to keep the sun from making you sweat. I stood on the corner for a minute sipping coffee and letting the sun warm my face. Warm coffee, warm stomach, warm face, ahh. I made a visor with my hand against my forehead and checked traffic both ways before crossing the street.

There didn't seem to be a good way to get from Wicker Park, where Ellie lived and where I stood, to my apartment over in Lakeview. You either have to take the three buses, or a bus and two trains, or walk for forty-five minutes and then take two buses or two trains. Either way, it would take an hour, unless you took a cab, which I couldn't afford yet, not until I got a job. So, I crossed the street to the bus stop on the other side going toward the lake.

A small crowd of four had already gathered when I got there, which gave no indication of when the bus might come, but at least I hadn't just missed it. An older lady with grocery bags was sitting on the sticker and graffiti-covered bench, a young couple standing beside it. There was a guy on his phone near the curb standing somewhat detached from the rest of the group. He had on gleaming white tennis shoes that were so clean and polished they reflected the sunlight like chrome hubcaps. And when I say he was on his phone, I mean he was *on* his phone, talking and listening and talking. They were separate acts, his talking and listening, happening at different times. He would tilt the phone to his ear, mouthpiece nowhere near his mouth, and listen for a split second, not even close to long enough for the other person to actually say anything. Then, he'd squeeze the phone in his fist like he hated it and yell into it from two feet away, like it was a lawn mower that wouldn't start. "Goddamn it. I told you. I told you that ain't what I said. And I don't know no *girl* you talking about. Quit asking me about that shit." Then he'd swing it back around to his ear for a millisecond, rocking on his shimmering white shoes, feet shoulder width apart. It was hard to tell if he was standing apart from the group, or if the group was standing apart from him. I stayed on the far side of the bench where I could still, plainly, hear everything he said.

The bus eventually came from the west, stuffed full of people. The older lady got on first while the rest of us waited, crowding into each other, reluctantly smelling the back of each other's heads. The aisle was obnoxiously full as the bus bounced onward, ready or not. I wished I'd finished my coffee and thrown it out before I got on. You needed both hands to navigate the constantly shifting space and hold on. Some hard rocker kid had a huge, old, tube amp sticking halfway out in the aisle. Everybody tried not to kick it as they shuffled past. Some tried harder than others, or just swore at it as they did.

At the next stop, a group of people got off. I scooted along to my new position by the back door, in front of the two steps going up to the back part of the bus by the engine. I could see two seats open in the back, but I couldn't get up there. The aisle was too filled with people and nobody wanted to push throw to the open seats. I eyed them with eager anticipation as we crept along to the next stop; looking at the people between me and the empty seats, sizing them up, wondering who was most likely to go for them, trying to predict who might get off. The lady behind me pushed into my back, jockeying into position before the doors opened again.

We all bumped against each other as the bus jerked to a sudden, complete stop. I held my coffee high, trying to keep it in the cup. The people getting off pushed into everybody else, clawing and fighting their way to the doors before they closed. I took the opportunity to scramble up the stairs, stepping on feet, muttering empty apologies in my wake.

When I reached the seats, I swung my butt wide around, claiming it for myself before someone else could sneak in there. I aimed for the first seat, closest to the aisle, leaving the open one by the window. I glanced down briefly before my ass hit. Something didn't seem right. The fuzzy upholstery looked too dark. I pushed at the last second, purposely throwing my aim. My right hand held the coffee. I landed on the hard plastic ridge where the seats come together and immediately scooted onto the seat by the window.

The bus pulled away and I adjusted myself in the seat, gathering my composure, nonchalantly glancing over my shoulder to see if anyone was laughing. Then I relaxed and inconspicuously eyed the dark seat next to me.

It was hard to tell with these seats. They were covered with dark patterned material most similar to that indoor/outdoor grass your grandparents have on their patio, except dark blue with little bursts of color to hide the stains. The one next to me, the one I'd almost sat in, was dark, like it was wet-dark. And wet, to me, being new to the city and all, meant homeless person, which meant homeless person pee. I suppose someone could have spilled something on it, but with public transportation, I automatically assume the worst.

I sat still, looking down at it out of the corner of my eye, trying not to make a face. There wasn't a puddle or anything, but it definitely looked wet. My free hand went to feel it, but I yanked it back, the coffee finally waking me up.

The bus stopped. More people got on. I forced my attention outside, watching street signs for my stop. At the next stop light, when it was safe, I took a drink of coffee. I felt a figure lean in too close, felt the warmth of it and turned instinctually. It was the yelling phone guy. I jerked back to the window. He sat suddenly, heavily in the seat next to me. I choked on coffee, coughed. He looked over at me like I was disgustingly contagious, leaning away.

I should say something about his seat, but I couldn't think. How do I tell him he just sat in pee, some bum's urine? Should I even? He probably wouldn't understand me because of how loud the bus was, then I'd have to explain it and he'd somehow think I'd done it and.... I crowded closer to the window, making myself focus my horrified stare out the window.

How long it would take for the wetness to seep into his clothes? How long it would take for him to feel it? At first it would probably just feel cold. Then, the cold would last too long and he'd start to get suspicious. Would he blame me? I *was* holding a coffee cup. He might think I spilled it, loudly blame it on me, cause a scene. I'd heard him yelling into that phone back there and I didn't want to be on the other side of that. I felt bad for him, but what could I do?

I watched eagerly as my stop came up. It was the transfer to the Red Line, so almost everyone stood to get off, including the phone guy next to me. As we stopped, I let a little gap open up between us, so I could look at his pants. I was morbidly curious. I had to see.

Sure enough, there was a small moist spot about the size of a golf ball on the seat of his jeans. I shuddered all over, a grossed-out smile pulling at my bottom lip. He had homeless guy pee on him and didn't even know it. It could have been me! And where he was going to take it? To his girlfriend's house? Spread it all over the Red Line? Would he go home and sit on his bed to take his shoes off? Eh.

I had to stop thinking about it. I glanced at the spot a couple more times as I followed him down into the subway before I lost him in the crowd. Really glad I'd looked down before I sat. I reminded myself to always look before I sat on any part of the CTA.

The train came back up into the beautiful sunshine at Armitage and I transferred to the Brown line at Fullerton. At Diversey, I left the train station to the smell of bagels and pizza. My coffee was empty and getting lonely in my stomach, starting to kick up a fuss. That and the bus thing were making me feel sick. The smell of food was everywhere. I couldn't stop myself from looking at signs for lunch deals I couldn't afford. If I waited to pay my phone bill until next month, I could eat out a couple of times now.... No, I had food at home. I had to wait.

It wasn't easy. There were restaurants on almost every corner and more in between. Somebody was renovating a bar a block up from my apartment and I'd gotten into the habit of looking in whenever I passed, hoping to see someone in there who might look at my resume. They were going to need a bartender when they opened up and it might as well be me, but no one again today.

The lady with the high-pitched voice, who always wore three coats, wasn't sitting on the stoop yet. It was too early, or too late maybe. I could hear the buzzer buzzing through the front door which meant it was stuck open again. I pushed through without my key and checked my mail before unlocking the second door.

My apartment is at the end of the long, grey carpeted corridor. The building was originally a hotel, a hundred-and-some years ago, and you could see where every other doorway had been plastered over, combining the old smaller rooms into bigger, full-service one bedrooms and studios.

The neighbors in 3C were home, fighting as usual. Today it was about... pay, paying something..., probably rent, but that's all I caught on my way by. All the way in the back, just in front of the door leading down to the alley, there was a recess on both sides, one holding my door on the right, the other holding Melanie's, the girl across the hall.

I looked down to switch keys as I got closer and tried not to think about the bank statement which I'd just taken out of the mailbox. I reached automatically for the door, key in hand, and stopped...

There was daylight coming from the door. The door was open, ajar...

I stood up straight and looked down at the doorknob again. The wood was splintered and brown under the white paint close to the lock.

My butthole tightened and my chest suddenly hurt.

Someone had forced the door! Someone had broken in!

I stepped back, wide-eyed in shocked horror. This is what they said would happen. This is what my mom had warned me about. Why you don't move to the city.

I couldn't stop staring at the doorknob, the crinkled trim. I tried to look around, up and down the hall, but my neck was stiff.

Then a slow thought started forming behind my wide eyes, something really important, something that I needed, something that someone would break in for.

No....No...Wait.

My throat went dry and my tongue got heavy. My stomach quivered and deflated like an untied balloon, bouncing against the rest of my guts.

I didn't know if I wanted to cry or poop.

Chapter 3

Standing shock-straight in terror, I forced one of my limp, jelly arms to push the door open. A whirled mess of clothes and paper and trash lay on the other side. The one framed picture I had was yanked from the wall, sitting cockeyed on the toppled night stand, lamp on the floor, the light bulb broken. And so much trash. So much that they must have brought some in with them to make the mess look more impressive.

Disbelief held me hostage at the threshold for a strong minute, my mouth gaping open, turned perfectly round like an empty cup holder.

Eventually, I got my knees unhinged and managed to step in slowly, pushing the door closed behind me until it cracked against the splintered frame. It sagged open. I pushed it in harder, with more crunch. It sagged open again, little wood chips falling on the carpet.

I looked around solemnly, horrified; my bed kicked sideways on the slatted frame, my desk cleared of all the books and junk mail, the drawers dumped. A milk carton, sitting in a grayish wet puddle on the off-white flecked carpet, headed up a trail of litter from the kitchen, butter stomped and molded with shoe tread, bag of chips pulverized and sprinkling out.

My brain was stuck in a what-the-fuck, what-the-fuck loop as I surveyed the scene. I didn't have much stuff and the apartment was small, but what little there was made a pretty impressive mess.

A warm breeze came in through the bars on the open windows. The blinds had been pulled from the windows and fell in crumpled piles like bones. A garbage truck beeped loudly, outside somewhere, down the alley, eight feet below. I followed the trash trail slowly into the small kitchenette where someone had thoughtlessly left the refrigerator open. Not to worry about anything spoiling though, its contents were lying stomped to death in a mushy pile on the black and white checked tile floor.

Slow disbelief gave way to shitting urgency as my mind snapped back into action. I'd forgotten the most important part. My head spun with fear as I reeled around, my shoes slipping in the muck. Please let it be there. Please let it still be there. Please let this be just a random break-in, having nothing to do with that. Please.

The sliding door to the closet was open, hangers and clothes, hiking boots and my only suit discarded in a heap. My chest contracted, my breath shallow. Standing on dumped dirty clothes, I pulled the string for the ceiling light. The clean lines of emptied shelves leapt out of the darkness like the ribs of a giant skeleton. My eyes stumbled as they climbed the shelves, panning up slowly like the camera in a horror movie, not wanting to know what lay on each shelf above. Finally, I forced myself to look at the right hand side of the top shelf.

My heart dropped like a ripe red apple and fell through a new hole at the bottom of my stomach. The burst of fearful nervous energy I'd had vanished. An avalanche of heavy disappointment fell on top of me. I felt exhausted. I couldn't hold myself up, or keep from sinking to my knees, enveloped by the sweet sweat smell of the dirty clothes.

I kept a lockbox on the top shelf. It was gone. It had everything in it. My face and shoulders started to sag. Everything...

But as soon as my head hit my hands, I jolted upright. I didn't have time to cry. I jumped to my feet. I didn't have time for this. I had to get it back. *Had* to. No way around it. I had to get it back now!

My eyes started flicking around like flies caught between the window and the screen. My mind racing. When had this happened? Could they still be around? Had anyone seen them?

Action. I ran to the windows in the back, stepping over trash and mess like a football player running through one of those squared rope things in practice. Straining my eyes to see further than the windows allowed, I scanned the alley like an old-timey prisoner looking for a ring of keys.

To the left a guy was unloading bags from a linen supply truck. On the right and moving, a few people jogged lightly to the bus stop at the end of the alley. Suspicious? In one of the back yards across the alley, a little kid chased a squirrel up a tree. He was never going to catch it. I made my eyes search the other yards, seeing around trees and behind garages, clear through to the tall apartment building on the other side of the block. Nothing! Shit.

Neighbors! Melanie!

I yanked my door open, looked both ways and charged across the hall. Bam, Bam, Bam.... Nothing happened. I knocked again, impatiently. Thunk, thunk, thunk. I could hear the TV through the door. She was home. I knocked again and stood there waving my hands in the air like a kid having to pee, picking my feet up and putting them down without going anywhere. Tinny voices of women screaming at each other came from the TV, muffled by the wooden door. I was too anxious, I couldn't wait.

Moving on. I crossed back diagonally to my side and raised my hand to knock on 3C. As soon as I made contact, a voice came through the door yelling, "Leave me alone." I stopped my hand mid-knock and froze. How could someone answer that quickly? I hadn't even been at the door long enough for someone to know I was there. Were they watching me? Knew I was coming? "You won't ever leave me alone," it said. "I can't even breathe without you there smelling my breath." Ok. They weren't talking to me. It was a high-pitched voice similar in whiny tone to the one I'd just heard from the TV. "I said leave me alone! I even have to eat my Pop-Tarts in the bathroom." I wished I hadn't knocked. I started to creep away with my hand still up in the air. I'll just slink away... maybe they hadn't heard me.

"Michael," somebody whisper-talked from behind me in a self-conscious voice, "what are you doing?"

I spun around letting my hand fall. Melanie's big eyes and wet head were poking out of the door across the hall from mine. "Finally," I said, gesturing with my hand and quick-stepping toward her, "What the hell were you doing in there?"

"What're you talking about?" she said. "Taking a shower."

I heard the swoosh of a door rub against the carpet behind me. Shit. I moved faster without looking back.

"Who the hell's knocking on the door?" The high-pitched voice blurted at the empty space in the hall where I'd been standing.

"Oh, uh, sorry," I said over my shoulder, charging on, "wrong door."

I hurried toward Melanie's floating head. She watched me approach with confounded concern wrinkled across her forehead.

"Come here. Look!" I reached in and pulled her wrist toward my apartment. I made it halfway across the hall before she pulled back, her wet arm slipping from my grip. What the hell? I spun on my heel to see her standing in the middle of the hall like a statue of a chubby nymph, dripping wet, wrapped in a towel.

"Hey," she said quickly, looking at the guy from 3C, clutching the towel tighter to herself.

"What's going on out here? What are you guys doing?" said the fourth grade voice, coming from the diminutive little man. "What are you playing at? Is this some kind of sick—"

"Oh shit," I let out, looking down at Melanie. I moved toward her, pushing her back through her own open door instead, closing it behind me. I fell against the door breathing heavily. "Somebody broke into my apartment."

"What? When? Just now?" Her eyes went wide, listening with excited intent.

"I don't know, I just came home. I'm trying to—"

"You scared me," she said, settling down prematurely, "I thought something had happened."

"Something did happen!" I said pleadingly, "my *place* was broken into."

"No, I meant...now, like an emergency." She took a step back further into the room and leaned against the high counter separating the kitchen from the living room. Her hands rang water down the length of her long hair and let it drip freely onto the carpet. Her full cheeks and shoulders were still tinged pink from the hot water of the shower.

"What are you talking about? It *is* an emergency." I clasped my head. "I don't think you understand...they," I paced in a circle. "They got my weed."

"Oh," she said, like it's no big deal. "That's what you're so worried about? They took your stash?"

"No," I said, "not like that. You don't understand. They got *two pounds*."

"What do you mean two pounds? Two pounds of what?" Ringing more water from her hair.

"Weed! Marijuana. I just said that."

She stopped ringing. "Wait, what? What are you doing with two pounds of weed?"

"Selling it. Or trying to."

"Selling it? Wait, you're a drug dealer?"

"No, I'm not a drug dealer. Not really." I resumed my pacing. "It's just weed. It doesn't count."

She smiled. "Huh."

"It's not like that. I don't sell it all time. It's not what I *do*. I'm not a *drug* dealer. I just couldn't get a job and needed the money and... Look, it doesn't matter. What matters is it's gone. They fucking took it."

"Who's they?"

"I don't know!" I yelled at her, and immediately apologized. "Sorry."

"Do you think it was just random? Just bad luck?"

"I don't know. I can't think straight. What am I gonna do?"

"Well, think about it. When did you leave? Weren't you here last night?"

"Why?" I turned to her expectantly. "Did you see anyone last night? Hear somebody at my place? Think it was me?"

"No. Not at all. I'm just asking," she said calmly. Then more brightly, "You weren't home?"

"No, I stayed at Ellie's," I said flatly, not wanting to change the subject.

"Ellie's, huh?" she said in a powdery voice, with a sly, head-cocked smile. But I refused the bait. I kept pacing instead, concentrating, walking around my left foot trying to calm down. Melanie shrugged patiently, started fluffing her hair with her fingertips, gathering it in the back, running a hand down the length of it over her shoulder.

"What am I gonna do? I have to get it back....It can't be gone. It just can't...." I pinched my temples and took a deep breath. When I looked back up, Melanie's towel had loosened a bit, yet was held in place by the moisture clinging to her full breast. My mouth filled with saliva, started moving, wanting to pose questions, but nothing came out, forgot what it was going to say. I could tell from the flat expression on her face she wasn't trying to distract me. Her head rolled sideways as she pulled fingers through her hair. Her eyes watching me vacantly, waiting for me to go on, ready to help.

It was the second time in a matter of hours I was standing next to a half naked girl. Melanie's figure was fuller than Ellie's and certainly no worse off for it. Her skin was lighter and had a soft tender look to it like she never went out in the sun. Little droplets of water on her neck and shoulders called for attention, shimmering in the afternoon sunlight coming in through the half-closed blinds. My mind clogged and stopped working.

She didn't hurry to pull the towel tight and it went on sort of hanging there, attracted to the wetness of her clean skin. I knew she wasn't *trying* to be seductive, it wasn't the time for it. Plus, we didn't have that kind of thing going on. We were neighbors. We'd have a beer sometimes, more often lately, at her place, or mine. She'd complain about her boyfriend working too much and I'd talk excitedly about Ellie. So why should her near-nakedness be an issue? It wasn't. Damn it. Snap out of it.

Urgency finally cut in and kicked me in the ass. I shook my head wildly and resumed my pacing. Melanie's apartment is bigger than mine with one window facing west into the bricked-in courtyard of the building next door and two looking north over the alley like mine. I started wearing a quick groove between them.

"You sure you didn't see anything?" I said, spreading the blinds apart, searching the courtyard next door. "Hear anything? Maybe this morning?"

"No, I've been here all morning," she said, matching my matter-of-fact tone. "But you know how it is, people are *con*stantly going in and out the back door. I wouldn't really know..."

I did know how it was. I barely slept my first week here because of the noise at night, and then trucks in the alley in the morning.

"And nothing last night? Maybe in the middle of the night? Thought it was me coming home? Anything? Nothing?"

"No, Michael," she said, holding her towel against her now. "You're being hysterical. I didn't hear anything, or see anything. Phil came over late, as usual, but other than that, it was noisy as always."

I came away from the window. "I can't be*lieve* it," I said, shaking my head, "I can't believe it."

"*I* can't believe you were dealing drugs."

"I'm not a drug dealer! I just needed the money."

"Uh-huh. I bet that's what they all say."

"Would you stop? You know what I mean. I'm just doing it till I get a job."

"So does that mean it was drug-related?" she asked, getting some of the seriousness back. "Does that mean it was somebody in the business? Not just some rando?"

It stopped me. The blunt reality of the question.

"Did they even take anything else?" She went around me to the closet next to the bathroom then, said, "Hey, look over there a second."

I turned around and heard the towel drop to the floor. "I don't really have anything else. Nothing else that matters anyway. Just a shitty laptop."

"And did they take that?"

"I didn't notice, actually. I doubt it. But they made it look random, tore the place up."

She came back around me wearing soft cotton stretchy pants and a loose t-shirt with the neck cut out. She flopped onto the couch and pulled her feet up, watching me pace along in front of her.

"So?" she said quietly. "Do *you* think it was somebody you know?"

"Hell," I said, somewhat fatalistically, "I wish I could say no…. But no burglar in his right mind would look in my window and then break in. I don't even have a TV." My mind was picking up speed again, without the distracting nakedness. "I mean, I would love to think it was just some random dude breaking in and getting lucky. But not my place."

"Yeah, I sure as hell wouldn't break into your place. The smell alone would distract even the most hard-up crackhead." She gave me a sweet smile, trying to lighten my spirits. But it wasn't the time for that either.

"You don't know how bad this fucks me. I got to get that stuff back." I wanted to laugh it off, wanted to kick back, cut my losses and laugh it off the way I usually do with important things. But whoever had broken into my place had seriously screwed me.

"Can you think of anybody that would do it?"

No was the quick answer and I said it. "But I only know about a handful of people in this city." Everything I said was getting heavier.

"Well then," she said, her tone getting some of the gravity into it. "I guess that makes your list of suspects pretty short, then. You know, unless it was just somebody random."

"Yeah, I guess so."

And so it did. The chance of somebody randomly picking my apartment out of thousands was pretty small. True, my windows do face the alley, but all three are at least eight feet off the ground and covered by iron bars that were set directly into the brick when the place was built. And, the front door buzzer does get jammed almost every day, but even then you have to get in the inner door, which is possible. The back door has an iron gate same as the windows. You might be able to climb it, but you'd have to go at least as high as the second floor, and then still get in the door itself.

I knew someone picked my place on purpose, but I didn't want to say it. And I knew it because *they* knew what was in there. And *that* meant it had to be someone *I* knew. It had to be someone who knew me and knew what I had.

It meant I had to go ask all of the people I knew, confront them. All of the people on that short list.

But how could I do that?

I didn't want to do that.

I don't want to confront anybody.

Chapter 4

For some good reason, Melanie gave me a long, sympathetic hug before I left. She was so soft and comforting, I had second thoughts about going. I could just curl up on the futon there with her, wrap myself up in her sweet smelling softness and forget all about this crap. Yeah.

No, I couldn't. I pushed her away with both hands, did my best to appear stoic, and purposeful, as I marched out the door.

Back across the hall, the depressive disaster scene brought faintness back into my knees. I really didn't want to admit that someone I knew had broken into my apartment. But my computer was still there, which sort of sealed the case, even if it was swept off the desk in a heap with a half rotten banana peel on top of it. Any random thief would have taken it for sure, no matter how out of date it was.

I had to face the hard fact that it was someone I knew. I had to, so I could start to figure out who. But I trusted *all* of the people I knew. Probably *too* much. Maybe that was why I was such an easy target. I liked to think of myself as a good judge of character, that I could spot someone trying to play me, but I guess we all like to think that. No one wants to think of himself as easily duped, easily snowed over. Shit, there was only one way for me to figure out who had done this. I had to go ask them. Fuck. All of them.

Or, I suppose I could pack up and crawl back to Indiana…?

I righted my desk chair and sat; elbows on knees, hand on chin, eyes looking over the mess. *Could* I actually go back home at this point? It would be a lot easier. I could sell the last of the weed to—Oh, that's right.

And besides, the last time I was in Indiana, I went to a bar downtown with some friends and before we even made it past the doorman, I saw four girls I'd already slept with. Four girls in one room! It wasn't even a big room. It was small, like the size of a garbage truck. That's enough to make any man run. Let alone all the talk of, "I thought you moved." "Oh, back so soon?" "Couldn't make it in the Big City?"

No. Going back to Indiana was not an option. There was only one option, goddamnit. It was to find out who stole my shit and get it back.

Like it or not, I had to physically go see everyone I knew. And by "knew," I meant everyone I was friends with. And by "friends with," I meant everyone I sold to. See this all happened a few years ago, before weed started being legalized everywhere. You had to have connections and shit, know people. And now, my depressingly short client list had suddenly become my depressively *long* suspect list.

The thought made my stomach hurt.

What was I even saying? "Go see everyone." Who did I think I was? Go "see" somebody, like I'm some sort of tough guy. I hadn't even been in a fight since I punched Thomas Glassburn in the stomach in fifth grade. And *that* was over fifteen years and all of puberty ago. I couldn't "go see" anybody. What would happen if they said, "Yeah, I took your money and your weed, so what?" Was I going to beat them all up? Go in with a shotgun, wave it in my friends' faces and demand my shit back?

Wooziness rode up my spine. I forced myself to sit up straight. Then stand. This wasn't going to fix itself. It wasn't. I had to act *now* while the trail was still fresh. And before I could talk myself out of it.

Before the break-in, there was a bottle of whiskey on top of the fridge. Watching my step, I went to see if it was still there. It was. I grabbed it by the neck and, at two o'clock in the afternoon, I took a gulp.

A different feeling shot through my gut and it stood me up.

"Ok," I said out loud, "I can do this." I nodded my head up and down, trying to drum up courage. "Yeah.... I can do this." The familiar burn of the whiskey soothed the acid in my stomach. I swallowed some air to cool my throat.

I wasn't really a drug dealer. I was a bartender. And I wasn't really only a bartender. I was a young-ish man armed with a college degree. I took another pull from the bottle. The burn followed. I smacked my lips after it.

So what if I sold a little weed to make ends meet? I couldn't help it if the economy sucked and the job market was flat. What was I supposed to do? Lie down and cry? No! I took matters into my own hands. Who cares if I dabbled a little in the drug trade? The government would wise up soon enough and start doing it themselves, so it couldn't be that bad. Plus it was easy, or it was easy-*ish,* and the money was good. My old hippie buddies from college were still growing the best hydroponic this side of the Mississippi. *And* they were still willing to front it to me. I didn't even have to put up any money! It was the perfect set up. Yeah. I'd have been a fool *not* to take it.

But then of course, I had to *have* the weed to sell it. And I had to have the *money* I'd made from selling it for it to count as profit. Plus pay the guys back, before they showed up at my mom's house asking her for it.

Yes, whoever stole that weed and the money really fucked me over. And I had to go find out who it was, damnit. I had no choice. I had to get it back.

Still reluctant, yet definitely encouraged, I waved the whiskey bottle out in a salute of promise to my disheveled apartment. "Ok," I said out loud again, "let's make this happen." I took another belt to drown the doubt rising up in my stomach. Then, returned the bottle safely back to its perch, so I'd know where to find it.

Chapter 5

My apartment door wouldn't stay shut all the way. I slammed it the best I could and went out the back, as usual, down into the alley. The sun was still high in the afternoon sky and the shots I'd taken made it brighter than before. Squinting heavily, I headed west down the alley, turned onto Pine Grove, then made a right on Diversey toward the train.

Sirens from an ambulance grew from loud to horrible, then screeched past, deafeningly, on the way to the hospital on the corner of Sheridan. Cars backed up for a few blocks every time the light turned red up at Clark Street, then slowly stretched out, only to bunch again at the next red. My feet felt a little loose down below my ankles. I shook them out as I walked to make sure they were still attached.

Classic rock blared out of a pick-up truck pulling two jet skis toward the lake. A big group of people in Cubs hats and jerseys jumbled and ran into each other at the corner where Broadway splits off from Clark like dead ends in a hair commercial. A couple stepped off the curb and a cab tried its best to run them down.

Drinking whiskey in the afternoon and setting out on business gave me a strangely urban feel, like I belonged. In old movies they'd call it a "bracer." I liked that idea. It was like admitting that the world we live in is hard to deal with and it was ok to brace yourself for it. In the small town I grew up in, only alcoholics needed a "bracer"; everybody else had Diet Coke. I certainly didn't feel like running around town, blaming my friends for breaking into my apartment. I didn't really care to know any of them were capable of it, let alone actually did it. And a Diet Coke sure as hell wouldn't have done much for my courage.

As I walked, I started clinching my fists, trying it out, thinking about punching someone. In boxing movies they're always talking about keeping your elbows in and your guard up. Or was it your shoulders in? I sized up a couple of guys on the street, pictured myself lunging at them with a stiff jab, or a shattering right hook.

And this time, it wasn't going to be like when that Anthony guy slashed my tire in college. He'd been running around town telling people I'd stolen his girlfriend, when my car tire mysteriously went flat from knife holes poked in the side. A couple days later, I confronted him at a strip mall, outside the record store where people used to hang out. I poked him in the chest, asked if he'd slashed my tire. People came out of the store, gathering, watching. He said, No, it wasn't him. I didn't know what to do next. I expected him to be more defiant, accusatory. I was prepared for him to insult me, try to hit me, blame me for taking his girlfriend away from him, but he didn't. He just said, "No." Simply like that. I didn't know what to do. I didn't have any real proof he'd done it. So, instead of punching him, I said, "Well you better not have" and that was it. I didn't want to look like an asshole, beat him up for something I wasn't sure he did. So, I pointed at him real hard with a stiff finger and walked away. Super cool.

But it's not going to be like that this time. I've grown since then, been let down more, had my heart broken. No, this time it was for real. I clinched my fists, walking past pizza places and nail salons.

A southbound train rumbled in overhead as I pulled the door open at the Diversey Brown Line station. Chatter and a stampede of footsteps came down the right side as I swiped my card and went up the left to the northbound track.

I had decided to try Tim and Chris first. They lived the furthest north and I could work my way back from there. One of the advantages of running a weed delivery service is knowing where all your customers live. I'd done it for more practical reasons at the time, customer incentive, privacy, that sort of thing, but now that my clients were suspects, it was paying off double.

Tim and Chris made the best starting point geographically, but if I'm honest, they also seemed like the least likely to be guilty. They could be my warm-up suspects, make sure I get the interrogating tone right. Plus, together they weighed about a hundred pounds. Not that I was planning on fighting anybody....

God, the whole situation felt ridiculous. Maybe it was the absurdity of it all, or the whiskey, but I caught myself chuckling into the wind as the train pulled in.

I got off at Damen and walked up past CVS, a dog grooming place and three hair salons with barred windows. As I went around the bar, Tino's, on the corner, I saw the door to their apartment building was propped open. I had thought it better not to call ahead and was even happier to see I was going to have the full element of surprise; walk right up and knock on their door, totally unannounced.

A hump-backed old lady in a long blue work dress and beige frock was working a broom out over the steps. Without looking behind her, she swept a cloud of dust in my face as I started to mount the stairs. I coughed loudly to get her attention while waving my hand in front of my face. The lady, bent with sweeping, jolted upright as if I'd goosed her.

"Excuse me, sorry," I said, with a foot on the first step. She reeled back at my closeness and got a look on her face like a pious Christian facing a voodoo demon. "I just need to..," I murmured pointing, moving awkwardly past her up the stairs. Clutching the broom in front of her like a crucifix, she inched as far back against the wall as the three-foot space would allow. I sidestepped along, keeping as far against the opposite wall as possible, until the carved wooden railing of the staircase dug into my back. Turning slowly around, I advanced up the stairs as quietly as one does when receding from a crazy person in the bus station, her stare turning to poison as I climbed further away.

The staircase, and building in general, was amazingly well kept and expensive looking for a couple of college kids to live in. The stairs and railing were beautiful, light brown hardwood, polished and obviously swept daily. After a short, left curve at the top, a small landing flattened out with a matching wood door. The dull thump of music with heavy bass barely came through the thickness of it. I knocked my standard three raps, listening consciously to the sounds on the other side as though they held clues. Nothing happened for a moment, then the music went off. I knocked again. There was a deep thud like something being dropped. The floor creaked slightly as the eyehole in the door went dark, somebody looking out.

I bent slightly forward, listening intently when the door was suddenly and completely pulled open wide. Chris, short and stringy, doorknob in hand, yelled over his shoulder, "Shit, it's just Michael."

I smiled uneasily and gave a single wave. He had a striped tank top on, flanked by bony arms no stronger than a little girl's. His dusty chinos were rolled halfway up his calf showing bright yellow socks. A thick tuft of wildly uncombed hair was pushed up over his forehead and off to the side like a crooked plume. "Damnit, man, you scared the shit out of us," he said, shaking his head as he motioned me in.

A waft of marijuana smoke floated out toward me along with the dead skunk smell. Across the room, Tim was climbing back in the window from the fire escape outside.

"Jesus, Mike, what the hell you trying to do?" he said, getting both feet on the ground.

Appropriately confused, I said, "*Me*? The better question is what the hell are *you* trying to do? Where were you going?"

Tim is just an inch or two shorter than me at six feet, but somehow gives off the impression it's a new development, like he just went through a growth spurt. His shirts are always a little too big, as if he expected to grow into them, and his pants are always a little too short, as if he's just grown out of them. He can't grow a beard to save his life and his hair is cut straight across his forehead as if cut by his mother. It all adds up perfectly with his future acting career, so long as there are plenty of high school parts for him to play.

"Well," he said, regaining his boyish confidence, "when you come knocking like the police what are we *supposed* to do? I can't afford to get arrested. Think of my career." He walked over with his hand stretched out reluctantly. I took it to shake. Tim grabbed my hand quickly and pulled me down into a headlock. I squirmed, completely taken off guard. He rubbed his knuckles hard against my head giving me a noogie. God, I hate dealing with college kids. I had to shake hard and use both hands to push him off.

"What the fuck?" I said, finger-combing my hair.

"Now we're even."

"Why would you think that?" I looked at him. "And why would you think I was the police?"

Chris said, "'Cuz somebody comes up out of the blue, banging super loud on the door. The landlady out there already warned us about smoking weed in here. What would you think?"

"Yeah," Tim said, then putting on an accent, "Don smoke-a da pot in heer. I call police."

"I didn't *bang* on the door."

"The hell you didn't." Chris said. "And she's always out there sweeping, man. Waiting for us to slip up. We come home late? She bangs on the ceiling. During the day? She's out there sweeping."

"I mean how dirty can the place get?" Tim asked me.

"She's watching, waiting for—" Chris stopped when he saw my attention pulled away. Something moved in the window. Instantly, I thought the old lady had crawled up the fire escape and really was watching us. A knowing glance passed between the two of them.

I moved in between, closer to the window, as a foot came through. A big right foot in Air Jordan's with the laces untied. A large, crooked beak-nose came through next, then an Adam's apple so big and pointy it beat out the small chin that followed. The skinny, lithe body of Ian, all baggy shirt, shoulders too sharp like a poorly made scarecrow, came in through the window from the fire escape. He pulled his left foot in last and hitched his skinny, tight jeans back up over his thin hips, before turning to face us.

But he didn't stop turning. His eyes, hanging to the sides of his nose like flittering deer flies on a sheet in the wind, kept turning, ticking nervously to look at the doorway to the kitchen, then back past us to the front door, then behind him at the window again to make sure no one had followed him.

I started to raise a question, but saw a reluctant look pass between Tim and Chris again and paused. Ian looked me up and down, his head moving in quick little pigeon bursts.

"What's up, Ian?" I said, "I didn't know you where here. You just come up the fire escape or what?"

His head swept the room again in the millisecond before he said, "What's going on, kid?" His voice had the rhythm of someone who had grown up mimicking hip-hop songs. "You bring the police or what?" Looking at the door again. "Had me on the run, son."

"I'm sorry, man, sorry to all you guys," I said. "I didn't mean to scare you so bad. Didn't know you were all so shaky." I was going to go on, but Chris was squinting his eyes at me, shaking his head tensely, and eyeing Ian. Warning me.

"What do you mean 'shaky?' What's that mean, Mikey? You think you know what's up? You know me? You think I'm shaky, like I'm spooked? Like I got something to hide? Why don't you search me? Ask me?" He thrust his hands up in a way that made me back up a step. "E'erybody thinks they got somethin' on me? Well ask me? Come on. People lurking around. What is it? Ask it." It sounds like he was attacking me, but he wasn't. It was directed at all of us, and none of us. I noticed, now, the strain in his eyes. At first, I had thought he was just red-eyed stoned, but I could see the bags under his eyes, strung out looking. "Everywhere I go I got to look over my shoulder? Fuck this. Thought I'd be cool here. Didn't think—"

"Hey, Ian," I said easily. "I didn't know you were here, man, that's all." I started to understand the looks coming and going between Tim and Chris. They were looks of desperation, not deception. I wondered how long he had been here. I could see they had hoped he'd actually left down the fire escape, not just hidden.

Tim started to put a hand on Ian's shoulder to calm him, but pulled back, deciding against it. Instead, he sided with him, I guessed so Ian wouldn't feel singled out. "Yeah, Mike, what's up anyway? Why didn't you call or something, let us know you were coming?"

"Yeah," Chris said, liking this strategy and joining in, "would have saved us all a lot of grief."

I backed up a step. "Hey, listen guys, I'm sorry. I didn't mean to cause a ruckus. I didn't realize it was such a touchy crowd around here."

"What's that mean?" Ian stepped forward. "What are you sayin', homey?"

I took another step back. It was hot in their apartment, even with the window open. I felt like I was standing on hot coals. But I was supposed to be the mad one in this situation. I was the one who came here accusing them, not the other way around. Ian was clearly strung out. He looked like he'd definitely been up all night. Perhaps breaking into my place? Stealing my shit? I couldn't let them bully me into backing away.

"Now hold on a minute here," I said defensively, "I just came over to ask you guys about—." My throat started to close up. "I just, well..." They were rattling my nerve. I had a good sting line I was going to use to try to trap them, watch their reaction, but I was losing it. The liquid courage I'd shot myself with was disintegrating. "I...I was just wondering if you guys needed any more weed?" Yeah, that was it. If any of them had stole my stuff, then I'd see the guilt flash across their faces when I mentioned it. "You know, I didn't want to come right out and say it." I measured each of their faces. "But since you guys are coming at me like this, I might as well ask now, be direct about it."

Tim and Chris looked mildly confused not knowing where to take it, not expecting the answer to be so innocent and simple. Ian cocked his head, scrunching his burnt-looking eyes.

"Aw, shit," he said. "If it's like that, why come so secret? Why not call?"

"I was up here anyway, looking for jobs in Lincoln Square. I don't know, I didn't think about it. Then the door was open downstairs, so—"

"Where at in Lincoln Square?" Chris said, interested. "Somebody hiring?"

"Yeah, a restaurant over on—"

"Where's your bag?" Ian shot in.

"What?" I said, assuming he'd misunderstood. "I don't have any *with* me. I just meant I'd—"

"No, your *bag*. Your backpack, whatever, you know what I'm sayin' with res-mays and shit," Ian said, looking at my empty hands. Damn. Why didn't I think of that. "You lookin' for a job, you hand out res-mays."

Tim and Chris agreed by continuing to look questioningly at me, but not wanting to draw attention to themselves.

"I just brought a couple," I said, trying to muster some insolence. "I gave 'em out. What do you care?"

"Uhn-uh. I don't like this, man," Ian said and edged quickly back to the window. Tim and Chris followed with their eyes and then together shot me a desperate look.

Ian, done with the window for a second, went to the door and looked through the eyehole. "Nah, I don't like it," he said as he crossed the room to look in one of the bedrooms. "Shit ain't right. He's lyin'. I can see it on him. You didn't come up here for that."

The room had the strange sensation of a kidnapping, of a bank held by terrorists. I was so confused I couldn't think straight. This isn't what I'd come here for. What was Ian even doing here? He came because it was safe? From what? And he was acting too weird. But somehow I didn't get the feeling he was the one who broke into my apartment. He seemed too out of it. If he had been on an all-night burgling spree, why would he be so freaked out? And why was he so suspicious of *me*? Could it be some mad plot to throw me off his trail? If it was, it was working. And since I was already the centerpiece of concern I decided, fuck it, throw it out there.

"All right," I said, in the tone of someone about to break down. I turned around with my head down, looking up before going on, "I came over here...I came to see if..." Tim put a hand on my arm. "Look, my place was broken into last night."

"Hah, knew it," Ian charged over to me. "You came to see if we *did* it? I fuckin' knew it. Everybody trying to blame me for shit, I knew it."

"No," I said, much more strongly. "I just came to see if Tim and Chris had any ideas about it."

"Oh, you didn't know I was here? You came to ask them if *I* did it? You think it was me?"

"No, man, no. That's not what I'm saying, I—"

"Really, Mike? Your place was broken into?" Tim asked.

"Last night?" Chris said.

"Yeah," I said hopefully. "You hear anything?"

"Who would they hear something from, Mike? Me? You think *I* did it. I swear to God. Nobody trusts me. Everybody thinks *I'm* the fucking asshole." Ian was pacing around in circles checking the windows then, the front door, the kitchen. I couldn't take it, didn't know what to do.

"Ian, what are you talking about? I'm not accusing you of anything. Hell, maybe I'm blaming these two guys. It's their house I came to, not yours. Jesus. And what the hell are you going on about anyway? All this shit talk? You that high?"

"Fuck you, Mike," was the surprisingly short retort. His eyes really started doing flips though, working back and forth across the room, back and forth, over and over.

I collected myself.

"Listen," I said, "I didn't mean to accuse any of you guys. I just wanted to see if maybe you had any ideas about my stuff. Or maybe, maybe you might have heard something."

"We all know *you* have ideas," Ian murmured, "just like everybody."

"Jesus."

"Um, we haven't heard anything, Mike," Tim said, doing his best doctor-informing-the-family-of-bad-news. "I'm really sorry though, that's tough."

"Thanks, man," I said, giving him and Chris a what-the-fuck look aimed at Ian.

"Did they really get all your stuff?" Chris said, "Like *all* of it?"

"Mostly, yeah."

"Damn," Tim said, visibly working through the scene, trying different poses and expressions. It was grating as hell.

Ian came out of the kitchen.

"I think I'm gonna go, leave you guys to whatever it was. This is stressing me out." I waved my hand around to include them all. "I'm gonna go ask around. Call me if you hear anything, yeah?"

I waited a brief second until Ian went back to the window, then slapped some sorry high fives.

"See ya, Ian," I said, moving to the door, "let me know if you see anything." As I pulled the door shut behind me, I heard him muttering something about "them" and "everybody."

The old landlady was outside, sweeping the sidewalk. I turned up the street before she could put a spell on me.

I'd never seen Ian like that before. He was losing his shit in there. Had to be pills, or something. But I wasn't really feeling him for the guy who broke into my apartment. His behavior was too obvious, too unfocused, like he'd been dealing with something else before I got there, something even more intense. And not doing a very good job of it either.

My head was spinning. That was some hell of a start.

That sucked.

I was glad to be away from there.

Chapter 6

Ian's place would have been next on the list, but I'd gotten lucky with that one. Who knows what he would have done if I'd have shown up announced, banging on *his* door. Shoot me? Shank me? Gouge my eyes out with chicken-claw-like fingernails, caw-cawing in my face? I don't know, but I'm glad I didn't have to find out. That kid needed to get some sleep, or to get laid, or something.

So, skipping Ian, Alex was up next, who lived over in Uptown, off the Wilson Red Line stop. Thankfully, I could at least count on Alex being stable. I'd never even seen him drunk, let alone paranoid and flipping the fuck out.

Of all the people I'd met thus far in Chicago, I'd liked Alex the best. A few weeks after moving up here, I was at a party full of college kids from DePaul, the perfect place for a guy like me to get rid of some illicit, if mostly harmless, drugs. The friend I'd gone there with was busy chasing some girl, so I was wandering around, drinking my beer and looking for someone to smoke a joint with.

See, I was having a hell of a time getting rid of *any* of my weed. I didn't know anybody. So, I'd worked out this little scheme for selling it off. I'd roll a few joints, cut with tobacco so it would go further, and hit the bars, or parties along the way, whatever I might run into. I'd get a beer, hang around looking over the crowd, then go out to smoke a joint when other people went out for a cigarette. I'd stand just far enough away, so as not to be obvious, but just close enough so someone would invariably wander over and ask either for a hit, or if I knew where they could get some. I did. Actually, I just happen to have some with me....

So I was wondering around this party, slowly drinking my beer, when somebody stumbled out of a nearby bedroom followed by the tell-tale cloud of smoke and laughter I'd been waiting for. I invited myself in.

There were about eight people in the room, mostly girls, all loosely gathered around this guy, Alex, in the middle, who was steadily rolling joints and passing them around, one after the other. I told myself, "Now, this is a guy I want to meet." I promptly joined the circle, dropping a little baggie on the tray in front of him. I could have just lit up my own joint and melted into the scene, but I wanted the look and nod I received.

When people eventually started to disperse, I nonchalantly brought the subject up and gave him a little dime bag of my Indiana homegrown and my number.

Sure enough, he called a few days later. He introduced me to a few other people and that, basically, became my "client list," which had now become my "suspect list," the same list I was very likely unraveling, traipsing around town throwing out accusations.

It hadn't taken long before I started fronting the weed to Alex. He'd pay me back right on time, easy enough, no problem. But it'd been taking a little longer lately. In fact, it had been about a week since I'd given him the last ounce. I wasn't really that worried about it, but seeing how things were going, I needed the money pretty badly. I mean, what if I didn't get my shit back? I had to have every penny I could scrape up.

So even though we'd become friends, this had to be more than a social call. He owed me money.

Being in Lincoln Square on the northwest side of the city, you would think it would be easy to get to over to Uptown by train. I was already close to the Brown Line. But Chicago's train system, as I was learning, had major flaws in cross town travel. Google said it would take almost an hour to get there, with most of the time spent waiting on two different trains, or half an hour if I walked. I walked.

I headed east down Lawrence, beside four lanes of ugly avenue traffic, blowing dust and cars going so fast I had to keep both hands up to bat down McDonald's sacks whipping up in my face. At Ashland, I cut over to a quieter street that steadily lost its charm as I went past Clark. The neighborhood changed from quiet-young-family to half-way-house-crazy. Whether they were drug abuse halfway houses, or mental health halfway houses, it was hard to tell. But either way, there were a lot more people hanging around on the sidewalk and I started to walk with a lot more determination.

And while I was walking, I practiced asking for the four hundred dollars Alex owed me, trying to keep desperation and suspicion out of my voice.

Not wanting to cause any more alarm, I decided to text this time, "Hey. Im by your place. You home?"

A block farther, he replied, "For a minute."

I had to go down to the Wilson stop first to find my way since I'd only ever been to his house by car, which did me no good, or by train. It was only a few blocks to his building on the corner of two small streets, Kenmore and Leland. I went past the stringy bush reaching hard for a little sun and climbed the stairs to push the buzzer.

All right, I said to myself: bring up the money nice and easy, watch his reaction.

I pushed the buzzer, got no response. I pushed it again. No response. Must still be broken. I called. He answered the call by hanging up immediately, which I knew meant he'd be down in a second. We'd done this before.

Looking through both glass doors of the foyer, Alex's apartment was just out of sight up on the left. His bare feet came into view, coolly bouncing down the half flight of stairs. Well-fitted jeans came next with white wear-lines outlining the phone in his pocket and capping his knees. His arms were long like mine, most of his chest covered by a black, deep V-neck t-shirt. His hair fell back down over his large, strong brow, which I thought made him look like a Neanderthal, but most girls disagreed. He pulled the door open with an easy smile and cool confidence that made you want to be his friend.

"What's happening?" he said, pushing hair out of his face and casting a quick searching look over me, which didn't quite match the friendly ease of his posture.

"Nothing man," I said, slapping his hand. "You know how it is."

"What are you doing up here?" he said, turning, moving lightly up the stairs. Music and low chatter came into the hall through the door he'd left open a crack.

"Aw, I was in the neighborhood, looking for jobs. Thought I'd see what you were up to. See if you wanted to get a beer."

"Can't tonight, man," he said, pushing the door open wide for me to catch and close. "We're gettin' ready to go out."

"Oh yeah? What are you getting up t—?" My question trailed off as we went in. The room was crowded with guys I'd never seen before; not that that was unusual, Alex seemed to know more people in Chicago than I'd had in my entire high school.

I'd seen a documentary once that told me exactly what they were doing. Three heavy canvas bags sat in the middle of the room overflowing with spray paint cans, tape and rags. World War II looking gas masks lay next to cheap, shop goggles and flu-style face masks. Being an art student at SAIC, Alex's apartment always looked like he was about to stage an art exhibition; canvases, four and five deep, always leaning against every wall, yet nothing hanging, bare white walls purposely not covered, as if being prepped. But this time the place was humming. The living room was filled with the various accoutrement of illegal spray painting activity. All of the guys wore variations on the dark-hoodie-and-black-jeans motif with enough visible tattoos showing to satisfy an album cover.

"Oh, hey guys," I said awkwardly, like I'd just stumbled into the private back room of a casino. A couple of nods floated in my general direction, but no one said anything, or stopped what they were doing. Alex left me standing by the door without any introductions, stepped over one of the stuffed canvas bags and walked off toward his bedroom.

One guy with black plastic glasses so big he could lick them was spreading portions of a large paper stencil out on the floor and refolding it exactly. Two guys were playing with, and pointing at, the computer on the DJ table. In the short hall Alex had gone down, another guy with huge white head phones on was invisibly writing his name on the blank wall in big, exaggerated loopy letters, going over and over it again, standing and crouching, without making a mark.

Obviously ignored, I crowded back against the front door and stood rocking back and forth on my heels trying to look as disinterested in everybody as they were in me. Behind the computer, the guy with the neck tattoo passed a blunt to the guy with the hand tattoos. The guy in the glasses spread another part of the stencil out, nodded his head and started folding it up again. When he paused to add more tape, I took a cautious step further in and twisted my head to see what it might be. The only thing I could tell was it was big, and maybe furry. A squirrel? Daniel Boone?

"Hey, how you doing?" I said to him. "Pretty big, huh?" Whether he didn't hear me, I don't know, but he ignored me, apparently not interested in my observations.

Somewhat encouraged by my newfound invisibility, I ventured further in to float around like a ghost and see what the others were doing. The floor was as covered in paper scraps, paint lids and discarded tape as a middle school art class before Thanksgiving. I tried not to step on anything as I moved from one clear spot to another like Frogger leaping from log to lily pad.

The new-looking, leather La-Z-Boy chair was similarly covered with papers and a backpack. I reached for the back of it to steady myself for a rather large stepping-hop. Of course, the chair rocked as I jumped. I wasn't ready for it. I reeled, my left arm whirling. My right hand grabbed hard to the back of the chair and I kicked one of the heavy canvas bags trying to catch my balance. Thankfully the over-stuffed bag was heavy as hell and didn't give much but the "tink" sound of metal banging together. My eyes embarrassingly shot around the room. Luckily, everybody was too enthralled with themselves to notice what I was doing. I played it cool, shook it off. Then I heard a faint hissing sound.

Holding my head still, I searched with my eyes for the sound like a buzzing fly. I was behind the stencil guy with the glasses, next to the DJ table, still holding onto the La-Z-Boy. The hissing fly-sound was definitely coming from below me. I looked behind me and behind the chair. Since I was close to the computer on the DJ table, I bent down casually to see if maybe it was the little fan running. That's when I saw the yellow spot.

Yellow spray paint was filling the inside of the bag I'd kicked. I could see the now-glowing, bright yellow tip of a screwdriver loudly pointing out of the bag. It must have punctured the can when I kicked it. And it was slowly spraying out in a faint yellow mist. AND painting the leg of the stencil guy still bent over, still folding his large paper cut out.

Oh shit.

I watched the computer guys looking at their screen. I watched the shoulder of the guy in the hall come in and out of view as he gestured with his hand. I watched the yellow spot grow on the pants leg of the stencil guy. How long will a punctured paint can last? No idea. I had to flee the scene before anybody saw it.

I nudged the bag with the toe of my shoe, trying to reposition the direction of the spray. It rolled slightly to spray on the La-Z-Boy too.

Damn.

I couldn't risk moving it directly without calling attention to it.

Alex came back into the room right then. I cringed inside, not letting it show.

Flee!

I stepped over the bag clumsily-on-purpose to push Glasses-stencil-guy out of the line of spray.

"Sorry, dude," I said, grabbing his shoulders and nudging him much harder than I'd meant to. I quickly let go, apologetically, with my hands facing him and stepped over to the side. My foot caught the edge of the stencil with a tearing sound. "Whoa," I said idiotically, "it's crowded in here."

"What the fuck, man," Glasses Guy said, pushing my hands away. "Watch it, bro, you're fuckin' up my shit."

"Easy, Michael," Alex said, sort of catching me. "Don't fuck up my guy's shit." I couldn't tell if he was mocking him or serious.

"Yeah," I said, trying to shake it off. "There's so much stuff in here." I was immediately sorry for referencing the room, encouraging them to look around, notice the spraying paint. "You guys going out soon?" I said quickly, changing the subject. "It seems kind of light out. I...I thought you did that at night mostly."

"What do you know about it?" Glasses-stencil-guy said again, trying to look tough, but looking mostly like a cartoon grasshopper.

His tone caught everybody's attention, though, like a fight in the cafeteria. Even the huge headphone guy heard it somehow and turned toward me. Alex smiled sarcastically, shaking his head as I backed away toward the door again.

"Now, now, come on guys. Michael's a friend," he said to the room.

"Oh shit, Zeke. What's that shit on your leg?" Neck Tattoo said, blunt smoldering between his fingers.

Uh oh.

"Damn," Hand Tattoo said. "That shit's on the chair too."

Glasses bent and pulled the back of his pants leg around. His eyes shot up at me with stunned anger. "You!" he growled and charged me, grabbing my shirt like a stunt pilot charging into a nose dive. He drove me against the wall. "The fuck, dude! What the fuck is wrong with you? You tryin' to—"

Alex jumped in and pushed us apart. "Hey, hey," he said quietly, but strongly. "Come on Zeke. It's not that big a deal. I know you didn't wear your good jeans? Take it easy, man." Then, pushing me further toward the door, "Come on, Mike, let's go. We're all leaving pretty soon anyway."

I didn't look back when I pulled the door open, but I could feel them staring coffin nails into me. Alex followed me closely into the hall. "Here, man, I been meaning to get this to you," he said, and slapped a wad of bills in my hand.

"Oh, yeah, thanks," I said, sounding like a jerk. "I didn't mean to upset those—"

"It's cool, Mike, they're just pumped up. You know how it is."

"Yeah, I guess."

"Let's get that beer this week, yeah?"

"Oh, uh, yeah. Yeah, we should." I said, sulking down the stairs and out into the twilight.

I was terrible at this.

At least I got the money Alex owed me. That was something. A start in the right direction maybe?

Chapter 7

On the way back to my neighborhood, I stopped at Clark Dog for a hot dog and a beer. Two stops in and four names scratched off the list equaled exactly two disastrous dead ends and one strung-out-crazy who knows what. I needed *two* hot dogs and *two* beers. But I couldn't even afford the ones I got. At least sighing into your beer is free and nobody can steal that.

After nearly three months, I was still trying to convince myself I liked hot dogs the way you're supposed to eat them in Chicago: no ketchup, that's most important, big slices of tomato, mustard, sweet relish, onions, pickle spear, peppers. It was too much like eating a whole meal, but on a small bun that wasn't up to the task. All the tomato falls over the side as soon as you take your first bite, the huge pickle slice inches its way out the back as you go, the bun splits and dumps relish on your jeans. But I was determined to love it, never to eat a hot dog with ketchup again.

I'd always wanted to live in a city known for its own type of food. That's how you know you're in a city that really matters; Philly cheesesteak, Boston baked beans, Memphis-style BBQ. Chicago has Chicago-style pizza, which is easy to love, and Chicago hot dogs, which are good, and I love them, but it takes time to teach yourself to like something a different way. You have to *believe* ketchup doesn't belong on hot dogs, of course not, who puts ketchup on hot dogs?

I didn't feel any more satisfied after I'd finished eating. The smell of dirty fryer oil stuck in my clothes after I left, trailing four feet behind me like a clinging fart. At the very particular coffee shop on Broadway, the guy who shaved his sideburns too short looked up his forehead at me without saying anything. I ordered a small coffee and sat down to wait the five minutes it took to make.

My reconnaissance mission was failing miserably. And it was almost over. I'd virtually found out nothing in the hours I'd been out working on it. I'd seen four "suspects", asked none of the questions I'd wanted to and surmised nothing. I *did* get the money Alex owed me though, which was good. Got to bolster your spirits where you can.

Broadway was crowded with people and slow meandering traffic. I watched them file past the window in front of me on the narrow sidewalk, sipping my single-origin, direct-trade, pour-over coffee.

None of the girls were prettier than Ellie.

There was only one more stop on my list, one final hope of a quick recovery: Sean and Gino's.

They lived conveniently close to me in an ugly building real estate agents call a 4-plus-1, or 4-and-1. It had four floors of apartments above one floor of parking. The color scheme was that of dentist's offices in Indiana; pale moss green, polyester brown. It reminded me of shelves in an old refrigerator, rusty, sort of moldy looking, all the oily, toxic crud dripping into the crispers below. There was Brady Bunch style landscaping out front though, which was a nice touch.

I went a few feet down on the shallow, curving, six-foot long steps to the double glass doors and pushed the button for 4D, then wiped my finger on my jeans.

"Yeah?" came the suspicious voice everybody uses when not expecting company.

"Hey, it's Michael." I couldn't tell whose voice it was.

"Ok. Michael who?" That's the other problem of showing up unannounced. My relationship with Sean and Gino was definitely a professional one. I came over when they called, that was it. We'd never even had a conversation that didn't directly involve me selling them something.

"Uh, you know," I said, not sure how to say it into a metal box standing outside, "Michael, your *guy*, you know."

"Oh, yeah, ok. Uh, I'll come down." I still couldn't tell who I was talking to. Sean and Gino basically sounded the same, even without speaking through an intercom. They were from the same town in Ohio, went to the same school and both dressed in whatever nondescript trend kept them from sticking out in a crowd; boot-cut jeans, or skinny jeans, or khakis, or plaid shirts, big, or too small. Gino was taller and skinnier while Sean was more square and muscle-y. Thinking of them and waiting to be buzzed in enhanced the bland, sterile feel of a college dorm their building gave off. The clicking sound of freewheel on a bicycle fit perfectly as a girl walked down the sidewalk behind me, helmet in hand. She wasn't very cute. Through the glass, I could see a row of tall narrow mailboxes and a community corkboard with names of moving companies and sublets.

It must have been Sean I had been talking to, because that's who came around the corner to push through the first set of doors. I reached out to grab the door, expecting to be let in, but he pushed through instead. I yanked my hand back just fast enough to leave it hanging in the air awkwardly, like when you try to swat a mosquito on somebody's arm you don't know, but it flies away and you try to turn it into a "Hey new buddy" back pat.

Only his head stuck out the door. He looked at my dangling hand. I looked at it. He decided to slap it gimme-five style. At the same time, I went in for a fist bump, then tried to pull it back, or read what he was doing and switch it? Our hands ran into each other uncomfortably. I looked down and away. Sean looked around to see who was with me.

"So," he said, not seeing anyone, "what's up? Gino call you?"

"No, uh," I hadn't prepared any lines. "No, I... just thought I'd stop by, see what you guys were up to."

"Uhh," he said, not in the stalling way I had, but in the purposely drawn out, none-of-your business kind of way. "We're just hanging out, man. Just got back from the ball game."

"Oh yeah? That's cool. We win?" The flood lights above the door tended to bunch and glare. I hadn't noticed the red rim around his eyes until he mentioned the baseball game. He'd definitely had a few.

"No, we don't win."

"Yeah," I said, as if I knew. "We'll get 'em next time." I put my hands in my pockets.

"Uhh, sure." His eyes lost me for a second. "So, what's up?" he said, with a small shrug of his thick knotted shoulders, hinting that I should get to the point.

"Oh yeah, uh...," I was hoping he'd invite me in. I wanted to get a look inside their apartment, to scope things out. I was trying to conduct an investigation here. "Well, you know, I was just wondering if, uh, if you guys needed anything?"

He nodded. "No, I think we're good, man. I mean, we got your number and stuff so...."

"Yeah, yeah, I know. I was just walking by, thought I'd see what you guys were up to."

"Yeah, that's cool, but I think we're good." He looked around again as if still not sure I was alone. "Or you know, one of us will call you."

"Yeah, cool..." What else can I say? Ask me in? "You guys doing anything tonight? Going out or anything?"

"Oh. Um...I don't think so. We kinda been drinking all day, pretty tired."

"Oh yeah, definitely." Shit. Nothing. "So you guys are good for now?" I tried getting a reading from his eyes, but the light was terrible. He looked tired. And not any closer to asking me in for a beer.

"Yeah, man, thanks for asking though." His body turned more away from the door. "Well, I think I'm gonna go back. Get some food."

"Yeah," I said, "I just ate. Had a red hot at Clark Dog."

"Ok. Cool....All right, Mike," he said, offering me his hand. "I'll see you later then."

"Yeah, definitely. You got my number."

He sort of smiled and went in.

I turned, shoulders slumped, to go home.

Chapter 8

I was in a quiet, side-street mood when I walked the rest of the way home. I meandered, zigzagged my way over to Pine Grove and followed it when it jogged the half block around a giant, newly redone apartment building on Surf. There was a street light out on my little half-block and the semi-darkness suited me just fine. A few steps in and my phone ruined the mood by lighting up and rumbling in my hip pocket.

I dug it out, looked at it, said "Hell-o," with an Eeyore inflection.

"Hey Mikey, it's Tim." Don't call me that.

"Hey," I said. "What's happening? You guys change your mind?"

"About what? The cheese, or the Siamese cats?"

"What? I don't—No about the needing stuff from me.'

"Oh, yeah. No. But we need to come see you."

"Sure, but if you guys need stuff, you know, I can't really help you out. Because, you know..."

"Yeah, yeah I know. It's not about that. Well, it is, but not like that. We want to talk to you about it, but not in the way you're talking about."

"Oh, ok," I said, somewhat confused. "Yeah, I guess not."

"Yeah, but that's what we want to talk about. Let's say an hour? That basement bar over by you on the corner?"

"Yeah, with the popcorn?"

"Yeah, that one. In like an hour."

I turned down the dark end of my alley and walked along the high brick wall closing in the picturesque courtyard of the building next to mine. The lights were on at Melanie's and I thought about taking some beer over after I'd showered.

Maybe there was a chance she'd still be in her pajamas. Maybe she'd let me lay my head on her breast while we drank and thought about my problems. Or maybe her boyfriend, Phil, was there, which wouldn't be nearly as much fun.

Up the back stairs, through the back door, and there was my busted lock with its sideways splintered grin to welcome me home. What fun.

I wedged the toe of a shoe under the door, keeping it mostly closed, and hit the shower.

Twenty minutes later, I felt measuredly better, but still not up to cleaning the looming mess that defined my apartment. Instead, I popped open the last beer in the fridge, sat down at the desk and threw my feet up, sipping gingerly, savoring the fine flavor of the cheapest beer I could get. Ahh. Then I got up again, turned out the lights and pulled the blinds open to stare out over the alley and the trees in somebody else's back yard.

When I was a kid, I used to sit in the dark and stare out the living room window at the lights going by on the highway a mile away over the newly cut cornfields. It wasn't anything as corny, or dramatic, as wishing to be in one of those trucks whisking me away to some other life. No, I liked living in the country when I was a kid. It was simply about someplace quiet to sit with my prepubescent thoughts while everyone else in the house screamed and laughed and yelled. Now, I liked living in the city. Or most things about it, anyway. I'd done the country thing, time to do the city thing. I opened the window a crack and put my feet up again to listen to city sounds and people walking by eight feet below.

That's when I heard something rustling outside.

It was quiet out, not much traffic in the alley. Nobody cutting through to catch the bus and too early for people to stumble back there to pee, puke, make out or snort coke, depending on the time of night. But it was still early and the bar next door hadn't started spilling smokers out the back yet.

There was a scraping noise. I held my breath and sat up, listening quietly. There it was again, like someone shuffling their feet slowly. Since the lights weren't on, I could look out knowing people couldn't see in. I stood up and tried to see into the dark shadows against the wall.

The sound was close. I moved off to the side and tried looking down, but it was coming from underneath my window by one of the cars parked tightly against the building. I couldn't see anything. I raised up on my toes for a better angle, my cheek against the glass, searching.

My phone erupted.

My heart jumped and my forehead butted against the glass as the suddenly bright phone vibrated and skated around, buzzing on the corner of my desk. The light reflected blue off the white paint on the walls. I jumped to silence it, quickly, as if afraid I'd been caught. But it was my house, I wasn't doing anything wrong. I controlled my breath.

The phone read, "Chris." I turned away from the window to answer it in a whisper, "Hey man, what's up?"

"Hello? Hey, Michael," he boomed. "You there? Hello?"

"Yeah, man—"

"What? Mike?"

I raised my voice an inch, cautiously. "Yeah, Chris, I'm here. What's up?"

"Oh, hey. Were you whispering? I thought you were there, but I couldn't hear you."

"No, why?" I said, at the ridiculousness of the thought. "I'm here what's up?"

"Anyway, we just got off the train. We'll be there in like five."

"Already? It's been like thirty minutes."

"I know, the train *actually* came right when we walked up. It does happen apparently. It's not just a myth."

"Crazy," I said, and he agreed.

I regretted having to slam the rest of my last beer. It tasted so good. But I did. I pulled my shoe from under the door and put it on my foot. When I pulled the door shut behind me, it sagged open again. I pulled it again. It sagged open. I slammed it. It sagged open. Fuck it.

Once in the hall, I thought briefly about going out the back way to check out the noise I'd heard. But it was probably just some homeless guy looking for cigarette butts, or a big rat looking to build a new home, lord knows there's plenty of them in that alley and plenty big enough to sound, and maybe even look human. Plus the bar was only halfway up the block on Diversey, going out the back would actually be the long way around. I turned down the door-studded hall, past the garbled yelling coming from 3C and out the front.

I used the front door so little that it gave me a kind of rush to step out into the immediate throng of activity. It wasn't New York City and I didn't have a doorman, but for a kid who grew up with cornfields on three sides of his house, it felt pretty damn cosmopolitan. It's true I preferred going out the back into the relative quiet of the alley, it's my nature, but I liked knowing that I had the choice. It was the reason I'd picked this apartment, in this neighborhood, before I realized I couldn't really pay for it.

The moment passed quickly though when a lady rammed into me while talking on her phone, almost pushing me into a guy asking people for change. I righted myself and walked on with purpose.

At the corner, I stepped a little out of the way and glanced down the street at the dark entrance to my alley. Had I heard something back there? Neh.

The basement bar on the corner is called Galway Bay, which might sound Irish-ish, but is one of the few bars in the area that wasn't trying to be. It's just your average underground dive bar peculiar in only one way; it has three very distinct smells. Down the steps is a large rectangular bar smelling like any other bar washed in spilt beer with a thin fog of burnt popcorn hanging in the air. Four guys sat on the far side facing the door, all of them a full generation older than Tim or Chris.

I got a PBR and carried it as fast as I could around the corner of the L shaped barroom, through the second area of smell; the bathrooms. For a place built in a basement, the bathrooms were strangely built on a rise, you had to go up a couple steps to get into them. And, once up and in the tiny bathroom with the cabinet hook in place to keep the door closed, you stood on soggy foot boards that seemed to float on a spongy substance of, well, I'm sure you can guess from the smell; piss soaked wads of flushed, dirty toilet paper sitting on top of logs of shit just strong enough to keep the floor boards from sinking under the weight of your footstep. Or that's what I imagined while holding my breath and trying to pee. I tried not to go at all when I was here, better to go out on the street and risk an indecent exposure charge.

Running quickly past that part of the bar, you turn right into the game area. A few people were playing Mario Kart on Super Nintendo projected against a square on the wall painted white. And the best part? The glorious smell of freshly baked bread wafting down through the floorboards from the bakery upstairs. An amazing contrast.

Tim and Chris were at a back table furthest from the bathroom, both facing me, watching a couple throw darts.

We shook hands and how-are-ya's and Chris leaned in resuming the conversation they were obviously having when I walked up.

"Look, here she goes again," he said, nodding his head toward the couple playing darts. He had white specs of popcorn dust stuck to the right side of his dirty plume hair. "She's totally sandbagging it. He sucks and she doesn't want to embarrass him."

"Kill his confidence," Tim informed me.

"Definitely a second date," Chris said.

"No," Tim said. "More like their fourth or fifth. They had sex last time and he didn't last long enough, got upset with himself."

"Why d'you say that?" I asked, turning around a bit to see better. "He looks alright to me."

"Nope, he sucks," Chris said, definitively.

"She's just doing a good job of making him think he doesn't," Tim said, absolutely.

I turned back and to face them. "How long you guys been watching those two?"

"Just a few minutes since we got here," Tim said.

"Look, it's obvious," Chris said too loudly. "She's way hotter than he is. Look how disappointed her face is when she misses."

"Totally faking it, poor shlub." Tim added.

"Anyway," I cut in. "What's up? What's the hot news? You guys hear something?"

Both of their faces went serious. Tim made creases in his childish forehead. They looked at each other deciding who would speak. Apparently it was Chris, who scratched at his sticky hair, grinding the popcorn bits in deeper. He leveled his eyes at me.

"We know who it was."

"Who broke into your place," Tim clarified.

"Ok. Who?"

They each looked around then, Chris leaned in, said, "Ian."

Tim followed quickly, "Yep," nodding his head, "Ian."

I let my neck relax and smiled thinly, not surprised. "Ok...what makes you think so, other than the obvious?"

"That's just it," Chris said, "the obvious, obviously. We all saw the way he was acting."

"Yeah, but—"

"But it's more than that," Tim jumped in. "You weren't with him as long as we were. You didn't see the way he was after you left."

"Did he hang around for a while after that? I would've thought he'd have left, after how awkward it all was," I said. "Hell, no offense, but I couldn't get out of there quick enough. And it's *my* problem we're talking about."

"I know, man," Tim said. "Believe us, we wanted him to leave. But he didn't."

"And didn't," Chris said, "and didn't."

"And you had to have noticed his eyes," Tim said to me. "They were all over the place, looking out the window and up the chimney and shit."

"And," Chris said, "the landlady was out in the hall sweeping or whatever—"

"Snooping," Tim put in.

"And she bumped the door with the broom or something—

"Slash microphone," Tim said.

"And you should have seen Ian freak. You would have thought a monster was coming to get him."

"He was running around, looking for a place to hide," Tim said. "It was weird. He's normally a pretty cool customer, you know that."

"Yeah," I said. "He obviously looked spooked to me too, but that doesn't mean he broke into my place. I mean, wouldn't he have been afraid of me?"

"He was acting pretty weird around you, man," Chris said.

Tim added quickly, "He was pretty defensive."

"And you hadn't even accused him of anything."

"That's why I think maybe something else was going on with him," I said, soberly. "Believe me, I want to think everybody did it. But something else seemed to be bothering him more than me."

"Yeah, but you didn't see the bag of weed he left at our place," Chris said.

"Well," I said, "in the state he was in, I wouldn't be surprised if he forgot his shoes."

"No, not like that," Chris went on. "He left it for us on purpose."

"Yeah," Tim said, "and it was what he said..."

They looked at each other nodding, letting it stretch out.

"Well?"

"He said, 'You guys keep this, for letting me chill. Been a long night. Think I can go home now.'"

"Guys, I don't—"

"It was like a quarter ounce, dude," Tim said. "Way too much to be courteous."

"Still," I said, with my thin smile in place. "I'm saying, *that* in no way means he broke into my place and stole all my shit. He wouldn't go directly to your house and give you a bunch of weed he just stole. It doesn't make sense."

Chris held his hand out. "Ok. Ok, but here's what we think," he said, getting confirmation from Tim. "He had someone else in on it with him. And maybe he came to *our* house to give himself an alibi. Like what you said. So we wouldn't suspect him."

"Or," Tim brought in, his eyes growing with conspiracy. "He was in with some other guys and he double crossed them."

"Shook them coming out of your place," Chris threw in.

"And came to our place to hole up for a while," Tim said.

Their theory hung over the table for a minute as they nodded, drank some beer and I mulled it over. It was a bit ridiculous, of course, but I guess I was happy to have someone on my side just the same.

"Well, guys, I tell you what," I said slowly. "That's definitely something to think about. And either way, I think I should probably talk to Ian again anyway, alone. There's definitely something up with him. And from what we saw, we should at least be worried, if not, suspicious."

Chris shook his head a bit, "I wouldn't want to go over there."

"Yeah," Tim said. "What if somebody's watching his place, waiting for him?"

I waved that off with the beer in my hand. "I don't think that's what's happening."

"Still," Chris said. "I wouldn't want to find out."

"Better be careful," Tim said. "Whether you think so or not, something's up with that dude."

We finished our beers and had another one. I tried to make some jokes about their theory, but they wouldn't budge. Around midnight, we headed out. They went down Diversey to the train and I went down Pine Grove toward the alley, not at all thinking about the noise I'd heard outside my window earlier. And especially not thinking about someone snooping, or watching my place. The street light was still out and the street seemed quieter because of it.

I rounded the corner in the relative darkness. Two bright lights jumped out at me followed by the glinting roof of a car.

Engine roared, tires barked.

I jumped out of the way as the car lurched up at me.

I didn't jump high, or far enough. The car clipped my left foot as it shot by, knocking my shoe off and spinning me in the air. My knee hit metal. I kissed the asphalt, landing hardest on my right shoulder. Tires squealed and barked again.

The car jerked to a stop right beside me. I could feel the heat from the engine. My left leg underneath. I twisted around and tried to scramble to my feet, but my sock was stuck under the wheel.

The interior light splashed out over me as the driver's side door swung open. I threw my hand up to shield my eyes from the light as Ian climbed out over me.

Chapter 9

"Mike! Shit! Fuck!" Ian's hands reached down at me, bent and bright in the harsh car light, dark shadows hanging from his palms. "You all right?"

A shrieking moan came out as I scurried back for the wall, my sock pulling off, stuck under the front tire like a dead rat.

"Jesus, you Ok?"

"Get away from me," I yelled. "You already got my money. What else do you want? You don't have to kill me!"

He stepped cautiously closer, gnarled hands still reaching. "What? Kill you? Money? What the hell are you talking about, kid?" He looked around, for witnesses probably. "What the hell you mean kill you? You Ok?"

I pushed away across the dirty alley as far as the brick wall would let me. My heart was fluttering too quickly, weakly. "Get away from me, Ian. I didn't do anything to you. I didn't tell anybody."

"Tell anybody what? The fuck you talking about, homey?" His narrow face was twisted up, confused. "I just want to talk to you, man."

"Talk? That's how you come to talk? By trying to kill me?"

"What are you talkin about, killin' you? It was an accident. I wasn't trying to hurt you."

"Bullshit! You just fucking hit me with your car, man. Don't tell me what you where trying to do. I'm walking along all normal, come around the corner and you punch it! You tried to run me over!" I pushed myself up the wall to a standing position, my hands at the ready.

"Mike! It was a accident! I didn't even see you. I didn' try to run you over. Would you chill? I need to *talk* to you, son. Not *kill* you."

"Bullshit."

"Mike, listen to what I'm sayin'."

"Then why try to run me over?" I said and stepped to the side, careful of the broken glass sparkling in the car light all around. "...You came to talk." I rested my naked left foot on top off my right shoe and surveyed the distance between me, my sock and my shoe. "You got a funny way of getting my attention."

"Would you knock it off with that shit. It was a accident!"

"Then why didn't you text me or call...shit. You didn't have to hit me."

"I did text you. And called.... Why would I call you to say I'ma come kill you?"

"Probably to cover up for it."

Ian relaxed his voice, put his hands out palms up, pleadingly. "Look, you know I ain't tried to kill you, man. Quit sayin that shit."

"You didn't have your lights on." I walked around him and yanked my sock from under the wheel and dragged it onto my bare foot. "You're waiting in the dark. I come around the corner. You charge me."

"I wasn't waitin' in the dark, damnit." He put his hands down. "I wasn't trying to kill you. Would you knock it off? I got something to talk to you about. It's serious."

"Oh, you mean more serious than getting run over by a fucking car!"

"Alright, man. Alright. I'm sorry." He turned around, closed the car door and leaned back on it patiently. "I did call and text. You didn't answer."

I hopped to my shoe on one foot like the ground was wet, not wanting to touch the pavement, or step on glass. After I got it tied, I checked my phone. One text, one missed call, no message. Oh.

My heart slowed and my fingers quit tingling. "I was across the street in the bar downstairs."

"I told you.... It was an accident. I really did come to talk."

"Still doesn't explain why you were driving with your lights out and punched it when I came around the corner."

"Jesus, Mike. Ok, I'll tell you....I was too restless, didn' wanna sit around waitin' for you to respond to my calls. So I come over and cruise by your spot. You ain't home. I wait. I was about to leave, started rollin', forgot to turn on the lights, checkin' my phone one more time. Bam! You pop out just as I hit the lights." He uses his hands to lay out the scene, one hand running into the other. "I freaked, hit the wrong pedal. Then slammed on the break..... Just like that."

I stared at his small eyes stuck in his long skinny head, looking for tells of lying.

"You understand me?" he said. "See how it happen?... We cool?"

I shook my head slowly. "I need a beer." I shook my head some more. "You want to park the murder machine there? I'll go get us some beer?"

"Yeah, Cool Mike. That's what I'm sayin'," he said, snapping his fist in his hand with a little clap sound. "And what's all this stuff about me taking your money. You think I'm the one broke in your place?"

"Forget it, just something somebody said. I was scared."

"Yeah, well, I got something to say about that."

"Yeah, yeah, let's get a beer first."

He held his hand out and I slapped it. He got back in his car and I went back around the corner for some beer. When I rounded the corner into the alley this time, I made sure to crane my head around to make sure nobody was coming at me. Ian was still parked in the alley, but further down behind my place with the flashers on.

"Fuck parking in this neighborhood," he said rhetorically, as we went up the back stairs into my apartment. "Damn, son." was the next thing out of his mouth. "You never heard of feng shui? Your mojo is way fucked up in here."

"Ha ha," I said, popping two beers. I pointed Ian to the desk chair and, while he sat, made a cursory motion of cleaning up, dropping a kitchen towel on the spilled milk. As I said before, I didn't have a lot of stuff, so I didn't have to work too hard. In a minute, the place looked basically like it had before my special visitors had arrived. I righted a stool, sat and pulled on my beer.

"Somebody really did bust your shit, huh?"

"Sure, pretend it wasn't you."

"Come on, Mike, that ain't funny. Who said it was me anyway?"

"It doesn't matter. People just talking...." He looked at me sideways. "But seriously," I said, "what was up with you today? You were tweakin' pretty hard."

He took a drink and shook his head. "Yeah, sorry 'bout that." He looked at the floor. "Ain't really been sleepin' much. Took some pills. Think it was the wrong ones though, know what I'm sayin'?"

"I guess...something up?" I said, gauging him. "You're usually a cool guy, you know. I was a little surprised."

"Yeah, well don't worry 'bout it too much. Nothin' got to do with you."

"Yeah, well, I've got trouble of my own...you know. Can't help but wonder if the two have something in common."

He looked at his shoes a minute. And at his beer, then shook it off. "Look, man, don't worry about that shit this mornin'. I was just kind of wiggin out, you know. Ain't been sleepin right." He rubbed his eyes for effect. "But listen, about your shit... That's what I came over here for. I got some ideas."

Do you now. My reconnaissance mission must have netted me a lot more than I thought. Here it was just a few hours later and this was the third person in as many telling me who had done it. I'd like to say my tone didn't change, but what came out was much quieter and had a few more ears on it. "Oh yeah? I'd certainly appreciate it."

"All right, check it." He perked up a little with the excitement of someone telling a secret. "Hear me out. I don't know how tight you guys are and shit, but I'm pretty sure I know who it was. I got my reasons."

I made the tumbling on-with-it motion with my hand, "Ok."

"I can tell you, without having anything on it..." He held it a second. "It was Alex."

I let out a breath. Alex.... First, Tim and Chris said it was Ian. Now, Ian is saying it was Alex. Ok. I scratched the back of my neck.

"Why him? Why not put it back on Tim and Chris?" Oh shit. I tried to pedal it back. "Or anybody else you—"

"Put it back? You mean them's the little bastards blamed—

"No, no. What?" Shit. Back pedal, back pedal. "No, I just meant," I fanned my hand around at the world in general, "like pick a name, you know, naming anybody else." Change direction. "Anyway.... So, Alex. Why Alex? I mean, what makes you say him."

Ian got that twisted look on his face again like he can't hear you. "I'm just sayin. I tellin you, it's him. I don't care what them other fucks say."

"What? No, they didn't say anything. It was an example, damn... But no, really, why Alex?"

"I told you to listen. You don't know him like I do. You can't trust him."

"But you're friends with him. Shit, you're better friends with him than I am."

He looked at his shoes again, and the side of my face. "Yeah, well. I'm just sayin, you should look into it. For yo'self."

"I already talked to him. I was over there right after I saw you guys."

"Yeah, and I bet he was really cool too. Probly even give you somethin to make him seem all straight, put himself ...above suspicion, or whatever."

"No, he didn't. He was cool, but," I remembered the money, "he gave me some money he owed me, but he already owed me that."

"See? Yeah. That's what I'm sayin."

"You got to give me something more than that though, Ian. You don't just show up and rat out your friends. I mean, what's up?" He started moving around in his chair. "You're acting all weird today and then you run me over. Now you're telling me Alex stole my shit. You got to give me something to go on, man."

I saw his face gaining color. The aluminum can made a small crinkling noise in his hand, but he wasn't looking at me. His eyes were seeing something on the wall that wasn't there.

"I'm trying to tell you, man. You can't trust that dude." The can crunched a little more. "You don't want to believe me, fuck it." He stood up. "Don't believe me."

"I'm asking why. Give me something to go on."

"Just check it out. I ain't saying shit, but I'm sayin shit, you know." He pointed his can at me. "And watch it. Word to the wise." He tilted back his beer and slammed it empty on the desk. "Whatever," he added and marched to the door. "Sorry I almost hit you." He crunched the door hard against the frame.

Almost hit me?

The blinds were drawn again so I couldn't see him, but I followed his footsteps out the back door, down the stairs to the slamming of the car door. I got up, turned out all the lights and pulled the blinds open. The alley was empty where his car had been. Wind blew the trees around in the yards on the other side of the wooden fence.

Chapter 10

Two beers later, my head started drooping. Leaning my chair back with my feet on the desk didn't seem like the best way to spend the night, waking from a bad dream like that could really hurt, or a good one for that matter. Plus, my feet were going numb.

I got up and pulled the blinds closed to keep daylight out until I was ready for it. Robotically, I pulled my t-shirt over my head, took my jeans off, let them fall on the carpet and stretched out on the low futon bed. It was *much* more comfortable than the desk chair and the sheets didn't dig in to the back of my ankles like the desk. Yes, I could sleep much better here.

Out in the hall, I heard someone's key grate in the back lock and then the suck of air as they pulled the door open. Simultaneously, my door kicked in its frame, clapping softly against the broken jamb. Damn. In my boozy sleepiness, I'd forgotten my door didn't close.

I slid off the bed, went to the closet mess, found the heaviest winter boot I could and used it as an anchor to hold the door closed.

Thirty seconds later, someone went out this time with the same kicking and clapping of my door. Damn, again.

I grabbed a flip-flop. It was thick enough to shove under the door and rubbery enough to catch and hold on the carpet. It was mostly better and I was back on the futon drifting off when two drunken idiots stopped at the back door to tell each other how much the loved one another. After a full minute of them confirming it, I yanked the door open, in my underwear, with red-ringed eyes, to kindly ask them to move along.

Please. Their faces puckered as they went out the door, then burst into laughter as they went down the steps.

The shoe-jamming business wasn't going to work. And drunk or not, I wasn't going to be able to sleep with an unlocked door in an apartment that had just been broken into. What options did I have?

I thought about knocking on Melanie's door, but it was pretty late, and maybe it was assuming too much to think she would let me sleep at her place. Or her boyfriend could show up and get the wrong idea. He worked weird hours. No, I decided I didn't want to impose on her like that. And it sounded a little bitchy to go crying to the neighbor girl because I was afraid of sleeping alone in my own apartment.

So, I decided to man up and pull my futon in front of the door. It held the door firmly shut and, though I still heard everything going on out in the hallway first hand, no one could get in without me knowing about it. I also decided another beer would probably go quite well with my new arrangements and took it to bed with me.

I propped myself against the wall listening to traffic in the hall and thinking about the absurdity of the whole situation. This time the night before, I was lying in bed propped up against a different wall with a delicate, beautiful, exhausted, sweaty naked girl lying on my chest. If Ellie were still up, maybe I could stay over at her place. That wouldn't be a sign of weakness, that would just be eagerness. I texted her, 'Hey you up? Out?'

I drank some beer, waiting. One of the problems with modern-day relationships is waiting for people to respond to text messages, especially early on. It can be a good thing if you're on the other end and don't feel like responding, you can always say you didn't get it until later. But when you're the one waiting it sucks. There was a good chance Ellie could be up, or out. She didn't have to be at work until nine.

I leaned back and pictured her, naked of course. Her thin arms and slight shoulders. Her palm-sized breasts with the nipples pointing slightly up. I drank my beer and thought of her neck, that was one of the things I'd been drawn to, her neck, so small, fragile.

Alex had taken me to a college party a few weeks ago. You can get rid of a quarter-pound at one of those things if you're lucky, which was mostly why I'd befriended Alex to begin with. But it wasn't a big party, more casual, so I abandoned my drug-selling endeavors and got down to enjoying myself.

I was working my country charm on a couple of doughy girls when Alex beckoned me over to sit with him and a girl twice as attractive as either of the ones I was busy impressing. I hated to leave them, but excused myself and promptly wiggled onto the couch next to Ellie. Alex informed me I'd be interested to hear how Ellie sold paintings in bulk to large hotel chains. I wasn't sure what to do with the information at first, but it was enough. He smiled his smile, satisfied with himself, and left us.

Ellie. She was everything I'd been looking for. For a second, I wondered how Alex could walk away from her. But I didn't think about it long. She had me going. Small, beautiful, coy for a minute, sassy the next. Delicate and strong. Stylish and worth listening to. She was every reason I had moved to Chicago incarnate, the exact kind of girl I'd hoped to meet. And there I was talking to her, Ellie, and she was responding.

But she *wasn't* responding to my text at the moment. My eyes were getting heavy again. The lovers came back, stopping outside my door long enough to mock me with slurpy kisses coupled with gross moans. It's amazing how repulsive it is when it's not you.

I thought some more about Ellie, clothed and naked, then naked some more. The night before was the first time we'd actually slept together. I couldn't wait to do it again. Her bed was so soft. She fit so well into the crux of my arm. I slid down onto my pillow. Her sheets were so soft and clean. Her skin was so soft and clean. She smelled so good.

Chapter 11

The next morning it took me three hours to chase down the building engineer, as they call them up here, to get my lock fixed. While waiting around for him, I decided I should get on Craigslist and send out some resumés. But after pacing back and forth and staring out the window for a while, I couldn't convince myself it was important enough to dig out the laptop my ever-so-thorough burglars hadn't taken with them.

I did manage to do a better job of straightening up though. By the time the maintenance guy showed up with a new lock and wood to replace the doorjamb, the place was back to its bare bachelor neatness that is easily achieved when you don't own anything. He was still there working when it came time for me to go meet Alex at a sports bar near his place in Uptown. The guy said my old key would still work the lock and I didn't need to stick around.

The bar was up near the Aragon on Broadway, a dozen, or so, blocks from Alex's apartment. It was a big place with a huge U-shaped front bar and TV's surrounding. They claimed it wasn't a sports bar and had motorcycle posters on the walls and framed pictures of Bettie Page and Vargas girls to prove it. But it was all thought out too much, too staged. And you could tell their busiest nights were game nights.

Alex was on the far side of the big bar playing with his phone, the way everyone does when made to wait more than fifteen seconds. It was still early evening and the bar was mostly empty, so they filled all the extra space with the properly themed music of Morrissey and early Elvis.

I walked around to meet him. He was wearing a '90s-looking shirt, three buttons undone, with faded geometric neon shapes and khakis; always comfortable and cool. I was wearing a v-neck t-shirt that needed to be washed two days ago. He didn't look up until I was almost next to him, though aware of me the whole time.

"My man," he said with a big warm grin and held out his hand.

I slapped it. "What's happenin?"

"Shit. You? What's the word?"

"Aw, you know," I said, "the usual."

The bartender finished texting before she turned pliable, soft eyes on me. I ordered a beer and was given a long view all the way down to her bellybutton when she leaned over into the cooler to get it, and leaned over again to get the glass. It was a practiced move and probably worked really well. I tipped her an extra dollar.

"Nice place, huh?" Alex said when I finally looked up.

"Yeah, good beer," I said, pouring beer into the glass. "You wanna get a table? Little privacy?" I motioned with my head.

"Oh. Yeah, alright," he said, then smiled again. "Sounded like you had something to talk about and I guess you do." He used his ring finger to swipe hair off his man-brow. It's a move that always looks feminine, but not with him. He pulls it off somehow, managing to only make it look cool, to make you think maybe you should grow your hair out too.

"It's nothing that serious. Just seems more, you know—." I let it trail off, leading the way.

We slipped into a booth and Alex looked at me levelly. "So, what's up, Mike? You look, I don't know...kind of tense." He said it like it was a disease.

"Yeah, well, I didn't say anything when I was by your house yesterday. You know, all the guys there and shit. But, well, I'm having a hard time." I paused, looked down at my beer before watching him when I said, "Yeah, somebody broke into my place the other night. Stole all my shit." His eyes went from warm expectant to soft concern and his eyebrows followed obediently. "And you know what I mean," I added more quietly.

"Shit man," he said, sympathetically. "That's tough. They get your money too?"

"Yeah, man, everything. That's part of why I came to see you last night."

"To see if I heard anything or whatever? But we were all getting ready to go out."

"Yeah, so I didn't bring it up, too many people—"

"Wait, you don't... You didn't come over last night to see if I had it?" He said, with no trace of the nice guy smile.

"No, no, no." I sort of lied. "I came over to see if you had the money, which you gave me, for that last sack. I mean, they took all my money and I need what I can get, you know? In fact," steering away from that, "what I wanted to talk to you about..." I glanced around the bar, more for effect than concern, and said, "You know Ian right?"

"What? You think he did it?" He said, in a strained whisper.

"I don't know, I don't think so, but somebody told me he was acting kinda weird. And that maybe I should look into it."

"Did you?"

"A little. I mean, he came to see me." Alex started nodding in expectation. "Came to see me and almost ran me over with his car."

"What? He tried to kill you?"

"Huh," I smiled, "that's what I said. But it wasn't as dramatic as all that. It was an accident. I think."

"Shit, someone tells you he broke into your place and then he runs you over? That's some kind of accident."

"Yeah, yeah, I know, but listen," I said, waving it off. "What I wanted to ask you," I paused to let the joke pass, "you know Ian right?"

His eyebrows got confused again. "What do you mean?" he said. "You know I do."

"Yeah, but I meant more in the way of, like, you *know* him, like, better than I do."

"Oh, well, yeah. Why? You want me to talk to him? See if I can find out?"

"No, it's not that, at least not right now... It's just, well," I squinted my eyes as if looking into a storm. "He said *you* did it."

A smile instantly broke fully across his face as he nodded in acceptance. "He did, did he?"

It hung in the air there, floating between us like an invisible balloon. We both watched it for a while before I broke it. "Yeah," I said with apology in my voice. "That's why I asked how well you know him."

It didn't take him long to decide what to say, though I did see a couple of other thoughts run across his mind. "I can't believe he'd say something like that to you." He said, slowly, "I'm not surprised he said it really, but to bring you into it isn't really—I just don't." He stopped there.

"What do you mean 'bring me into it?' I'm in all the way. This shit's my life right now. I mean, bring me into what?"

"It's not that. I don't," he said, all suspicious like, "I don't know how much I need to tell you."

If it's got to do with my money, I wanted to scream. "Look, Alex, my apartment was broken into and all my shit was stolen. This is pretty serious to me, about as serious as I can get. Now, I'm not trying to stick my nose in and shit, but if whatever you're talking about affects me, than start talking."

"Ok," he said. "Ok. Don't get all excited." He took a second to show me he was collecting his thoughts, then it was his turn to squint at me. "Alright. I'm just gonna lay it out, then you can put it together.

"I've known Ian for a couple of years, basically since I moved to the city for school. A couple of months ago, he came to me with an offer, like a business deal, to go in on a bunch of weed with him." Hmm, language I could understand. "He's from Arizona, if you didn't know, and he says this friend of his can get bulk weed at ridiculous prices, good shit too, not shwag-type stuff. So, I think about it for a couple days and, fuck it, about a month ago, we go in together to buy fifteen pounds."

"Wow," I said, wide-eyed, "that's a lot of weed."

"Yeah. It's not big time or anything, but for a couple of dudes, yeah, it's a lot. And supposedly good shit too."

"Supposedly? Why supposedly? And where is it now? You guys still buying from me. Didn't you get it?"

He squirmed in his seat a bit, suddenly uncomfortable and his neck seemed to go stiff. "I gave him the money, twelve thousand dollars, but I never saw a damn thing from it."

"Oh. Ow…. What happened?"

"He said his guy got busted coming across the border."

"But you don't believe him?"

He shrugged.

"Did he have money in it too?"

"Supposedly. He said he had ten grand in."

"But you don't believe him?"

"Well, I can't exactly check the tracking number, can I?"

"Shit."

I sipped my beer feeling uncomfortable. What had I stepped in? I'd only known these guys about a month. They never let on like anything this big, and divisive, was going on within their little circle. But I guess I was just the new guy, the guy they got weed from.

The barroom floor started to feel sticky under my feet. I started thinking about Ian's performance yesterday morning and wondering if anybody else was involved. Ian's nerves had seemed pretty raw. Was there a third party? Someone pushing harder, asking more questions than Alex was? There was some shit going on. My mouth felt dry and the beer wouldn't fix it.

"So, are you saying you think Ian did this? And now he's trying to put it off on you?"

His eyes didn't change, but a slight shudder rode over his broad slumped shoulders.

"I don't know, man," he said, humorlessly, "but I'm not so sure my money ever made it to Mexico. I'm not sure my money ever left Chicago. How could I know? I trusted him and I got fucked." There was some emotion behind that word. "So just take that into consideration. That's all I'm saying."

"Did you confront him about it?"

"Of course, I asked. But there's nothing that can really be proved. I can't go to the police. And, he says he lost ten thousand on the deal too, so?..."

"And you guys are still cool? I mean there's nothing between you guys?"

"I mean, of course, there is. I'm suspicious. And he keeps coming around trying to smooth things over. Talking about saving up more money and going again...." He was trying to get his smile back. "But there isn't any more money." When it came, the smile had an edge on it. "And now you say you lost some."

The focus in his eyes changed. "Aw, well," he said, and raised his glass, "you know what they say about friendships and business."

Yeah, I guess so. I needed to go think this through. We shook hands and mumbled see-ya-laters.

I had Tim and Chris telling me Ian did it. Ian telling me Alex did it. Now Alex telling me Ian stole twelve thousand dollars from him.

Who was I supposed to believe?

The lake was only a ten-minute walk from the bar and I needed it. There was still a touch of fading blue in the dark sky, but the lights were taking over. I stood on the concrete ledge looking south over the blackening water at the twinkling downtown skyline.

Waves came in, touched the wall and went back out, running into each other. It's amazing how pretty the city looks. And it's crazy how separate the idea of it is from the lives of the people in it.

Chapter 12

My gut feeling was to take these new accusations straight back to Ian, but when I called, he didn't pick up. I pulled myself away from the tranquility of the shoreline and made my long, canoe feet take me back to the train. The sooner I got this whole mess over with, the sooner I could go back to enjoying my new city with slow strolls along the lake, maybe with Ellie next to me, sharing a bottle of champagne, sitting on the edge with our feet dangling over the water...

I needed to talk out the new situation and see what it had in it. I couldn't talk to Ellie about it. She didn't know about the weed, or my recent troubles, and I liked it that way. I liked having her separate; floating up there on her peaceful, serene little cloud of wonderfulness. Melanie didn't answer her phone when I called either, probably still at school. So, it was back to Tim and Chris. I'd never spent this much time with them in so few days but, they seemed to always be around and I didn't have enough friends to be picky about it.

The sandwich board outside the bar below their apartment in Lincoln Square said it was trivia night with a thirty-dollar bar tab as top prize. I rounded the corner, no smokers out yet, and buzzed 2A. The door buzzed open without any word from the metal box. I'd called ahead this time. And as soon as I'd pushed the door shut behind me and raised my foot to the first stair, the door to 1A opened. The land/cleaning lady stepped out carrying a tiny CVS bag of trash, like from the bathroom, and eyed me with her voodoo stare. I made my steps lighter and crept on, telling myself not to look back.

Tim opened the door at the top of the stairs wearing a baggy button down shirt, untucked and wrinkly. It was checked in the sort of out-of-date pattern you find in thrift stores. He beamed a shining white smile at me and said, "Brooksy!" then sang out, "Brrookseee," in a stage-musical baritone voice with a trill on the end of it. I shook my head, where do I find these people? No wonder the landlady thought they were suspicious. He stuck his hand out. I took it and he pulled me in close to give me the one-armed bro hug. But instead he stuck two rigid fingers into the soft spot on my side just under my ribcage. Damnit.

I buckled reflexively, but straightened quickly, pulling my hand away. He laughed hugely and stepped forward at the same time to close the door behind me. My knee unconsciously jerked up to protect my balls from attack. Tim backed up on his toes and threw his hands up in a whoa-buddy gesture.

"Hey, easy now," he said, still chuckling, while I looked around embarrassed.

"Jesus Christ. How old are you?" I said, between head shakes.

"Aw, come on." He put a hand to his heart as if hurt, then laughed again and clapped the friendly hand on my back. "So what's happening? Did you talk to Ian?"

"Actually, I did. He came by my place late last night and he—"

Right then, the door opened up again. I had to step to the side to get out of the way.

"Hey hey, Mike," Chris said as he came in.

Tim didn't move to make room for him to get in. Chris shut the door behind himself out of habit. I stood squished between the two them looking for a place to step. We were all stuck in a little huddle too close for comfort, Tim obviously the cork. I thought for a second he was going to wrap us both up in a big family bear hug, but Chris leaned forward and sort of moved to come in farther. Tim stayed fast, smiling dopily at us both like nothing was happening, enjoying the company. I stepped to the side a bit, but couldn't really move much because of the wall Tim had already backed me up against. Chris inched between us politely, careful not to step on my toes. He hoisted the six-pack he was carrying in a plastic bag in front of him, and finally broke through saying to me, somehow without showing annoyance, "Did the landlady check you out? I saw her coming back around the corner when I came in."

"Yeah," I said, following him into the room. "Right when I hit the stairs, she came out with some trash."

"Yep," he said. "Little tiny bag? With, like, three Kleenexes in it? That's her move. Every time somebody buzzes.... She's so paranoid it's amazing."

"So," Tim yelled and clapped his hands. "Our old friend Ian paid our buddy, Michael here, a little visit last night."

Chris's eyes opened wide. "Oh, yeah?" he said, anticipating a juicy story. "No shit? What happened? You guys duke it out? Fight to get your stuff back?"

"No, I didn't get my stuff back," I said, quietly to tame the sudden fanfare. Then more loudly, "But...he did try to run me over with his car."

"What?" Chris said, exaggeratedly.

"Hah! So he did do it" Tim yelled, and smacked Chris on the arm. "You owe me twenty bucks!" Then back to me, "He did it and then tried to rub you out?"

"Rub me out?" I said. "No. But that's what I thought too, when I saw it was him."

"You saw him? You know it was him for sure?"

"Yeah," I said, "he stopped."

"He stopped?" Tim said, "Did he try to stab you too?"

"What? No. He didn't stab me. He—"

"So, he denied it? After you knew it was him?" Chris said, giving it pause. "How could he deny it after that?"

"Actually, I don't think he really denied it—"

"Hah, see," Tim said, again.

"But he said hitting me was an accident. And I believe him about that."

"But what about him breaking into you place?" Chris said.

Tim said, "Did he say that was an accident too?" Then mimicking Ian, "Yo, son, I knock on yo' do' and it jus open."

"No, Tim," I said. "In fact, he told me somebody else did it."

"What? Who?"

I waited long enough to get their full attention. "Alex."

"Oh," Chris said, without surprise.

"Huh," said Tim, blinking, not ready to buy it. I thought they'd be more excited. "He say why Alex?"

"Yeah, what's Alex got to do with it?" Chris said, still in a flat expressionless voice. "Did he give you a reason? Or just pulling names out of a hat?" Then he clapped his hands brightly. "To cast doubt on himself!?!"

"Well, he did give me a reason, but I wanted to ask you guys something first, before I get into it."

"Ok," Tim said, making get-on-with-it hand circles. "What?"

"Let's sit down second," I said. "I might have more than one question."

"Jesus Christ," Tim said, impatiently. "Would you like a pillow for your back too. Put your feet up maybe?"

"No thanks, but I would take one of those beers," I said, pointing to the bag as Chris turned toward to the kitchen.

We sat down at the long, six-person dinner table that designated the end of the large, open living room as the dining room. It was a beautiful, big table and matched the built-in hutch so well it could only have come with the apartment. No one in their right mind would ever try to move that thing in, or out.

Chris came back, passed beers around and put down a small metal tray with weed and papers spread out on it. He sat and busied himself with rolling a joint.

"Alright," Tim said, all things now in place, "You were saying...."

"Let me ask you something. Did Ian ever sell you guys weed?" I said, as we all unconsciously looked at the tray of weed in front of Chris. "Like before I came along?"

"Yeah, sure, all the time," Tim said. "He was our guy."

"Well, when was the last time? I mean, why are you guys getting it from me now? And Ian too, along with the rest of you guys?"

They looked at each other trying to remember, not seeing the importance. "I don't know, I guess it's been more than a month, or so," Chris offered, breaking up weed.

"Yeah," Tim agreed, "it seems like a while, but I guess it's been six weeks anyway. Why? What's it matter?"

"Do you know where he gets it from? I don't mean names or anything, but like around here or...?"

Chris said, "Oh, you mean, was he getting it from back in Texas or wherever?" There was a pause. We all watched Chris's fingertips twisting nuggets of weed into crumbs. And finally I saw it; a knowing glance passed quickly between them. I couldn't tell if they knew where I was going with this, or if it was a suspicion of their own confirmed.

"Yeah," I said, watching them both stare at the weed Chris was dropping in a line on a folded paper. "Alex told me he was bringing it in from Arizona, where he's from."

"I heard that once," Tim said, looking back at me again, "but you don't ask too many questions about that sort of thing, you know."

"No, I know. I'm just trying to get a feel for what Alex told me." I paused again, feeling out the room. There was definitely a hit on something surrounding Ian and his weed. But I couldn't tell if they knew something, or if they had only suspected something, and I had piqued their interest.

I took up a different line. "Do you guys know if Alex and Ian are, like, good friends? Like, do they hang out or whatever? Pick up chicks together, or?"

Chris licked and twisted the joint. "Sure, I mean, I don't know how much they hang out, but we all chill at parties and shit."

"And I know Alex used to get weed from him too," Tim said, "'cause we've all talked about it. How good it is and shit, you know. "How it makes your wig float.""

Ok. "Have you noticed a change lately in the way they are to each other?" I asked. "Like, recently, since, say around the time Ian ran out of weed and you guys met me?"

"I don't know...," Tim said, and sat back to think about it as Chris lit the joint. He puffed on it a couple times to get it going and passed it to me.

I waved it off. "I'm good, man. I have to keep my head straight. I can't figure out what to do, but I have to do *something* after this."

"I don't know," Tim said, staying surprisingly on task. "They came to that party together the other night. Didn't they?" he asked Chris.

"Yeah, I guess," Chris said, kind of looking off. "But they didn't really talk that much though."

"But they did come together," Tim confirmed.

"But what are you getting at?" Chris asked me, directly. "I mean, what did he say?"

We were at the heart of it now.

I took a breath and said, "Alex told me, ...and don't go splashing this around," I pointed a cautionary finger at each of them. "Alex said Ian screwed him out of a bunch of money, like thousands. He said they went in together to get some weed from Ian's buddy in Arizona, said they'd been working on it for a while, then, when the deal went down, the dude got busted." I paused, for effect. "That was it. No weed, no money."

"No shit?" Chris in a squeaky voice of inhaled smoke.

"Really?" Tim said. "Like how much?"

"I don't know, but it must have been a bunch."

"Jesus," Tim said. "And he doesn't think it's true? He thinks Ian stole the money?"

"Or his buddy did," I said. "Or they split it. I don't know, I want to ask Ian about it, but I can't get ahold of him. I mean, he probably lost a bunch of money too."

"Fuck," Chris said, sounding high and astonished. Judging from their reactions, I was sure they hadn't known, but had suspected something was up.

"Huh," Tim said. "So he took Alex's money and if he stole your money…. Or?" He gave it squinty-eyed emphasis, "Maybe he did lose a bunch of money too and that's why he stole your shit?"

"Yeah," Chris agreed. "Maybe he was trying to get back his losses and set Alex up for it. 'Cause I'm sure he knows Alex thinks he should get his money back."

"Yeah, and that's a weird position to be in," I said with obvious self-pity. "What do you do when you put money in and the shipment gets busted, or stolen, say? You can't exactly go to the police with it."

"Exactly," Tim said. "But you can't really expect the other guy to pay you back. I mean, this isn't the mob, this is business between friends."

"Yeah, that's why you don't do business with your friends," Chris said.

"Or you accept the loss," I said. "Drug dealing *is* kind of like gambling after all, there definitely aren't any guarantees." We let that sink in. Then I reminded myself that someone had actually *stolen* my money and weed, there was no gambling involved. The two situations were very different; one was taking a risk, the other was straight-up malice.

Then, I got back on track.

"But wait," I said. "What I really want to ask you guys is this: Do you think Ian would do it? I mean, you already think he broke into my place, but do you think he would purposefully screw someone over like that? I mean, he says some corny shit sometimes, the way he talks, but I never got a bad feeling from him, like I couldn't trust him."

"I don't know," Tim said, visibly thinking. "He's never shorted us on a bag."

"Yeah," Chris agreed, "he is always honest about that, that's kind of why we stayed friends with him on the side."

"But you ratted him out to me?"

"Yeah, but that's different," Chris said, waving it away with stoned indifference. "He was acting all weird. You saw him. And he was definitely jacked up on pills, or something. You never know about people like that. Hell, he left his bag here." He picked it up to show me. "Said we could keep it, like it was no big deal, like it was free."

"Yeah," I challenged, "but if he was a dealer before, he would be in the habit of giving a little away here and there, like a bartender buying people drinks. It *is* basically free to a point."

"And," Tim said, with his head down, "we told you because we were... maybe a little scared of him after that. And we thought if we helped you out, we might get, you know, a little reward." He looked up at me with a boyish smile on his hairless face. "You know, if you got everything back all right."

Chris added, "That, and we were pretty stoned, and it sounded sort of exciting."

I shook that off. "Alright, but anyway, seriously, do you believe what Alex said? Do you think Ian would do that?"

After some red-eyed consideration, Tim said, "I don't know, man, I guess I don't trust Alex any more than I trust Ian, probably less."

"Yeah, I'll agree with that," Chris said. "Something always seems kind of fake with Alex, like he's putting something over on you. Ian will come over and hang out, chill. Alex wouldn't do that. You're *his* friend, he isn't *your* friend. You know what I mean?"

I weighed those things in my head.

"Yeah. I don't know what to think."

I finished my beer and stood.

"Well, thanks guys. I'll keep you posted. I'm gonna try to track Ian down. I think I should ask him directly, give him a chance to defend himself. And hopefully not get myself killed in the process."

Chapter 13

Ian's apartment was a stop back toward the city on the Brown Line. His building was on Wolcott, but the back of the building, and presumably his back door, faced the train as it came rumbling and screeching into the Montrose station. I sat on the right side and tried to guess which apartment was his, but seeing as I'd never been back there, coupled with the fact that the backs of all the buildings basically looked the same, though alternately equipped with wooden fire escapes and newer, black-painted steel ones, it was impossible to tell which one was his. I had tried calling him and texting and had gotten nothing back. I don't know what his deal was, but I could feel pressure building behind my eyes, could feel my pulse thumping in my temples.

People always say the first twenty-four hours are the most important in kidnapping cases. With stolen money, it can only be worse. I had to start getting somewhere. Like now. Ian had been pulling some weird shit. I had no way of knowing which version of him I was going to get. And if he wasn't home, I was going to have to do *something*. I couldn't wait around anymore. I don't know.

If I let my imagination go, it didn't have to go far before I could see the opportunity in Ian's not being home.

Could I really get in anyway?

Every kid tries to pick a lock, or use a credit card to let himself in somewhere he isn't supposed be. We've heard about it too much to not be curious enough to try. Half the kids on my basketball team knew how to get into the school gym on Saturdays when no one was there, even though most didn't have the balls to actually go in. And I'd found out multiple times that there was always a window unlocked in my house growing up. I'd lock myself out, or lose my keys hunting crawdads in the creek and have to get creative, be resourceful. Or wait the four hours until my parents came home to find me sitting on the steps and my chores not done.

The thought brought a childish grin to my face, whether it was nostalgia or anticipation I couldn't say. Maybe just plain stupidity. The idea started to stick in my mind like a game, like a challenge almost. It was time for a ground mission, a covert mission. Clandestine operations in the face of wrongdoing!

Yeah, a covert mission to recover my stolen goods. Covert, I like that word. It's so loaded.

I couldn't let it go. It was stupid. Of course I wanted Ian to be home. I needed to ask him directly. No more hearsay, no more beating around the bush.

He wasn't going to be home though. He hadn't answered any attempt to contact him. Was it possible? Could I let myself in? That larcenous grin tickled my mouth again.

Light from the street lamp on the corner faded as I turned down Wolcott. Hollow tugs pulled at my nerves. Once I cleared some overhanging trees, Ian's building came fully into view. His apartment was on the third floor, the top floor on the far side. The windows were all dark.

A short, black, iron fence ran along the front of the building with an archway leading into the courtyard. One central cement walkway bisected two sundried, dog-piss-scorched brown lumps of grass in the center of the U-shaped, yellow-brick building. Shorter concrete paths ran off to four doors, two on each side and two at the T that bent to the main doors in the bottom part of the U. I took the first small path on the left, nearest the front.

There was no foyer and, having been here several times to drop weed off, I knew a hard push on the front door worked just as well as a key. I glanced quickly at the street and behind me, a couple of professional types walking past on their way home, talking and looking ahead.

Without hesitation, as if I belonged, I pushed through the door and started to climb the short turning flights of stairs. The stairs were carpeted and shallow with just five stairs per flight. The going was quick and painless. By the time I got to the third floor, I was barely even breathing hard. I gathered myself and knocked softly on 3F.

I knocked harder.

He wasn't home.

I tried to stop myself from rubbing my hands together, manically, like an evil, mischievous bastard, shoulders hunched up, hands close to my face. But I couldn't. Something about the gesture really does help you concentrate and give you courage, especially when you're doing something you know you shouldn't be.

Sure, I didn't know if Ian was the one who had actually broken into my apartment, but I needed to get some answers, to start clearing things up. Ian was just as likely to be the culprit as anyone else. *And* he wasn't home.

Had I wanted this all along? Had I known I was going to do this from the first time he didn't answer his phone? It wouldn't surprise me. I'd always loved sneaking around in the dark, breaking into city pools, TPing the principal's house.

And I just didn't know who was telling the truth, or half of what was even going on, apparently. I mean, I wasn't going to steal anything, just have a look around. There's no need to feel guilty. Or like I was even breaking the law, really. I was just here looking for something I'd lost. That's it. If I didn't find it, no harm done. And who knew? Maybe he had fallen down, or choked on something and was in there dying, waiting on someone to rescue him. Maybe I would end up a hero?

I took the jiggly old doorknob in my hand and turned it as hard as I could, hoping it might pop. I leaned my weight into the door and shrugged against it a couple times to test its strength, but the dead bolt was fastened and held it steady. I took a step back and sized it up. The door felt solid enough, but if I could get that little strip of wood on the inside to give, I might be able to break it open.

I waited a second, listening down the stairs to make sure no one was coming or going. Satisfied, I squared my shoulders, positioned my feet and reared back. I kicked the door hard beside the top lock.

Nothing. Not even a shudder.

Immediately, the lock in the door behind me, across the hall, rattled and turned.

The seriousness of the situation congealed all around me in that one, quick instant. The reality of it crowded around me thick and heavy like humidity. The close, grey-carpeted stairway with its beige-turned-pink walls closed in. I had been like a kid playing at breaking into your own house, with no consequences, and imaginary danger, make believe trouble with your brother playing sheriff and your best friend breaking into the garage to set you free.

But that sound. The clicking of a lock behind me, a sound *I* hadn't made, brought the reality of the situation banging in.

Real life and a real person, who could call the real cops. Fuck.

In slow motion, before I could bolt, the door opened and a middle-aged guy in sweatpants stuck his head out.

Act quick!

With no place to go, I shivered and leaned in to knock on Ian's door, again, as if that was all the guy had heard. My arm was solid as steel with nerves and fear. I knocked loudly, as loudly as I could. The sharp hardness of the wood jarred my knuckles, and helped ease the tension coursing through my body. I banged again, much louder than necessary, but with each knock convincing myself I was supposed to be there, that nothing had happened, that I had every right to be there. I hadn't done anything wrong at all. I just came over to visit my friend Ian, see how he was doing. Nothing wrong with that at all.

So I turned to look at the guy the way anybody would and let indignation roll in across my brow, astonished at being interrupted. He squinted his eyes at me, then closed the door, slowly and suspiciously, angry without saying anything.

A long sigh ran up my throat and out my nose and mouth. Conscious of probably being watched through the eyehole, I turned slowly away with an oh-well shrug and reached for the stairs. But I was not done. I'd let the sweatpants guy think I was going home, but I hadn't exhausted my options yet. I couldn't get in through the front door, and Ian wasn't home, but I wasn't giving up. It would have been a lot easier if he was there, I guess. But he wasn't. And I still needed to know if he had my shit. I didn't want to steal anything. I'm not a criminal. I just wanted back what was mine.

I'd had my first scare. That guy opening the door had shattered my world in a way, but it was my first time, adrenalin had me going. I'd gotten wrapped up in my imaginary world and the guy in the sweatpants had brought me out of it. Had shown me, theoretically, and in my own mind, that this thing was for real, that real stakes were involved. Hell, for that second, when the lock was twisting and my world breaking, *I* had felt like the bad guy, expected to be sent away and punished the way bad men are. But fuck that. I was here to get my shit back. Someone, probably Ian, had stolen stuff from me and I was going to get it back. *He* was the bad one, *I* was the one setting it straight. Sure, the police might not see it that way, but they weren't here, were they? So, *whatever*. There was another way in this place.

I stumbled, determinedly, back down the steps to the sidewalk. Around the block, a wide alley ran between Ian's row of buildings and the train overhead. Warehouses backed up to the underside of the tracks and loading docks ranged among parking spaces between the huge, dirty- steel supports.

A car turned down the alley at the other end, bathing me in headlights. I tried to walk coolly along, one foot in front of the other, to Ian's back gate. Nothing unusual happening here. It's easy to blend in in the city, people are always out and about. Walking in alleys is just something people do, especially in an alley with parking.

But I couldn't shake a nagging guilty feeling. Before I was giddy with innocent anticipation. Now, I felt suspicious like a filthy criminal, dirty with just the thought of breaking into someone's house. Damnit. I was the one who had been wronged. I wasn't going to screw anyone over who hadn't done anything to me. If Ian didn't have my stuff, I sure as hell wasn't going to take his. But I had to find out. Now. And those damned car lights felt like x-rays seeing right through me. Boring clear through my confident façade and exposing my naked intentions of breaking and entering, of committing dirty crime. I threw my hand up to block out the light like a vampire disgusted by, and shielding himself from, the sun.

Finally, the headlights swerved off of me into a parking spot just on the other side of Ian's building. The interior light came on. I slowed my pace, watching the lady inside collect her things, then climb out ahead of me. I lagged back long enough to watch her walk the opposite way to a building further down the block.

There was a six-foot tall, chain-link fence running the length of, and across the back of Ian's building, but the gate was missing. Two sections of new, wooden fire escapes stood tall above me; one section down the length of the building with a staircase in the middle and another smaller section at the end for the forward-facing apartments, like Ian's, with a separate staircase. Bright white, naked porch lights shone beside every door.

I paused to see if anyone was around, looking down at me from the second or third stories. I knew this was the right building because I had counted, so Ian's apartment was at the top of the far, smaller section. I nodded in determination and strode forward confidently. I climbed the wooden stairs up to

Ian's place hoping something would come to me by the time I got up there, a great plan, a way in.

Nothing did, but a lot of heavy breathing. These stairs weren't as easy as the ones in front. And I swear there were more of them. No wonder people in the city are skinny.

Once I got to the top, I put my hands on my knees and looked back in the direction I'd come. Past the train tracks, which ran about level with where I stood, lights flickered in buildings as far away as Uptown. It was impossible not to notice the sky and the steady row of airplane lights lining up, jaggedly aiming for what must be O'Hare Airport. And as a harsh reminder of my near heart attack, the Sweatpants Guy's back door was just a few feet behind me again, staring at me with its stupid flat face. But I'd had the shit scared out of me already, tasted that first realization of what I was doing wasn't legal. I was going to check this place out.

First things first, I licked my fingers and, with quick touches, turned the light bulb in the porch light beside the door enough to make it go out. I waited a second for my eyes to adjust and watched Sweatpant's door. Then, for simplicities sake, I pulled the screen door open and tried Ian's backdoor. Locked. I cupped my hands against the kitchen window to see what I could see. Nothing really, except a golden opportunity. The window was closed, but it was unlocked. Hah.

I had done this before. With one of my house keys, I poked a hole in the corner of the nylon screen, then scored the edge repeatedly until I had a nice long rip I could get my hands into. If I could get the screen out of the way, I could slide the window open and climb in. I tore the rip wide enough to get both hands in. With my palms flat against the window, I tried to use friction to slide the window up. It wouldn't move. I tried different angles, but my hands kept slipping. I wiped them on my jeans, but no good.

A northbound train pulled into the station. Because of the building, I couldn't see it until it pulled out and rattled directly across from me at eye level. I stood still with my back to the window and waited for the commotion to settle. A car went slowly down the alley, looking for a place to park.

I turned back to my work. The window was about chest high and I couldn't get any good leverage on it. I tried running my fingernails in along the seam and lifting from there, but the angle was no good. Next to a bag of charcoal, there was a rusty metal folding chair in the corner of the porch. It wasn't much to sit on, but I didn't have time for that anyway. I tore the screen away from the top of the window so I could get my fingers in under the metal frame for a hold. Careful to keep my weight toward the front, I climbed up on the chair. I tried to get a hold with my fingers, but they were too stubby, kept slipping. My fingernails had to do all the work. I stood up the best I could and pulled cautiously. I could feel the nail pulling away, ever so slightly, from the cuticle, or nail bed. If I used just enough pressure they wouldn't break, the window just might...

A door opened below me. I froze mid-lift, but my left hand slipped, catching the nail on my ring finger and tearing it sideways. The rusty chair creaked. I started to moan, but caught it midair. A guy and girl came out laughing onto the porch one floor down. Damn.

I shook my hands out and stuck my left ring finger into my mouth where the nail had torn. The chair creaked again. I cringed. My finger throbbed in my mouth. I could taste blood.

As loud as if they were next to me, I heard the flick of two lighters and smelled cigarette smoke floating up between the wooden boards toward me. I tried to stay frozen and keep my balance on the rickety folding chair and suck my finger. Cigarettes take, what, five minutes to smoke?

The girl below said in a forced whisper, "Julia's fucking nuts."

"Yeah," the guy said. He wasn't as good at whispering. "I don't know how your brother can stand it."

"Seriously...Maybe if we stay out here long enough they'll leave."

No.

I steadied myself with my right hand, turned and sort of sat on the brick window ledge. The chair creaked and I stiffened. The people below me, who had apparently nothing else to say, smoked, silently hating Julia. I was sucking my finger trying to figure out what to do. The best plan was to stand there quietly until they finished, then continue what I was doing, despite my injury.

So I sat/stood/leaned quietly, keeping my balance mostly on the front part of the seat. Then, my phone went off.

I couldn't believe how loud it was. It's amazing how loud something can vibrate. The girl below me said, "Is that your phone?"

I heard the guy pat his pockets. "No, mine's inside."

Fuck.

I wiggled my hand into my pocket quickly to silence the phone. My heart was exploding, thumping, thumping in my temples.

After a minute, or so, of silent smoking going on below me, my heart rate went back to normal-ish. I got curious. I pulled my phone out and looked at the missed call. And of course, when my attention was diverted, the folding chair I was standing on, the folding chair holding all of my weight, folded.

My feet pinched inside the chair as I fell backward. My shins grinded on the rusty metal as my right elbow smashed against the brick window ledge. I bit my finger and yelled. I grabbed a handful of window screen for balance, which ripped away in my hand as I clamored to the ground.

"Jesus," someone said below me as feet hit the stairs coming up.

Damn it.

I wrestled my legs from the chair and painfully got to my feet.

As heads appeared on the stairway, I pulled my phone to my ear yelling, "Yeah! I'm on my way! Yeah, yeah! I'll be right down," and ran-limped down the stairs past them. I was a full flight down before I stopped yelling.

Chapter 14

Out through the back gate, I turned right and fell against the brick wall panting. I hadn't run that far in at least five years. I stood up, wheezed, bent down again to steady myself with hands on knees. No footsteps followed me. I breathed and coughed. Jesus, that was awful. I shook my head as I stared down at the gravelly asphalt. A total failure. I accomplished absolutely nothing except definitely establishing that Ian was *not* at home. Damnit.

Recovering slightly, I moved to standing with my hands on my hips and limped around in a circle, favoring my right leg. I poked my head back around the corner. The smokers weren't there anymore, just Ian's blacked-out porch light and torn screen. And a flattened, metal folding chair was lying flat up there somewhere with scraped-off skin and leg hair stuck to the side. I reluctantly lifted my right pant leg. Blood was running into my sock from a series of gashes and cuts, long and short, like bloody Morse code. The train started making noise a few blocks away. I looked up, but would never make it in time. A car turned into the alley. Police? My eyes went wide and my heart rate spiked again. No, thank god. I blocked the lights with my hand. This time it didn't feel like x-ray vision. I had no intentions of anything. I was deflated. I was going to have to get better at this.

The car went on past swirling the mild, rotten-trash-can-smell of the nighttime alley air around me. I sighed and started walking toward Montrose as the train I needed loudly pulled away. The call I'd missed was from Melanie. She hadn't left a message. I needed some cheering up, so I called her back.

"Oh my god," she answered in a frantic whisper. "Where are you?"

"Up by Lincoln Square, by a friend's place." I said, keeping the discouragement out of my voice. "Why? What's going on?"

"Mike there's somebody outside."

"What? What are you talking about? Of course there is, we live in one of the busiest neighborhoods in town."

"No, you know that's not what I mean, damn it. There's somebody, like, snooping around."

"Why are you whispering? Where are you?"

"At my house. I don't know why I'm whispering. I'm scared. What if they hear me?"

"Alright. Ok, chill out," I said, reassuringly, then almost laughed. I don't know why. Maybe it was nerves catching up with me, or the continued absurdity of everything. One ridiculous thing was piling on top of another. I covered my mouth in case a giggle escaped. As soon as I was out of one stupid situation, another was plopped right down into my lap. It was fucking ridiculous.... I held it together, cleared my throat and said, encouragingly, "It's fine. You're inside right? Door's locked? They can't get you." I bit down another chuckle.

"Yeah, I'm inside, fine.... Are you laughing at me?"

"No," I smiled, "of course not." I cleared my throat again. "Of course not. Ok. Tell me what's going on. Why do you think somebody's outside."

"Mike, don't laugh at me. This is serious. Somebody's fucking outside, snooping around."

"I'm not laughing. Promise." Saying it made me smile again. This shit..."Ok, seriously," I said, getting control again. "What happened? What makes you think somebody's outside?"

"Cause they're out there, I know they're out there. I can hear 'em moving around out by the cars. I think I heard them over by your place too."

And just like that it wasn't funny anymore. I remembered the shuffling noises I'd heard below my window the night before. I started walking faster toward the train station.

"Can you see anything? Did you look out the window?"

"I tried, kinda, but I didn't want them to see me. But I think I heard them, like, knocking, or tapping around your window. Trying to break in or something, I know it."

She was obviously exaggerating that part, imagination filling in.

"No, nobody's trying to break in my place from the outside. We have thick iron bars on the windows. You can't get around that."

"Oh, yeah. I guess that's true."

"Listen, turn your lights off and peek through the blinds. You'll be able to see out, but they won't be able to see you."

"I don't know, Michael. What if they do? I'm seriously scared. What the fuck are they doing out there?"

"Melanie, it's fine. Turn out the lights and look out. Let me know if you see anything. Did you call the police?"

"No, I didn't think about that. I called you first. Should I?"

"I don't know," I said, being realistic. "They might not take you too seriously. I mean, it's a pretty busy area with all the bars right there. And you're safe inside."

"Yeah, but what if they get in somehow, like, if somebody leaves and they sneak in the back door."

"Keep your door locked and keep your lights out. Maybe they'll think you aren't home."

"That's no good! Then they'll break in for sure!"

"Melanie, it's ok. You're fine. Nothing's gonna happen." I leaned over the tracks and watched for train lights in the distance. "I'm waiting for the train now. Hopefully I'll be there in like twenty minutes or so. Watch out the window. Let me know if you see anything."

"Fine, but hurry."

When the train finally came again, it was basically empty; the Brown Line at night. It took twelve minutes to get to

Diversey and another seven for me to walk quickly home. Instead of going all the way down Diversey, I turned down the street before Pine Grove and picked up the alley a block before it ran behind my house.

On the way through, I found a broken Swiffer sticking out of a dumpster with the green attachment head hanging limply down the side. I yanked it out and broke the mop head part the rest of the way off. I whished it through the air a couple times, trying it out. It wasn't much, but it would put some distance between me and whatever shady characters I might have to prick and prod out of the shadows.

I moved cautiously along the alley, the narrowness of it enhanced by the height of the buildings. A cool damp smell swirled around my feet like fog from a smoke machine. I crept along concentrating on the dark section of alley past where the light spilled out down Pine Grove from the corner. I lurked on across the street with my Swiffer-bat/spear held at the ready, careful to stay in the dark shadows for defense. Nobody was out smoking in the patch of security light behind Doofy's Bar. Rats raced ahead of me as I moved past the row of trash cans right before coming to my building.

I crouched, stepping slowly, carefully. I glanced quickly up at Melanie's dark window to see if she was looking out, but there was no way to tell. A muffled grunt and a scuffling sound drew my attention to a dark spot near the ground. My breath caught and my heart jumped out ahead of me. I hoisted Swiffer and...

Ian rose up out of the shadows and fell into me with a wet gurgling grumble.

"Aaaah," I yelled hoarsely, like a bad actress. The Swiffer stick fell from my hands as I caught him under the arms, instinctively, before his head hit the ground. I swayed and struggled to hold him up.

"Ian, what the fuck?" I burbled, before he slid down my torn-up shins to the ground.

His hair was matted down with blood, stuck to his forehead. His left eye was completely swollen shut. He looked horrible. Blood and swollenness described everything; mouth, teeth, crooked nose, ear, eyes.

I waved frantically at Melanie's dark window. Ian made a terrible gurgling coughing sound. And did it again. I propped his head on the toe of my shoe, talking lightly. "Ian. Hey, man. Ian, buddy."

Lights went on in Melanie's apartment. A second later, she came bounding down the back steps wearing jeans, Toms, and a white, ribbed tank top. She came out with her hands in her mouth.

"Oh my god," she cried. "What happened? What's wrong with him?"

"I don't know. Help me get him inside."

"Inside?" She looked at me like I was crazy. "Inside? Why do you want to take him inside?"

"Melanie, come on." I motioned frantically for her to come closer. "Come on, I know him. He's a friend of mine. Help me get him inside."

Chapter 15

Ian was basically unconscious by the time he hit the ground. He wasn't totally out, but he didn't do much to help me get him inside either. Melanie went ahead holding doors while I carried/dragged him up the back stairs and through the door.

The building engineer had finally finished with my door, leaving a "Wet Paint" sign taped near the eye hole. Melanie had some trouble getting the new lock to open and I got a few extra seconds of holding my bleeding, beaten buddy up in the hallway for everybody to gawk at as they went by. Though no one did, thankfully.

Once inside my apartment, I really wished I'd had a couch, or a recliner, or soft chair of some sort, anything other than my own personal bed, where I slept every night, to lay my bloody visitors down on. But I didn't, so I had to lay him out on my bed and gather the two pillows I had to prop him up against the wall, so he wouldn't choke to death on his own blood if he passed out.

"Hold him up while I get some water," I said. "I don't want him to fall asleep."

"What the hell happened to him?" Melanie asked as I went into the kitchen; her cheeks and forehead flushed with worry, contorted with sympathetic disgust.

"I don't know, but it doesn't look good. Why don't you ask him?"

"Hey," she said, shaking his arm, then over her shoulder to me, "What'd you say his name was?"

"Ian." I filled a glass.

"Hey, Ian," she tried again, shaking him lightly. "You ok? You still with us?" She took his wrist in her hand and made an attempt to check his pulse, though she obviously didn't know how.

"Really? Checking his pulse? Making sure he's still alive?"

"What? That's what you're supposed to do."

"You can see his chest moving. You can practically hear him breathing," I said and motioned for her to move over. "I don't think he's dead yet."

"Well, what the hell are we supposed to do?" She said, not moving. "We have to do something. He's in bad shape."

"I know. If you'd let me get in there, I'm trying to give him some water. Ian," I said loudly, as she gave me an inch, "here. Have some water."

I lifted the glass, careful not to touch it to his cracked lips, and poured water in the direction of his mouth. It ran down his chin, wetting his shirt at the neck where blood hadn't. Three quarters of his face was swollen huge and fleshy, red and pink. His left eye was swollen shut, but the right was relatively untouched in a little patch of normalcy about the size of ten-minutes-to on his puffy pink mashed-up clock face. He was a long and slender guy, but you couldn't tell it to see that face. It was swollen almost flat, even his neck looked swollen. His thin, long nose had an extra bend in it I hadn't noticed before.

"Jesus," Melanie said, to herself out loud.

"Grab one of those white t-shirts would you?" I said, nodding to a pile by the closet door. "Put some water on it. We should try to clean him up a little."

I poured some more water at his mouth. Melanie wet a t-shirt at the sink and gingerly touched the wet cloth to his face. His legs went instantly rigid. He moan-barked, "MmWHa-ya-dyamM?" The good right eye rolled around like a one-eyed fish trying to look up.

I steadied his shoulders. "Hey, man, easy now."

He lopped his head around, checking his surroundings. His left eye wouldn't open. The wobbly right one finally stopped on me, then skitted to Melanie.

"Wer an I?" he said through a space at the corner of his mouth without moving his lips.

"Easy, man, take it easy," I said in a calming voice. "It's cool. We're at my place. You came to my place. We brought you inside."

"Alet's," he groaned, pinching his eye shut. "Alets."

"Alex? ...What?"

His head rolled to the side. He almost lost consciousness. I reached out to steady his chin, but didn't know where to grab it. I tried for his head, then his jaw, but the whole thing looked so tender and sensitive, so pulpy and puffy, so raw and exposed.

"Ian," I said, not knowing what to do. "Take it easy, man. You're all right."

"Alecks..," Ian mumbled, "He...Is he...?"

Melanie said, "Who's Alex?" to me. "What's he trying to say?"

"I don't know, maybe Alex was with him? Maybe they got jumped."

"Al...he..he."

"Was Alex with you Ian? What happened to you guys?" I said to Melanie, "Maybe Alex is hurt too. We should call him. Or maybe he knows." Ian moaned something unintelligible. I dug my phone out of my pocket and scrolled through to find Alex's number. Ian grabbed my arm weakly.

"Alex—"

"Yeah, man, I'm calling hi—"

"NO!" He gasped through his teeth, "He di thi."

Melanie put her hand over my phone and looked at me. "Wait. He's saying Alex did this to him."

"Nah, that's not right," I said, looking back at Ian. "Just let me call and see what happened."

Ian pushed my hand away. "No," he grunted weakly.

"I told you," Melanie said, hitting my arm. "This guy Alex did this to him."

"Ian," I said. "Alex did this? He did this to you?"

"Yeth," he said. "Don't...Aleth?" He tried to grab my hand, but his head flopped again and his arm went limp by his side.

"Jesus, man." Melanie stared at him shaking her head. "He's fucked up. What should we do?"

"Alex." I said under my breath. "Why would Alex do it?"

"I don't know," Melanie said, "but this isn't good. He looks bad."

"Yeah," I mumbled. If Alex had done it, it obviously had something to do with whatever was between them. And did that mean it had to do with me too? They both blamed the other for what happened to me and there was no way this wasn't tied in. Ian definitely didn't trust Alex, that's why he came to me in the first place, to warn me. But if what Alex said was true, Ian could be lying. Could this be another plot of his against Alex? Seemed a little excessive. OR was Alex really as suspicious, and apparently dangerous, as Ian said?

"Michael, what should we do with him?" Melanie asked, pulling me back to the situation at hand.

"I don't know. Should we take him to the hospital?"

"Yeah, probably. Look at him. There's one down the street," she said with questions in her eyes.

"No, that's like a specialty hospital." I'd seen that somewhere. "I don't think they have a regular emergency room. We'll have to call an ambulance."

Ian's head came up a bit. His one eye rolled around. "No," I think he said, "—Poliss."

"You want me to call the police?"

His right eye strained. He made an attempt to grab my shirt. "No," he hissed, "no. No, hoss—"

"I don't think he wants to go to the hospital."

"Yeah, I guess not."

Melanie said, "But what if he has a concussion, or internal bleeding or something. He looks pretty fucked up."

"I don't know," I said, thinking. "I mean...he probably doesn't have insurance...I mean, I don't, so if this happens to me don't take me to the hospital either. I can't afford that shit, just so you know. But, I don't know."

Ian's head wobbled around some and his eye squinted open. "Hone," he said in a raspy, scratchy voice, "I be... fine. Juss..home."

I looked around the room trying to decide what to do. Then suddenly something occurred to me. Maybe it makes me an asshole and I don't wish ill on anybody I know, but if a situation arises and you have an opportunity to help someone out and get something in return, then, well, everybody wins.

"I don't know," Melanie said, shaking her head. "I just don't think we should leave him here like this."

"I don't know what to do," I said, even though I'd just decided. "We can't take him to the hospital.... Maybe I *should* try to get him home." I watched Ian for a response and listened to him breath roughly, but evenly. "I mean, I don't really want to leave him here in my bed and maybe he would be more comfortable at home."

"That's terrible," Melanie said, looking hurt. "You can't just take him home and leave him there. You're just trying to get rid of him." She gave me a challenging, disappointed look.

I had to get her to go along with me without making it obvious. "I mean, I don't want to leave him here," I said, grasping at straws. "Where am I going to sleep? And he's bleeding all over my bed." I immediately felt guilty, lowered my voice, and went on. "It's not like I have a couch to sleep on. At his place—"

"Sleep with *me*." The sudden shock of the command made my head swim a bit. She caught it, clarified, "At my place," with a smug smirk.

"No," I said, wanting to. "I can't leave him alone. Listen," my thoughts clearing up again. "I can get him home, put him to bed, then sleep on *his* couch. Here, we can't both sleep on my bed. We wouldn't even fit. Plus," motioning with my head, "he is sort of bleeding all over my stuff. At his place, he won't have to feel guilty about it when he wakes up." Then, another beautiful thought occurred to me, "Let me borrow your car."

"My car? Then what am I gonna do?"

"You help me get him in the car. Then, get a good night's sleep knowing everybody's safe and comfortable."

"No, idiot, what am I gonna do without my car?" She whined, "I have class tomorrow."

I shook that away. "You don't need your car and you know it. Besides, I'll bring it back first thing in the morning. I just want to make sure he gets through the night ok. And maybe I can find out a little more about what happened."

"But he'll bleed all over it," she said, then looked guilty for having said it. She said more quietly, "I mean look at him. It's gonna get all over the seats."

"Nice. Such compassion," I said from my high moral ground. "I'll put a towel down. ...And besides, I've seen your car. You afraid it'll lower the resale value?"

"Screw you, Mike. I just don't think you should move him. And I love my car."

"Really? That much?"

"When it runs I do. And I hate it too. But, well...," she looked at us both for a second. "Maybe I should come with you, help you get him inside."

"No," I said plainly. "We'll be fine. I'm sure I can manage. But help me get him to the car."

Chapter 16

"Think my ribs... is broke," Ian said. He was slumped between the seat and car door. The renewed pain of us helping him out to the car had woken him up.

I squinted forward in the driver's seat trying to read the road sign up at the next intersection. "Shit, man," I said, with a quick side glance. "That sucks."

"My knee too." His words came out of the far side of his mouth mixed with lots of air and breathing. "They sma-smashed it.., or s-somethin'."

"What happened, man? Can you tell me? I mean...yeah, what happened?"

"I-I, I told you." Heavy sighing. "Alex. And his...his fuck cronies."

We were up past Wrigley Field on Clark and I knew Montrose was coming up. I had to sit forward and lean out over the wheel to see the road signs, driving every bit like the tourist I was in so many ways. Melanie's car crunched and creaked. It was an old, silver Toyota Corolla pockmarked with rust around the tires. There was an exhaust leak somewhere under us that rumbled faint and airy like an old-lady fart.

"Yeah," I said. "But, I mean, you guys are friends. I don't get it."

Heavy breath. "Damnit, I—"

"I know," I cut in. "I know he's not what I think. You keep telling me. But why now? I mean, why do this now? If it's what you're sayin, or if it's about your guys' weed deal?" As soon as I said it, I realized he didn't know I knew. I had been on my way to ask him about it.

I looked at him quickly; bowed heavily against the passenger door, hand slung across his ribcage. He didn't even budge, excepting it.

"Yeah," I said, cautiously. "Alex told me about it. I was gonna ask you...." I paused, giving him a chance to get a word in on it. He let it go. "But anyway. If this is about that, then why do something about it now? Why not then? ...Or any other time? He could have done this any time."

Ian moved enough to ruffle a cigarette out of a wrinkled pack and light it; holding it an inch from his face as his head bobbed and drooped next to the window. A long brick wall stretched on beside us, ringing in a huge cemetery. Montrose had to be coming up next.

"It just doesn't make sense," I said softly. "And if you knew he might do something, if you didn't trust him, then why would you go meet him?"

I thought he might have fallen asleep, but his left eye crinkled as he drew slowly on the cigarette in front of his face. "I...I was tryin' keep it..cool. You know, 'tween us." He rolled his head to the side as if trying to lift it to look at me, but it drooped, failing. "He said meet 'im at Jake's... You know," he breathed, "kinda by yo...spot."

I made the turn and followed Montrose past Ashland.

"He's cool, normal," Ian went on slowly, cigarette burning down. "We go out...to-to the alley.. smoke." His voice getting softer, trailing off. "His buddies roll up." Then quietly, almost finished, "He says, 'Better watch yo'self, spreadin' rumors.'"

A few people jogged ahead of us across the street, under the bright lights of the Montrose train station. I slowed to make the turn into the alley I had just come from, behind Ian's building. I double parked, the Toyota giving off a sick, old-car electronic whine when I opened my door without taking the keys out.

Ian fell completely out of the car in one lump when I opened the door next to him. I watched his cigarette tumble, still burning, onto Melanie's floorboard as I scooped my arms up under his shoulders to catch him. I got him back in the seat, held him stiffly with one arm and snatched the smoldering butt off the floor, flicking it out behind me. The next series of moves weren't elegant, or graceful, but I managed to get Ian out of the car and down the walk to the bottom of the fire escape without dropping him, or me, on our teeth. He grunted a lot and came somewhat to life whenever my hip dug into his tender, broken ribs, or banged his injured knee. But other than that, he didn't have enough strength to help much.

I dumped him at the foot of the wooden stairs and went back to the car to move it. All of the parking places were full, so I left it next to a loading dock that was cluttered with cardboard boxes and litter and didn't look like it got much use. I planned on being up and out early enough to beat the ticket lady or tow truck anyway. The train rumbled overhead as I walked back across the alley silencing everything else.

When I got back to Ian, he was lying back on the steps with his feet out, sleepily smoking again.

"Didn't want to sleep," he said and flashed me his cigarette.

I stood over him and looked up at the three flights of stairs grudgingly. I hadn't liked climbing those things alone, let alone half-carrying someone else.

"Alright," I said with a huff. "Let's get this done."

He threw his cigarette and I helped him up, wrapping his arm around my shoulder. The stairs were new and sturdy and I got a much better look at them this time up, my head bent with the effort. It was the second time in a matter of hours I had been up those stairs to his place, and luckily, the physical excursion kept me from being awkward amidst the mixed pangs of confusion and guilt I was feeling.

"Hey, your light's out." I said, as we hit the last flight. Setting the stage for what came next. Ian didn't have the energy to notice, but I said, "Shit, man, your screen's ripped too." I stood him up straight. "Shit," I hissed dramatically, "you don't think someone tried to break in, do you? Think it could have been the guys that jumped you?"

Ian didn't seem interested at all, or much awake for that matter. He rummaged his keys out of his pocket and unlocked the back door while I held him in place. The door opened into the kitchen obviously, I'd seen this much through the back window earlier. We squeezed through a tight doorway into the short hallway. The hall was too narrow for us. I had to crab walk, pulling Ian along beside me into the small bedroom. His bed was entirely too big for the space, allowing only a twelve-inch gap between the foot of the bed and the wall. I side-walked into the space and let him fall back manly, but gently, onto the huge bed.

Here I was in another awkward situation. We hadn't been friends that long, but we'd gotten a lot closer on that climb up. And now I had to perform the helping-a-hurt-person-to-bed scenario we've all seen a dozen times in movies: shoes off, covers over, moist wet beaten pulpy swollen head on two pillows. His eyes began to shut almost immediately. I went to the kitchen for a glass of water. And one for him too.

Satisfied with a job well done, I stood back to survey the scene. Ian was home safe, in bed, and snoring horribly through his shattered, blood clogged nose.

And I was inside Ian's apartment.

I didn't know what else to do for him at that point, so I closed the door most of the way, leaving it open a few inches and went to the living room.

Now then. Did Ian break into my apartment and steal two pounds of marijuana and ten thousand dollars in cash? Tim and Chris had thought so. Alex told me as much, but there was really only one way to find out. And here I was standing in his living room, knowing exactly where he was, with no danger of him busting in on me. That dubious grin found its way back onto my face. I rubbed my hands together. Where to start first? Am I a terrible person?

His apartment was much bigger than mine, a proper one-bedroom, but still sparsely furnished. Two framed posters, scenes from Scarface, were on the wall above the couch, opposite the TV. I turned the TV on with the volume just high enough to drown out any noise I might make without waking him up, if that was even possible.

Ian was beaten pretty badly. He says Alex did it. But do I think that? I couldn't tell.

It was hard to believe Ian would steal from me, then come to me, bleeding, for help. Then again, he had just told me himself he went to meet Alex, who he may have stolen from, to "keep things cool" between them. So, Ian could've stolen from me, gotten jumped by someone random, and come to me for help so I'd feel sorry for him, thereby casting doubt on my suspicions.

He could have even been spying on me when he got jumped, in the alley creeping around my place, trying to see if I was onto him when, *Boom*, he gets mugged. He could be blaming it on Alex to confuse me even further, putting more blame off him.

I'd never searched someone's place before, but there really was only one way to get to the bottom of this. If my stuff was here, Ian did it. If not, I'd think about that after.

The first thing in front of me was the coffee table. I bent over and pulled open the wooden drawer: a glass pipe, a one-hitter and a small bag of weed, but it wasn't any more weed than I would expect him to have. I was looking for almost two pounds. You couldn't keep two pounds in the drawer of your coffee table.

There was a small coat closet next to the bathroom. I turned the knob completely before pulling it open silently, listening to Ian's rough breathing from the bedroom behind me. Light from the standing floor lamp next to the couch wasn't bright enough to see into the dark corners of the closet, but a thorough sweep of my hands let it pass inspection.

The bathroom was simple with no place to store anything except the medicine cabinet, which didn't contain ten thousand dollars. I pulled on it as well to see if anything could be hidden behind it, but it was securely in place.

I looked in on Ian, like the good friend I was, on my way by and made sure he was still out, and not dead.

Next stop: the kitchen. I had read once that people always hide their money in the freezer, so I checked there first. Just some Eggo's and Ben & Jerry's. Nothing in the cupboards. Nothing under the sink. I already knew what was on the back porch, so there was only the bedroom left unsearched.

First, I went back out to the couch to bolster my nerves. Even though Ian was passed out in there, snooping around someone else's bedroom just feels wrong and shady. And this wasn't snooping around my parent's room for hidden Christmas gifts either. If Ian had my shit, he wouldn't be too keen on me ransacking his room while he slept. But then again, he probably wouldn't have let me come over here at all. I wouldn't. But it still had to be done.

I stopped at the bedroom door and listened to his rusty breathing. Satisfied it was the breathing of a sleeping person, I pushed the door open to let in as much light as possible from the hall. It was still too dark. Hearing him breathe made me feel kind of sick, the choked roughness of it. I could picture his right eye all bloody and swollen shut. His big, thin nose with an S-bend running along the ridge, his snoring, heavy breath trying to work its way out, getting caught on fragments of gross shit. It felt a bit like standing outside the cave of a sleeping dragon, but after you've stuck your sword in him, waiting around for him to die, waiting until just the right moment to slip in and steal the key from around his sleeping, dying neck to open the treasure chest.

Without getting closer, I crouched down in the hall and used the flashlight on my phone to peek under the bed. I could see two old pairs of high tops and a backpack. Damn. There was no way I could leave without checking that backpack. I turned the flashlight off and used the dimmer light from the screen to guide my hand. On hands and knees, I stretched my arm out as far as possible to keep as much distance as I could. Ian snored above me. I reached the backpack and could tell immediately by the lightness of it that it was empty. But I pulled it back out into the hall and unzipped it to be sure.

Having been in the bedroom once calmed my nerves a lot. I poked my head in to see what else there was, just the dresser, dangerously close to Ian's head. Under the guise of "checking on him," I decided it was safe to go all the way in. If he woke up I'd just say, "Good, you're alright." So, I actually did check on him, I'm not a dick, and then quietly turned my back to him to riffle through his drawers.

Knowing how loud *my* dresser drawers are, I closed my eyes and held my breath as I, very easily, pulled slowly on the top drawer. A scraping of wood on wood was the only sound as the billowy contents of an underwear drawer came into the light of my phone. Going through an underwear drawer is definitely not a good experience, especially another man's. People keep things in there they don't want others to see, and I don't want to see them either, but I had to check. The drawer was shallow and wider than long. And besides a couple of pictures of twenty-somethings naked – old girlfriends, I assumed – there was just underwear. With a backward glance at Ian, I had another look at the pictures before sliding them back down into their hiding place.

I repeated the closing-of-the-eyes, pulling-slowly-on-the-drawer routine three more times and decided the dresser was clean. Ian snored on.

Back out on the couch, I stretched out and relaxed. The dirty work was done. Nothing found.

Ian slowly started to fade off the suspect list in my mind. Either he didn't do it, or he stashed the stuff somewhere else. And while still considering the facts, I settled uncomfortably down to go to sleep. I couldn't really see Ian doing it, I decided.

Happier thoughts drifted toward Ellie and the last time I'd seen her. She was lousy at texting. I wondered if she liked me as much as I liked her. I really liked her.

Chapter 17

In the morning, the sun came through the front window unhindered and shone brightly off the undecorated white walls. After only a few hours sleep, my back felt so stiff I had to roll off the couch to get my feet under me. I splashed some water on my face in the bathroom then, checked on Ian one last time before I left him alone.

He had rolled over in the night putting his good eye against the pillow and leaving the bloated dead-cow-looking right eye up to greet me for breakfast. Part of the sheet had dried a reddish brown color and clung to his cheek just under the swollen eye. It hung there stubbornly, crustily. I couldn't bear to look at it for long and was contented by listening to his raspy breath come and go. He wasn't dead and there wasn't really anything else I could do for him. Plus, I needed to get the car back to Melanie.

The early morning air was bright and crisp, no humidity yet. Melanie's Toyota was quietly growing rust exactly where I'd left it. I'd beaten the parking guy and the tow truck, thank God.

Feeling groggy, but somewhat at ease, I stopped at a diner for eggs and bacon, no coffee, then retraced my route from the night before amongst ten times more traffic. It took me fifteen minutes to squeeze Melanie's little car into the even littler parking space behind our building, just in time for the person beside me to pull out, leaving a huge gaping hole.

Melanie had class in the mornings, but I knocked on her door anyway to let her know I was back and got no response. My apartment was cool and dark. I pulled the sheet back where Ian had lain bleeding and dropped down face first.

Lying on cool sheets on my stomach after a hard night on my back and a too-short couch was amazing. My eyelids felt heavy as lead. I didn't try to hold them open.

My cheek was wet with drool when I woke up for the second time that day around noon. I wouldn't say I was any less stiff and I still had my clothes on, but at least I was home. I shat, showered, shaved and made some coffee before doing any real thinking for the day.

Like a pinball stuck between two bumpers, my mind was bouncing back and forth: Ian, Alex, Ian, Alex, Ian, Alex. Ian was pretty much off the suspect list. There was some lingering doubt that could only be cleared up by going to talk to Alex again. Ian, Alex. What was the real connection? Who was telling the truth? And where did I fit in? And who had my stuff?

Alex was up to bat. I wasn't going to call before I showed up this time. With any luck, I could get into his building and knock directly on his door before he knew I was there, like I'd done with Tim and Chris. That way he couldn't come up with some smooth-as-silk statement ahead of time.

I waited until quitting time, around 5:30, to head up there. I knew he'd be home from school by then and there would be a lot of foot traffic in and out of his building. The train was packed. Out of the station at the Wilson stop, I fell in line with a group of people walking in the appropriate direction and only broke off when I could tell no one was going directly to Alex's front door. It took less than a minute of me pretending to search for my keys until someone came up the steps behind me, keys out, to open the door. I followed him in, climbed the flight of stairs, took a deep breath and knocked.

Alex opened the door a sliver, peeking out suspiciously. "Mike." The irritated look melting into a weak smile. "Back so soon?" He pulled the door open to let me in.

"Yeah," I smiled back, stepping in past him. "I been all over lately. Thought I'd see what you were up to."

He was barefoot and relaxed as ever. He had on light khaki pants and a well-worn white linen shirt unbuttoned half way down. His hair fell in his face, required repeated tucking behind his ear.

"Sure, man," he said, smiling through professionally whitened teeth. "What's up? You want a beer or something?"

"Nah, I'm good." I unconsciously pulled at my lower lip, not wanting to begin. I looked for scabs on his knuckles, or bruises were Ian had maybe gotten a couple of blows in, but didn't see anything. "So what's going on? You busy?"

"Nah, man, just working on some shit." He walked over to his laptop on the DJ table by the window. I followed obediently. "You remember when you were here the other day? Me and some guys were about to go out?"

"Oh yeah, you were going *bombin'* right?" I said it like it was some new catch phrase and immediately felt self-conscious.

Alex's smile got bigger. "Yeah, right." He shook his head. "But anyway, we went out, threw up some tags and shit, but I got some nasty footage. Here check it out."

There were a bunch of windows open in layers on the screen; pictures of the guys in full gear, bandanas or masks over their mouths, spray painting, but without the walls or images they were painting, guys spraying at nothing.

"So I got these images, see. Then I got these other ones," Alex moved windows around showing me pictures of politicians and famous people making various disgusted, or surprised looks. "Then, what I do is paint a realistic, like, nature scene on a canvas then, set these images up on the computer and print them onto the canvas."

"Oh, ok. Like a collage or something."

He snapped his fingers. "Exactly, it's all about collage now, the only way to express anything in these mashed-up times, you know what I mean. But not like collages grade school kids make out of magazine pictures and shit. They've got to say something more interesting, you know. Give a bigger picture."

Alex had never shown me what he was actually working on for real, what he was doing in school. Up to that moment, I'd assumed he was bullshitting his way along, majoring mostly in being cool and getting laid. I mean, that's more or less what I'd done and it worked out for quite a while. My suspicions softened. I was interested in the possibilities of what he was doing, wondering if I'd see it done before, like in a Coke commercial.

"Yeah, that's cool." I said, nodding along. "I'd like to see it when you got something put together."

"For sure." He shut the computer and looked at me with a questioning half-smile as he stood. "But you didn't come here for this shit. What's up? Something on your mind?"

"Well, actually...," I paused, decided to sit first. I went around to the love seat. Alex followed, sitting in the leather La-Z-Boy across from me. I looked down at the bright spot of spray paint on the side, then wished I hadn't. My palms got sweaty.

"I just came from Ian's house," I said, looking him in the eye. No reaction, not even a flicker. If Ian was telling the truth, I expected *something*, a look away at least. "He's fucked up. Bad. Got the shit kicked out of him last night."

"What!? Really?" Surprise made his eyebrows bunch then lift. He looked down for a second, but more uneasy than suspicious. "Like, bad?"

"Yeah, man, it's pretty bad. He's all purple and shit. His eye's swollen shut."

He crimped up one side of his mouth, shaking his head. "Damn. That sucks," he said, slowly. "He say what happened?"

This was the part I had been thinking about. "No, he doesn't know. He said some guys came out of nowhere, blindsided him."

I couldn't tell if he relaxed, or if I inferred it. "Damn.... Does he know who it was? Or see 'em or anything?"

"No. He said he didn't see 'em. They just came outta nowhere."

"Shit. Do you know where he was?"

"Not exactly, but he must have been somewhere by me. I came home and he stumbled up and, like, fell into me."

"Jesus." He twisted around and got up. "That's some serious shit."

"And since he came to me," I said, looking uncomfortable. "I feel kind of responsible, you know? Like I should at least ask around?"

"Yeah, shit," he said, considering it.

"Yeah. I thought I'd come see if you thought anybody might do it." I watched him pace in a small circle, staring at the ground. "You know, like what you were telling me the other day. Maybe he had somebody else in on that thing you guys had. Only maybe they didn't take it as well as you."

"Yeah, I know what you're saying." Now it was his turn to pull on his lip, only he added the circling movement to it. "That's some shit, Mike." He relaxed. "Let me think for a second. I'm gonna get a beer, you sure you don't want one?"

"Yeah, sure, all right," I said and got up, went over to the window. People streamed by on their way home as Alex went to the kitchen. I waited. I didn't know what his reaction would be. Maybe Ian was lying and Alex was legitimately thinking of people who would attack him. He hadn't shown any sign of guilt, or nervous reaction whatsoever. He was obviously thinking up something to say, or do. I just didn't know what it would be, what his angle was.

Did he do it? Was he protecting the people who did do it? Or was he suddenly scared they might do the same to him, thinking it could be a double-double cross?

He brought me a bottle of Bell's. "I wish I didn't think this," he said, as he handed it to me with a grave look. "But I might know who it was."

Huh, not what I expected. "Yeah? You don't sound too happy about it."

"Well...I'm just wondering. If it *was* them, what does it mean, you know? Is it about the old thing? Or does it have something to do with you and your thing?"

"Ok. Who's 'they'?" I said, cautiously, "Somebody I know?"

"I don't think so...." He sipped on his beer with a far-off look in his eye. "Well," he said with a resigned, inevitable tone, "we might as well go in on it together." He gestured at me with the end of his bottle. "You know that kid Paul I'm friends with? Kind of weird."

"That pill-head kid?" I blurted out too quickly and got a sorry look on my face.

Alex huffed a small smile. "Yeah, him." Then went grave again. "Well, him and his roommate, they had a little bit of money in with Ian too."

So he was definitely tying it in with the old thing. I looked thoughtful. "And you think they did it?"

"Well, I could see it, you know. They could have done that to Ian, yeah. They're kind of intense dudes."

"Do you think it was about that old shit? Or do you think they could have busted into my place, and maybe it was about that? Like a dispute or whatever."

He raised his eyebrows, "Or both?" I didn't like the inclination in those eyebrows. "Only one way to find out."

"How's that?"

"Ask 'em." He said it point blank like that, and looked directly at me. There might have been a challenge in his eyes.

Chapter 18

"What," Alex said. "What is it?"

"What, what?" I said from my dark corner of the taxi.

Alex smiled, always smiling. "What's up, that's what. You haven't said a word since we left my house."

"Oh," I smiled fakely back at him. "I don't know, nothing. Just a little nervous I guess."

Alex's smile brightened even more, like the smile of a friend who knows you're scared to go on stage, but knows you'll be great. "Look, Michael, it's no big deal, we're just going over to have a chat. No big deal."

"I guess. But I don't even know these guys. I'm gonna show up and be like 'Hey you beat up my friend. You shouldn't do that.'" I shook my head and looked out at the lights going quickly by down Ashland. The cab driver kept braking too hard and changing lanes abruptly, ratcheting up my general anxiety.

The smile continued almost mockingly. "It's cool. I know you don't know them very well—"

"Don't know 'em at all."

"Yeah. But they're my friends, I'll do the talking."

Parked cars whipped by shockingly close. My skin felt electrified, my nerves hot. I like riding in cabs, love the idea of being in a city where I could just stick my hand out and a car stops to pick me up. I was trying to focus on that, let it soak in, except for the fact I didn't want to be going where we were going. Cabs are supposed to mean fun things like going to clubs, getting too drunk and magically being driven home by a stranger. Not going to a couple of shady dude's house and accusing them of beating up your friend. Then waiting to see what they say. That was the worst part of it for me. Sure Alex does the talking and asks them if they beat up Ian and why, and what, I just sit there invisible? No. I'm there too. That's the part I didn't like. They'll be eyeballing me, assuming it was me who ratted them out.

"And," Alex continued reassuringly, "it's not like I'm gonna go in there and yell at them 'Hey, you beat up Ian. You're assholes.' I'm just gonna sort of feel them out. Then once we know if it was them or not, then we can figure out what to do about it. Come back later or something."

"I still don't like it." We came to the intersection of Chicago and Ashland. Alex leaned forward at the light, giving the cabbie instructions. He pulled through in the left lane and did a quick U-ey, stopping at the curb on the opposite side of the street under a Coor's Light billboard in Spanish: *Llevate la Cerveza Mas Fria de la Ciudad*.

I had only met this Paul guy once. I remembered him being scrawny and crazy looking like a meth head in one of the trailer parks off my old school bus route. Apparently, he lived here in a light blue coach house behind a three-story brick building. But the way the property was situated, the side of the house faced Ashland, behind the billboard, with a little scabby patch of trash-strewn grass separating it from the sidewalk.

Alex and I stepped through the strip-of-grass/dog-shit-mine-field and down onto the concrete patio between buildings. Amber colored halogen light spilled from the billboard, cut across the dark spaces at different angles, and dimly lit the brick wall of the building next door. Irregular black shadows nestled in a blacker walkway between the buildings.

A cement staircase, with rust showing on the white railing, led six feet up to the front door. A large bay window with two side panels stretched across the front of the house and another one on the floor above. From the ground, I was surprised to see the top of a big plant in the window. I never would have thought Paul, suspected pillhead, could keep something like a plant alive. Beyond it, blue and white flashes of light played on the ceiling from a TV screen.

I don't know if it was the trash whirling around my feet, or the darkness, or the absence of people walking by, or simply the obviousness of the situation, but a tight nervousness hung around my spine. Alex climbed the steps ahead of me and, instead of knocking on the door, reached over the railing and tapped a knuckle on the big window. The TV was so loud we could hear it outside. Paul's beady eyes popped through the gaps in the big rubber plant just inside the door.

That's what it was about him; his searching little eyes. They made you want to keep your hand over your wallet and put the fine China away if he ever came to visit.

The smell of weed blasted us in the face as soon as the door opened. I followed Alex in through dense smoke-colored blue and green from the television. The flat screen was absolutely the center of attention in the room, all else shrank from its mass and volume like minions before the high priest. Guys ran around on it shooting and jumping behind cars. I shook hands with Paul whose palm was, of course, cold and greasy feeling.

Pratt would be his roommate, the one in the pleather recliner. He didn't offer to shake hands, or introduce himself, which was just as well because the TV was so loud I couldn't even hear my own heart beat pounding away on the inside of my ears.

Alex stopped to talk to Paul leaving me oddly stuck next to the TV, next to Pratt, whose flat-billed, brand new baseball hat jerked slightly up as he handed me a short brown blunt.

It seemed like a welcoming gesture, so I took it and sat on the short brown couch behind the coffee table. The blunt was fat, flat and soggy. Pratt's eyes watched heavily as I turned it over in my fingers. Somehow, under his watchful loaded stare, the blunt felt more like a test to see how I'd handle myself than an invitation. But I wasn't new to this game. I pinched it expertly between my fingers, puckered my lips and hit it without touching the soggy end to my lips.

I hit the blunt again and passed it to Alex who sat next to me. Pratt sank somehow further down into the pleather, apparently accepting of my behavior. I guessed he wasn't big on pleasantries, which was fine with me. But pleasantries looked to be about the only thing that wasn't big on him. He had huge tan work boots, which had never seen a day of work, baggy dark denim shorts that covered his knee, even while sitting, and a black t-shirt so big he was sitting on it. I was trying my best not to stare at him and keep my eyes on the television, but considering the reason we were here, I couldn't help but size him up.

Paul pulled a folding chair, the card-table type, over to the end of the couch and took the blunt from Alex, then got up again to pass it back to Pratt. I kept my head pointed at the television, but could feel Paul's eyes on me, wandering through my pockets, the contents of my wallet. The whole scene had an uncomfortable surrealism to it, from the blaring TV and dim lights, to the waiting room like quality in the air. Or maybe it was just me anticipating what was coming, the anxiety distorting my perception.

Alex sat still next to me. Even while watching TV, Paul's eyes seemed to move all over the screen searchingly, looking at the guy with the gun, the girl behind the car, the guy in the window, the vase on the shelf behind the guy in the window, how to pick the lock on the front door after the scene was over and the cameras moved on...

But it couldn't hold his attention. He jumped up, fidgeting, offered us all beer using sign language; the hang-loose sign with thumb and little finger out, putting it to his mouth. He really didn't wait for a response and loped off to the kitchen. He came back, handed bottles of Miller High Life around and sat back down on the edge of the card chair, resumed his watch at the TV, counting the number of shots fired, the value of the ring on the girl's finger.

Then, Alex abruptly picked up the remote from the coffee table in front of us and hit the mute button, causing a resounding silence and the word "mute" to appear in green near the bottom of the screen.

Shocked by the sudden quiet, we all turned to look at him. Alex slowly turned to look at me with a shit-eating grin on his face.

"So guys," he said, pleasantly. "Our friend Michael here, has something he wants to ask you guys. Don't you, Mike?"

I blinked three times.

"He thinks you beat up his good friend Ian. Isn't that right? And... I think he thinks you guys broke into his apartment and stole a bunch of shit from him."

I dropped my beer.

The bottle didn't break. Beer gurgled out of the bottle as it rolled under the couch. I watched it disappear. I moved my head quickly, looked up at the waiting faces.

Alex goddamned set me up. He brought me here on purpose. The scheming bastard. He really did beat the shit out of Ian. He swindled me. It *was* him who broke into my place. The bastard! And this is his attempt to get rid of me, to scare me off, leave it alone. He dumped me here, in the lion's den, with these two crazy fucks. One as big as an iron worker and one a probable sociopath. Fuck.

Various degrees of recognition and understanding crept and crawled onto the faces of Paul and Pratt like insects crawling under fake skin in a horror movie. Alex stared back stiff and challenging with the same smug smile he'd been giving me all along. I sat there long enough for the significance of the statement to really hit home. Then, I bolted for the door.

With one foot on the coffee table, I jumped up and over in one motion. If I could get to the door first, I would have a shot at getting away unharmed. I leapt over Pratt's outstretched feet like an Olympic hurdler as one huge boot shot up, perfectly in time, and scrambled my legs around like eggs.

Momentum carried me forward, but my swirling legs couldn't keep up. I went down face first onto the dirty hardwood floor.

Paul was suddenly, somehow, there. Quick and nimble as his eyes were, his feet were just as fast. He planted two kicks into my ribs before the rest of me even hit the ground. He was little though and his kick weak. I pushed up, moving for to the door again. I lunged forward from all fours like a leaping frog. But my shirt stayed put. It's hard to run when your shirt is nailed to the ground.

Pratt yelled, "Come here!" in a deep Mortal Kombat voice and yanked me back by the collar. This time the momentum went with my legs and my torso stayed put, tipping backwards as my back, then head, smacked the floor. A white flash banged from the back of my skull to my eyes.

Paul was standing over me the next second, fidgety with adrenaline, whether real or pharmaceutical I don't know. Pratt jerked me across the floor and up in one motion. My neck was pinned to the wall. My legs flailed. From the weight pushing against my windpipe, I knew my feet were dangling six inches above the ground. Skin stretched, straining at my neck. Blood was percolating in my head. My eyeballs bulged out as I frantically groped at anything in front of me. Blurry shapes.

"You got questions?" A muffled voice said. "Here's your answer." But I couldn't hear anything. I saw Alex standing across the room, looked like he had a smile on his face.

Then from somewhere behind Pratt's huge fuzzy head, I saw something start to come into view. I tried to see what it was. It got bigger and bigger really fast and I felt the white flash crack behind my eyes.

Chapter 19

I came to back outside at the bottom of the concrete stairs. I could taste cement in my mouth, and blood. Murmuring was going on above me. It hurt my head to roll over. My left eye didn't want to open all the way. But I still wasn't alone. The three of them stood at the top of the stairs; the stairs reaching six feet up, a mile up, stretching out away from me, insurmountable. I could see them laughing, laughing down at me like villains in a cartoon, pointing their long fingers, their chests heaving in staccato motion, up and down, hands on their hips.

I scrambled to my feet, over the grassy shit-strip to the sidewalk under the billboard. In a sudden monolithic rush a bus roared by, spinning me around in my dazed confusion. It came to a sick-brake screeching stop on the other side of the glowing orange intersection across Chicago Ave. I wanted on that bus. I wanted on anything that could get me away from the blue fucking coach house.

I stumbled toward it and flicked my hand in small pathetic gesture that was supposed to say, "hold the bus," but it didn't listen. The street was desolate in its wake. Trash and dust blew after it.

Once I was past the alley, stores began to line the street. They were all closed, but at least the coach house was no longer in view. I hobbled along like a hunchback with only enough strength and energy to hold my knuckles off the ground.

At the corner, I slumped into the bus stop shelter and sat back heavy against the glass. It smelled like pee. It felt really good for a minute, then it smelled like pee and poop. Then, it smelled like stale pee and fresh poop and blood. My mouth tasted like blood.

I got up and threw my hand out at a cab. It was full. Another cab: full. Empty street. A cluster of three cabs went by the other way, but they were all full too. Standing inside the bus shelter wasn't the best place to catch a cab, they'd think I was waiting for the bus. I stumbled a few feet up the street. A small taco place was open. Its lights were really bright. I wasn't hungry. It seemed like more cabs were going by on the other side, but I didn't feel like crossing the street.

With a little more distance between me and Paul's house, I was starting to feel a little more aware, the banging in my head quieting down. I leaned against a brick wall hoping the dizziness would subside. But I still didn't like being this close. I didn't want Alex to come out and find me limping around in the street like an idiot. I needed to get somewhere.

I was on Ellie's side of town. I was on Chicago and Ashland. Ellie lived at North and Wood. Only about a fifteen-minute walk. But I was in no shape to walk it. I had to get a cab. Suddenly, I thought about money. It would cost at least five, six dollars. I reached in my pocket for my money clip. Not there. My hand patted around for my wallet. Ssshew, I still had wallet and CTA card. The next bus stop was two blocks up. I was moving. I sure as shit wasn't going back towards Paul and Pratt's.

My mind was thick and fuzzy. It felt like I was in an old black and white movie, back when the effects were cheap; everything had a blurry ring around it, a small area of focus in the center. Footsteps and street noised came at me too fast and too soon. I couldn't get my head to clear. I felt obvious on the street and tried to stand up straight, to not look broke like a mugging victim. I leaned on a wall, shook my head.

My sweatshirt was torn, dirty and had blood on it. I decided it would be better to turn it inside out, but peeling it over my kicked-in head, past my swollen eye and busted nose was not as easy as it had been when I put it on that morning.

I kept finding new scrapes and bruises. Twice, I almost gave up, sweatshirt halfway over my right arm, but I persevered and succeeded, looking instead like a mugging victim with his shirt on inside out.

The next bus stop didn't have a shelter, or bench. I sat on someone's doorstep. I had no idea how long it had been since the other bus went by, nor did I try to think about it. One would come. I had to rest a minute.

I called Ellie to tell her I was coming. She didn't answer and I didn't have the energy to leave a message. But I did learn, in the process of digging my phone out, that my right hand was tight across the back and swollen. Hopefully I'd hit somebody with it and caused them great pain.

Finally, the bus came. I dipped my card and the driver barely even noticed I was a mess, was probably used to it. I bounced along the aisle to a seat by the back door. Ten minutes later, I pulled the cord and tilted my heavy head out the door at the corner of Ashland and North. I don't remember the walk, but somehow, as if in a drunken stupor, I made it to Ellie's door.

She still hadn't answered my call. I called again. She didn't answer again, until I leaned on the buzzer.

"Yes?" came her suspicious voice through the metal screen. "Who is it?"

Oh sweet safety. "It's Michael," I said, breathing a soul-deep sigh of relief.

"What?"

"Ellie, it's Michael." I breathed. I was, and sounded, out of breath. "Let me in."

"Oh. Oh, o-ok."

The door buzzed and I fell against it pushing it open. I looked far up the impossibly long staircase and half-expected to see three hideous laughing monkeys.

Looking for Ellie's face, I tripped up the first stair. I caught myself on my swollen right hand, which didn't want to hold the weight, and went on falling down.

A voice gasped, "Michael, Jesus!" Footsteps started rushing down toward me. My ears picked up the descending sounds of feet, but unless Ellie gained weight, or grew extra legs, it wasn't just her coming down.

I steadied myself on my good hand and looked up again to see Ellie floating toward me on a whir of knees and sock feet, while Sean came following in even, steady footfalls. What was he doing here?

It was just as well. I got back to my feet just as they reached me. Sean immediately hooked my arm over his muscle-y, lumpy shoulder and began pulling me easily up the straight two-flights-in-one staircase to Ellie's apartment.

Any uncomfortable feeling there was in being carried so far up stairs by a man I hardly knew was overshadowed by the pounding in my head and throbbing in my face and knees. Visions came to me of carrying Ian up stairs, trying not to hurt him more. Sean had more of a handle on it than I'd had. I kept trying to get my feet under me, but he was shorter than me, making it too hard for them to cooperate. Plus, my mind kept trying to think and complicate things. I didn't know what he was doing there making time with my lady, but I sure wasn't going to ask until I was lying down comfortably with an ice pack on my head.

Which was exactly where I was about five minutes later, but even then, Ellie wouldn't let me get a question in until I'd told them both what had happened.

"I..I went to...," I wanted to talk, but my mouth wouldn't loosen. I hadn't realized I'd been clinching it. This business of being knocked out had really fucked me up. I was feeling better with ice on my face, lying back, but I had to work out the kinks in my brain. The blurry edge to everything was gone. Now, there was only a whip lapse when I turned my head like a digital camera refocusing; turn, blur, image, turn, blur, image. I quit turning my head.

I actually *wanted* to talk to them, tell them the story, but my brain kept interrupting, causing me to stop and squeeze my temples. I was having a hard time remembering who I'd told what. I don't think I'd told Sean about my place being broken into and his being here muddied things up. And I hadn't told Ellie about the weed, because I didn't want her to know I was selling drugs, didn't want her to think of me that way.

So, I decided to moan and rock back and forth in pain for a bit, instead of being straightforward. But while my body rocked in pain, I kept my good eye peeled and sorted out my thoughts.

"I was over by Paul and Pratt's place," I squeezed out, pausing slightly as Sean snuck a glance at Ellie, who ignored it. I wasn't sure if either of them knew those guys, or how well.

"Yeah," I went on, "I stopped by to talk to them," pause, watch, nothing, "but, nobody was there."

Ellie stared through me with a plastic face, eyes blinking. Sean let out a breath, said, "So what happened?"

"Then, a couple of guys jumped me when I was leaving."

Ellie came back to life. "Oh my god, that's terrible."

"Shit." Sean said, standing behind Ellie. He was standing with arms crossed, a vacant stare growing behind his eyes. I could see this wasn't what he had come over here for, boredom was showing through the cracks in his hollow sympathy. "I didn't know that kind of stuff happened around here."

"Yeah. Jesus," Ellie said softly and touched my knee tenderly.

"Yeah, I told them to fuck off," I said, "but think that made it worse."

"Ha ha, tough guy." Ellie purred.

"They take your phone and shit?" Sean said, all compassion.

"No," I went on lying, "a car pulled down the alley, right then, at just the right time."

"Wow," Ellie said. "At least that was lucky."

"Yeah, I guess. Little late though." I said, repositioning the ice bag on my eye. Water ran down my chin. It felt good.

Story told, I didn't know what else to say. My face told the rest and I wanted to know why Sean was there. More awkwardness spread between us. Sean leaned back on his heels.

"Well, shit, man. I'm glad you're ok." Sean said, ready to go.

Ellie noticed and looked up a little too quickly, surprised.

"What," I asked, innocently, "what were you guys doing?"

"Oh," Ellie said, without a thought, "we ran into each other at the coffee shop." She smiled. "Came up here for a smoke."

"Yeah," Sean put in. "Wasn't expecting so much excitement."

We all chuckled weirdly.

"Yeah, me either."

"Well, I should get going," he said. Finally.

Ellie's head snapped up at his looming figure again. "Oh yeah?" she said, like it was no big deal. "It was good running into you." Then looked at me, kindly, and back to him. "And thanks for helping. I never could've carried him up alone."

"Yeah," I agreed on that, and waved my bag of ice. "Thanks."

"Yeah, no problem. Glad I was here." He lingered for a second, then turned and left. Ellie locked the door behind him and came back to the couch.

"I can't believe this happened to you." She touched my cheek. "Does it hurt too bad?"

As soon as Sean was gone, Ellie's touch made my belly tingle. "Nah," I said with a smile. "It's not so bad anymore."

"I couldn't believe it when I saw you laying at the bottom of the stairs. I thought you'd been shot or something."

"Hah," I fidgeted and sat up some more, suddenly feeling silly. "Guess it was pretty dramatic. I was just trying to get you to feel sorry for me."

"Well, you definitely put your all into it. You should take it to the stage."

"Oh, I don't think so. It hurts too bad to do it every night."

"You feeling any better?" She slid closer, her body coming against my arm, but keeping her weight off it. "Anything you need right now?"

I thought of a couple things. My eye met hers and slid slowly down to her mouth then, along her slim neck. And then self-consciously, her body closed off just enough. I wasn't supposed to notice. She sat back slightly and poured more honey into her voice to make up for it. She said slowly, "Anything you want me to do for you? Make you more comfortable?"

The warmth cooled in my groin, but I didn't want her to know it. "You know what I need." I said, matching her tone. "But I guess I'd take a drink for now. If you got one."

She sat back further, still eyeing me beautifully. "You sure you should drink? With a concussion and all?"

"Ehh. I'll be fine."

"Alright," she said, "but don't let it go to your head. In fact, I think you'll get some water in it too. I don't want you passing out on me."

"Fine." I watched her get up and go to the kitchen. Tinkling sounds came from glass as the faucet ran. I looked at the chair where Sean had sat.

When she came back, I couldn't help saying, "It was nice Sean was here. You guys hang out a lot?"

She brushed it away quickly. "No, not really," she said, shaking it off, "you know, at parties, or whatever. Lucky I ran into him though, huh?"

"Yeah, it would have really been embarrassing if you had to carry me up here all by yourself."

"Aw, I would have been fine." She nuzzled in beside me. "I would have figured something out for you. But you're here alone with me now, so what's it matter?"

I sat up again and took a full drink of whiskey. It stung like hell on my busted lip. I winced as it went down. Maybe it wasn't such a good idea.

"Why haven't you answered my calls?" I said, as the burning subsided. "I texted you a couple of times."

"You have?" She sat up straight. "My phone," she said, shaking her head, "it's been fucked up lately. I keep missing messages, or getting them too late."

"Yeah? Something wrong with it?" I kept my voice cool, accepting.

"Yeah, for the past couple of weeks. Sometimes it's fine, then it's not. It's frustrating."

The old fucked-up-phone routine, always so convenient.

"Oh," I said, smiling at her again, forgetting it. "I just wondered is all. Thought maybe it was my phone or something."

"No," she relaxed again. "It's been happening. I need to get it fixed."

I tried some more whiskey, but it hurt too much. This time it was me who rubbed her leg.

"Are you feeling better?" She put her hand on top of mine. "I'm getting tired. You want to get in bed?"

"Absolutely."

Ellie got me out of my pants, pulled down the covers and went back to the kitchen for a fresh bag of ice. I laid back in her billowy, cloudlike heaven-bed and tried to relax, let my cares drift away, at least for the next few hours. I heard water run in the bathroom and the toilet flush. Ice cubes fell into the sink. Lights went out in the living room and Ellie appeared in the bedroom doorway with the short silk nightgown on that ended just below her butt. She came around my side of the bed with the fresh bag of ice followed closely by hard little nipples. My whole body felt instantly better.

She paraded back around and crawled in on her side, though I'd hoped she'd crawl over. I hadn't thought about it until then, but my left eye was the swollen one. Meaning in order to spoon I'd have to endure the pain. I'd been through worse. I rolled over slowly, clinching my mouth tight and scooped my hand under her nightgown against her soft, soft stomach.

Ellie gently rolled on her back causing me to move over and softly pushed my hand back to me.

"I think you better sleep," she said, kindly. "You need to rest."

"Uh-huh," I mumbled.

She rolled back over. I endured and rested my hand on her hip, letting my fingers find the soft spot just inside her pelvis.

She ever-so-easily took my hand away and rolled toward me, nestling her head and knees between us, with the rest of her out of reach.

The hurting came slowly back into my head and body. Eventually, I rolled over giving up hope and managed to fall asleep.

Chapter 20

I slept hard and heavy that night with dreams of stampeding elephants, their dust clouding everything around me. My left eye was sore and gritty the minute I opened it. And the further I strained into consciousness, the more my jaw hurt, and then my neck, and my left leg. I felt pummeled and dried out.

Not only was everything sore, but as soon as I rolled over, I realized I'd missed the best part of waking up at Ellie's. She was already up and fully dressed. Her hair whipped around the corner as she hurried in to lean over me.

"Gotta go," she said, hair dangling on my cheek as she kissed my forehead. "You can go out the back way. Make sure you pull the door shut all the way, it'll lock. Bye." And she was gone.

I blinked after her, trying to get that dust out of my eyes and moaned "Good Morning" to the empty room. My head hurt and my body hurt. And it wasn't just sexual disappointment, though that was part of it. Ellie had been one part nurturing and one part distant. She would stroke me tenderly like a lonely field nurse at war time caring for the one patient she longed for, then turn icy cold when I pushed it.

Hmm. Women.

I knew I'd think about it more later, after some coffee. And probably thirty more times, until I saw her again.

But more immediate matters first. I needed to go see Ian. If nothing else, I owed him an apology. I also needed to find out more about what had happened to him. Everything he said to me the other night had been clouded by my suspicion. He'd told me it was Alex. And I was more concerned with *why* he was telling me than *what* he was telling me. Now, Alex's hand in everything was undeniable. I knew who.

And now that I knew who, I had to figure out what to do about it. I wanted more on who was with him when he hit Ian and how it had actually happened. Did Alex use the same 'hey buddy' plan on Ian? Probably. Were Paul and Pratt with him? Or did Alex have other guys he used as well? Was it a whole gang of dudes, or just a couple? Alex wouldn't do it alone. He didn't go anywhere alone. He liked an entourage, to be the leader of a pack.

Alex had basically admitted to me last night that he was the one who'd broken into my apartment. And I was going to have to do something about it. But I couldn't do it alone. I needed Ian to help me. He'd been hurt too and together we'd stand a better chance.

In Ellie's bathroom, I did a more complete job of cleaning myself up; wiping caked blood away, probing for loose teeth, digging dirt, I hoped, out from under my nails. Besides the black eye, I didn't *look* too bad. I couldn't breathe out of my nose though, and my mouth felt like it was full of ripe cherries, really juicy ones with hard pits in them.

The back stairs leading down to the alley behind Ellie's place were enclosed with cheap particleboard and vinyl siding. Judging by the rotten stains, gooey chunks of cardboard cartons and empty cans lying around it probably smelled like trash, if I could smell. The steps felt rickety under my feet. The two-by-four banister wiggled in my hand. The door stood open at the bottom and I was glad I didn't have to touch it. Outside it was warm and the sun was bright. It hurt my left eye to squint. I tried not to, but I couldn't help it. It was too bright. I used my hand as a visor.

The coffee shop on the corner probably still smelled like motor oil too. I could hear the coffee roaster wheezing and squealing in the corner. The girl with no bra wasn't there and I knew how the DIY process worked now. I got the Nicaraguan Blend this time and decided granola and yogurt might be easier to eat than a bagel. When I went to pay, I remembered my hand was sore. And that I didn't have any cash. There was a credit card minimum, but the guy behind the counter took pity on me and let it slide, or maybe with my black eye I looked like the sort that might make trouble.

I ate and couldn't help brooding.

Alex. Alex was *not* the friend he'd appeared to be. I probably would have felt ashamed if I wasn't so fucking mad. He'd led me straight into the lion's den and goaded the lions to make them angry. Maybe it was a stretch to call pillhead Paul a lion but, you know what I'm saying.

Goddamnit.

And what was worse, I couldn't go straight at him for it. I couldn't run to his house, drag him out and shake him by the boots. He'd be ready for it. And from the looks of it, he had a whole bunch of people in on it with him. Who knew which ones had my shit? Did *he* have it? Had I been in his apartment, *twice,* and not known I was standing right next to my own money?

First, I needed to go see Ian. Talk to him. Maybe he would have an idea.

The same Ashland bus that brought me to Ellie's took me up near Ian's. It was crowded and my sinuses had cleared enough to smell somebody's liquor-breath enveloping the whole bus. I stood in the aisle, holding the pole above me, bouncing along as the neighborhoods changed going north. Store fronts streamed by; liquor stores with neon lights challenging the sun from behind bars, auto parts stores, Chinese buffets. They thinned out for a while where nobody got off the bus, then, became more dense again closer to Ian's neighborhood in Ravenswood. I had to bend over a bit to see out the window and up at the street signs until I saw the right one.

I was around the corner and halfway up the sidewalk when I saw Ian come out of his building with a backpack on, carrying a duffel bag. Following his thin, forward leaning gait,

I noticed the taxi waiting at the curb. I had to jog to catch him before he got there.

"Hey! Ian!" I yelled, loudly. "What's up? Where are you going?"

His face was only slightly less swollen than the day before, turning from pinkish-red to purple. We must have looked like abused twin brothers, or like we'd beaten each other.

"I'm goin' home, Mike."

"What do you mean 'going home'? You can't leave."

"The hell I cain't," he said, pulling open the trunk. "I'm out, son. Ain't dealing with this shit no mo'. Goin' home for a while an' let this shit blow over." After tossing his bags in, he stopped with one hand on the trunk, noticing my black eye. He jabbed his chin at me, said, "So you didn't believe me huh?"

My hand unconsciously went to the eye but I stopped it halfway. "Yeah...Well no," I said, defensively. "I went to go see what he'd say."

"And? What he say?" he said, sarcastically, mocking my bruised face and slamming the trunk closed.

"That's what I'm here about. I need you to help me. You can't just run away. I need your help with this."

"Look kid, I'm done with this shit. I been tellin' you. Alex is fucked up, I don't want nothin' more to do with it."

"Look, but I got a plan. We can hit back. But we got to do it quick, before he expects it." I caught the door and held it shut as he pulled on it. "Come on, Ian. Help me out. Stay around for a few more days, see where things go."

"No way, son. I'm *done*. And what do you care anyway? As far as you're concerned, I was the one broke in yo' place. Ain't that why you were goin' through my shit the other night? Tryin ta see if I had yo' shit? Stashed away somewhur? Huh?"

Oops. "No, man, that wasn't it. I didn't think it was you but, I had to be sure. And after you tried to run me over—"

"I didn't try to run you over!" He threw his arms up in frustration, then tried to pull on the taxi door again. "Get out the way Mike, I'm leavin'."

"Ian, help me out. We can get back at Alex together. I can't deal with him on my own. He has too many people. You're the only one with me on this." I had already lost, he wouldn't hear me. "Come on, after it's all over I could hook you up with my guy back in Indiana, you could make your money back."

"No, Mike. I'm done. Look at my face, man. You think I *like* lookin' like this? No. An' this is just for talkin' shit about 'im, tellin' you the truth." He shook his head. "Don't fuck with him, son, he ain't right." I let him push me out of the way and open the taxi door. "Go ask Tim or Chris, or whoever else you got. I'm outta here. Let this shit blow over." He climbed in the car and looked up at me around his golf ball sized purplish left eye. "Let me know when it's done, maybe we *could* go in, like you said." And slammed the door.

I watched the cab go to the corner and stop at the light. I was stuck standing there, deciding what to do, as it drove off toward O'Hare.

Chapter 21

If it's possible for a sigh to last fifteen minutes, then that's how long it lasted. One long seemingly endless sigh lasting all the way to Tim and Chris's apartment, peppered with a few helpless hand-raises to the sky. How were these two guys the only people I had to count on? They weighed a hundred and twenty pounds each and wielded nothing but personality as their weapons against the world. Brawn was not a word they had ever heard, except maybe in a paper towel commercial, and I didn't think they even watched TV.

I needed help. That was it. And like it or not, these guys were always around. I sighed again.

The bar on the corner below their apartment had its windows open to the warm summer wind, the Cubs' game booming through the sound system. A group of red, white, and blue smokers sprawled across the sidewalk in front of the door, yelling in loud afternoon-drunk voices. The noise of a mower was coming from somewhere, the landlady out of sight. I waded through the smokers, holding my breath and buzzed up.

"Jesus, what happened to your eye?" Tim said, keeping his distance with both hands palms out, as if it were contagious.

"Whoa, no shit," Chris said, coming across the room to see the spectacle. "Did Ian do that? Weren't you going to talk to him?"

"No, it wasn't Ian. It—"

"So, you didn't go talk him," Tim said, now moving in too close to examine the black eye like a doctor on a bad TV drama, or at least his take on one.

"Yeah, I did," I said, pushing him away. "Just, just give me some room. I'll tell you."

"Ok. Ok." Tim said, stepping back, hands out again. "Take your time."

"So it *wasn't* Ian? Who was it then?" Chris said, impatiently.

I went and sat at the kitchen table. They followed. Chris pulled out his obligatory sack of weed and started rolling a joint. "No, Chris, don't do that yet. I need to talk to you guys first."

"Whoa. He comes to us again with the talking," Tim said. Chris looked at him briefly and pulled back a little, chastised. Tim gave a little shrug, sitting straighter in his chair.

"I need your help." I said quickly, as an explanation for my bluntness, no pun intended.

"Ok," Tim said neatly and spread his hands out on the table in front of him. "This sounds like it's going to be serious. Should we get our notebooks? Take notes?"

"No," I said flatly, not in the mood.

"Oh," Tim said, "I guess this *is* serious. No jokes allowed." He leaned closer, more serious. "Are we going to get hurt? Looks like we might get hurt."

"You're not gonna—"

"Yeah," Chris said, "and what's up with your face? *Did* Ian hit you, or what?"

"Yeah," Tim followed quickly. "Don't you think you need tell us what's going on?"

"Ok. Listen. Ian didn't hit me," I said and put my hand out to calm them. "But I did go see him. And I'll tell you guys. But more importantly, I need you guys to help me with something."

"Well, I don't want to get hurt," Tim said.

"You're not getting hurt. Nobody gets hurt. I just need you guys to stand lookout for me."

"Why?" Chris said, squinting at me suspiciously. "What are you gonna do?"

"Ok," I said, hand out again, and paused to pique their attention. "I'm going to break into Alex's place. And you guys are gonna be the lookouts."

They looked at each other, before saying in unison, "What?"

"Yeah."

"No," they said.

"That's who did this." I circled my face with my hand. "Well, his buddies did mostly, but he was there. And, now, I know he's the one who broke into my place."

"Wait, what?" Tim said. "What about Ian?"

"He's gone. He went back to Arizona this morning."

"What?"

"Yeah, I just talked to him, watched him drive off in a cab."

"Wow. Ok."

"So, you didn't go see him the other night?" Chris said.

"Yeah I did. And I found him beaten all to shit."

Both of their faces hung in confusion. "And Alex did that too?"

"Yes."

"And now you think Alex broke into your house and you want to break into his place to get your stuff back?

"Exactly."

"No way." Tim said, speaking for the group.

"Obviously, No," Chris said. "But more importantly, what does it have to do with us? What makes you think we're getting into it?"

"Getting into it? I need you guys to help me. And you've already been in it. Remember when you came and told me, wrongly, that Ian did it? You're already in it. And we're friends. And Ian's your friend. And mainly, I can't do it alone. I need you guys to stand watch. That's all. Nothing's going to happen to you."

"Yeah, that's definitely the pattern—" Tim said weakly.

"What if he comes home?"

"Or is already there?"

I said, "That's why we have to do it now—"

"Now!? It's daytime."

"Not now now. Later. Tonight. He does his DJ thing tonight at The Billington. And we need to do it quick, like today, before he thinks I'll try to do anything, while he's still proud of himself being the big shot."

"No way," Chris said. "I'm not doing anything to get my head beat in. No way."

"I wouldn't ask you to do anything crazy, not even break the law. Nobody's going to see you, or know you where even there."

"Then why not just do it yourself, if it's so safe?"

"'Cuz I need a lookout. I can't be inside *and* watching the street."

"I don't like it."

"I don't know, man," Tim said. "I don't think so."

Chris shook his head in agreement.

"Just...Look, it'll be fine. Nothing's gonna happen. Help me out guys, come on." I looked them both in the eye. "I need your help. A friend asking. Just lookouts. I'm not asking for anything dangerous, or illegal. Just be a lookout. If anything happens, you have my permission to run. I'll buy you a beer afterwards, two beers...."

Chapter 22

We waited until later, when I knew he'd be gone, to take the train over to Alex's. On the way, I told them, with words, about going to Paul and Pratt's place, but they could see on my face how well it had gone. Telling the story actually encouraged me, stiffened my nerve. I rode along determinedly, like a stolid sea captain, holding onto a pole while the train rocked gently and the city rolled by underneath us.

But the same could not be said for Tim and Chris. They both jittered visibly, looking alternately out the train windows, at me, to each other, at the cemetery going past below us. When we left the station at Wilson, walking out into the particularly grim-looking street scene around Broadway, the anxiety was boiling behind their eyes.

"I'm just gonna call him and found out where he's at, make sure he's not at home." Chris said.

"I'm telling you he isn't home," I said. "You *know* he always goes to The Billington on Tuesday nights. He plays music there, DJs or whatever. You've *been* there with him."

"Yeah, let's just call and find out," Tim agreed. "There's no harm in making sure."

"But there is," I said. "Listen. Guys. He won't be home! There's nothing to worry about. If we call him, now, he might wonder why, you know? But," I calmed my voice. "Ok. Tim, you go to the front door and ring the bell. Me and Chris will go around back and see if any lights are on or anything. That way we'll know he's not there. Ok? And make sure you ring the bell a couple times, to be sure."

We came to the corner, time to separate.

"But what do I say if he's there? If he answers?" Tim asked. "What, did I just randomly show up? I need some kind of motivation."

"I don't know, man, you're the actor. Make something up. Improvise."

He finally went on, shaking his head, not feeling good about his level of preparation. Chris and I turned down the alley, casually glancing behind us to see if anyone was paying attention. Well maybe we looked around a bit more than casually. Chris's head was swinging back and forth like a loose weather vane out on Lake Michigan. But I didn't want to say anything, didn't want to chastise him and cause what little confidence he'd mustered to recoil.

And maybe I was feeling it a little too. The way the two of them were carrying on was freaking me out a bit. We didn't talk. Deeper down the alley, Chris dragged a joint out of his pocket and flicked his lighter.

I smacked his hand away. "What the hell are you doing?" I whisper-barked.

"Come on, Mike, I don't like this shit. Look at my hands, they're shaking like crazy."

They were shaking. He wouldn't have been able to light a grill, let alone a joint. And for some reason, the sight of his shaky hands, and the slumped way he held them out for inspection, bolstered my resolve. Watching his hands quiver in the dim street light was like physically seeing the butterflies fluttering in my own belly.

I stopped, grabbed Chris's small shoulders, looked him square in the eye and said firmly, "Come on, man, this is no big deal." And repeated it inwardly. "We aren't doing anything wrong. Your just gonna stand out here, as if you were just another regular guy standing out back smoking a cigarette." Then I realized that could be misconstrued as telling him to smoke the joint. "But don't actually smoke. Not that thing anyway," I added, pointing at the joint.

"Why not, Mike? If I'm just another guy, nobody will notice."

"Are you kidding, you can smell that shit from a block away...I should know, I sold it to you."

Feeling somewhat more determined, we walked slowly on, trying hard not to tiptoe, or creep like bandits.

Tim texted, saying "No answer. Coming to meet you."

"See? I told you," I said to Chris, holding my phone out for him to see.

When we came to the right place, we pulled up short to wait for Tim. Alex's building was recessed from the others creating an alcove. We stood close behind the building next door, hidden from sight. With quick, pigeon-like head moves, I poked my head around the corner, slightly up at his back window. No lights. Tim crept up behind us and made bird movements of his own to check out the situation, only he moved his whole body, getting into it like some kind of acting class exercise, be the animal, his arms tucking back.

Alex's apartment was the first floor up on the right side. You could tell, even from the back, that his building was more expensive. The old wooden fire escape had recently been replaced by the stronger, black painted steel. The ground floor apartments had little concrete patios built into the ground a few steps down from the alley with flower boxes lining the edges. Alex's back porch hung about eight feet up with the staircase, and everything else at ground level, enclosed in sleek, six foot iron fencing protected by savage spikes on top.

In order to get onto Alex's porch/balcony, I simply had to climb the iron fence, step over the eight inch spikes and hop the railing. It was easy, except that there was no foothold on the slick fence. Tim, being the taller of the two, had to give me a boost.

I leaned back over the rail. "Stay close," I whispered to him, "to help me down. And if you see something call. Don't text. Call."

"O.K.," they both whispered back, looking from side to side. Ok, so far, so good.

The fire escape, or mandatory excuse for a balcony, was much wider than Ian's. There was enough room up here for a table and chairs, which the neighbor was taking full advantage of. Alex, however, only had two white plastic deck chairs, like you see everywhere, and a big, red and white Igloo cooler on two wheels, like airplane luggage, to rest your feet on. There was a glass ashtray balanced on the brick windowsill and....

You know, it's funny how everyone's always talking about crime in the big city. How afraid everyone is of crackheads and cat burglars, of being mugged, or robbed. People put four professional grade locks on their front doors and blaring security alarms in their cars and those metal bar things that lock the steering wheel in place. Yet, it's amazing how many of those same people leave their back windows open at night, or when the go out; windows cracked open to let the breeze come through and save on electricity by not running the air conditioner.

Alex's kitchen window was thin and rectangular and open, covered only by a screen. I guess there's security in a window screen? I mean, it *seems* like your window is closed. Only, screens are made out of vinyl, which is basically like cotton, or something. Needless to say, it doesn't do anything to keep anyone out. It was wonderful.

On the side of caution, I put my ear against the screen to listen hard for movement inside, or music, or any other signs of life. Nothing but faint street noise behind me. And something smelling like a dead skunk. Weed?!

Shit, weed! I smelled weed!

My chest tightened. Icy adrenaline started in my gut and raced through to the top of my head, standing the hair up on my neck. He was home! And I was on his porch unannounced. Shit!

He must have been sitting in the dark, puffing a big spliff. Maybe listening to Bob Marley softly and burning Nag Champa!

Shit!

I had to get out before he heard me. I pushed back from the window and spun around. I went this way and that, then to the side of the railing. I threw one leg over and looked below me at Tim puffing hard on the joint to get it burning.

"God dammit, you idiot!" I whisper-yelled. "Put that thing out!"

Alex wasn't home. It was just these two idiots.

Tim looked up at me with a question in his eyes, holding smoke in and shrugged his shoulders.

I wanted to yell so badly but I couldn't. There were still neighbors. I flailed my arms around silently instead, wildly signing, "You idiots. I can smell that" in big arm circles and pointing at my nose. Chris shrugged and mouthed "What?" I made jail bar signs like a mime and whirling police lights with my hands, pointing at myself and to them. Tim and Chris did more exaggerated shrugs and kept silently smoking the joint, while looking around to see what I was so excited about. Idiots!

A car revved its engine out of sight down the alley, then went whipping past like it was a drag strip. I checked my breathing. The best way to get this done, I told myself, was to get it done. Try to forget about my idiotic friends for a second.

I turned back, letting my heart slow down and focused again on the window. I was here for a bigger reason. A more important reason.

With my recent window failure at Ian's still fresh and sorely in my mind, and shins, I pulled the cooler beneath the window; not the one of the white plastic chairs, we've all seen those chairs buckle under some fat girl singing and dancing to "Chicken Fried" at some shitty Fourth of July party. The cooler was much sturdier, even if somewhat shorter.

Like last time, I poked one of my house keys through the screen over Alex's kitchen window. I scored it repeatedly until the small tear opened enough to get my hand in. The rest was a cinch.

A minute later, I was alone, out of sight, standing in the dark inside Alex's apartment.

The stillness inside and the sound of my heart beating in my ears gave me a strange sensation. I had just broken into someone's house. I was a burglar. Hah. I'd done it.

Sure, I had thought about doing it before, and even tried at Ian's house, but this time it was real. And it wasn't even that hard! Hah! I wanted to poke my head out the window and wave to Tim and Chris, triumphantly giddy, give a big thumbs up and a wave. But there was no time for that. This was serious. Really.

A nervous, tight smile broke on my face as I tiptoed out of the kitchen. Using my phone as a flashlight, I picked my way through to the bedroom, careful not to step on canvases leaning against the walls on the floor of the short hall. I was looking for two things, a two-pound sack of weed and ten thousand dollars in cash.

I hit all the usual places in the bedroom first; under the bed, nothing, dresser, closet. I searched the front room next, and then bathroom. I checked the bedroom again and the closet for anything I may have overlooked before going back to the kitchen on the way out.

I stopped to think. I *knew* Alex had broken into my place. I knew he had my stuff. Whether it was him directly, or if he had someone else break into my place, I knew it was him.

And BAM! There it was! Hidden away in that small cabinet above the fridge, the little one that's too hard to get to, where people put their croc pots and blenders they never use. That's where I found the small, worn, overstuffed manila envelope with the green rubber band around it and masking tape. The exact one I kept my money in. Except with a few more miles on it.

I looked quickly inside with almost watery, longing eyes, to make sure it was what I thought it was then, stuffed it down the front of my pants. I didn't really care if it was all there, I could worry about that later. Most is better than none. I made a quick search of the rest of the kitchen for the bag of weed that went with it. The big, fluffy, couch-pillow-sized bag wouldn't be as easy to hide, and it wasn't there, which was just as well, because my mind was already doing flips.

I'd found the money. I had my money! My hands were shaking and my brain was spinning like a top. I had to get out of here. Nervousness mixed with excitement and relief and dread and paranoia, I had to get out. Screw the window, I went out the back door, purposefully leaving it unlocked and open. I rushed to the side of the railing looking out for Tim to help me down. But he wasn't there. Christ.

Chris wasn't in the alley either. Shit, did they leave? I ran two steps back and two steps forth, my mind hemorrhaging. I quickly dug out my phone and called Chris. Bouncing with impatience, I went back to the rail waiting for an answer. Shit. Did they see someone? Did the cops come and scare them off? Did they get high and forget? The idiots wander off to get chips? Bastards!

The fence and spikes were the problem. I'd seen an internet video of a guy that skewered himself on spikes like that. No time. I swung my legs over the railing, tried to secure my feet against the iron fence away from the spikes. Hoping and praying, I jumped/slid/fell to the ground. Still, no sign of Tim or Chris. Damn. I booked it.

I made it to the alley in three long strides and rounded the corner of the building at full speed.

There was something there.

Something hard. Something I didn't really see, because something else got in the way. Something hard got in the way. Something very hard hit me in the side of the head. There was a flash and then darkness. The world went out from under my feet, sideways, I think.

Chapter 23

I woke up drenched in bright light cuddling a board. It was a long board and it had blood on it. I was holding it like it was my board and no one else could have it, like I loved it. The blaring light was pointed, coming from somewhere down by my feet. I squinted hard and shielded my eyes. A sharp pain shot up my neck when I tried to lift my head to the source of the light. Someone was saying something in a strained raspy voice.

"Hey, you ok? You hurt? Why you lying in the street like that? What are you doing with that board? You shouldn't be laying there like that. It's dangerous." His shape was a hazy blur, but it was an old man's voice. He kicked the bottom of my foot. "Hey, buddy, you can't lay there like that. You ok? You hurt?"

I could hear him, but his words were sort of muffled. I put my hand to my ear and it came away bloody. My nose was bloody too and I could taste it in my mouth, again.

I put a hand out to stop him kicking me. "Yeah, yeah, fell...got hit..."

"A car hit you? Hell, *I* almost hit you. Laying in the street like that, it's no wonder. I should—I should get the cops."

"Uhn-uh, I...I ok." I got up as far as my right elbow.

"Well, you got to get outta the alley. I almost hit you. Somebody else *will*. You're lucky I'm still sharp, coulda run you over." He kicked my foot again. "Can't you get up? You ok?"

"Yeah," I said, moving my legs under me, letting the board fall away.

The old guy backed away, untrusting, as I got shakily to my feet. The ground dropped away again and pulled at my head like a giant magnet. I staggered hard to the left catching the brick wall to hold myself up.

"You, yeah, you look alright now," the old man said, backing behind his open driver's side door. "I should get going. I—I'll tell the police you're back here. Let 'em know you're hurt."

I stretched out a hand trying to mutter "no," but he was gone before it came out. I put my hands to my head to steady it a minute. I looked up and down the alley after him. I turned to look up at Alex's back window. Still no lights on. I looked down at the board lying on the ground next to the trash can and felt for the money in my waistband. It was gone. Perfect.

Up, down, throbbing in and out. I took a few deep breaths and tried standing on my own, away from the wall. How quickly everything had looked up and up, then went crashing down again so hard. My head pounded. My heart sank down, beaten down by the pile driver in my banging skull.

I pushed off the wall and tilted my swollen, swelling head in the direction of the street. Cars went by, their headlights washing out the orange-brown street lights briefly. I scuffed my big tennis shoes on the sidewalk. I hated it when people scuffed their feet and I make it a point not to, even when I'm drunk, but who cares. There was a convenience store at the corner across from the "L" station at Wilson. I got a bottle of water and some napkins from the coffee machine.

On the train platform, some kid with his pants falling off was singing off key under big, DJ-style headphones. Another guy was smoking a Black and Mild further down. I could smell the sweetness of it. It's illegal to smoke on the train platform. But who cared about that either.

I sat down. The train came. I transferred. I went home.

A cold shower cleared my head up more than I thought possible. In the bathroom mirror, I realized, thankfully, it wasn't my ear that was bleeding, but a small cut under the hair, above my ear, on the left side. Miraculously, my muffled hearing started to clear up with the realization. An ice pack on back of my neck did wonders. And although my spirit was still in pretty bad shape, I felt, surprisingly, better.

There was an antsy, uneasy feeling tickling my stomach. I'd been so close. I paced around thinking in circles. The third time I caught myself staring unconsciously out the eyehole in my door, I realized I didn't want to be alone. I was looking across the hall waiting to see if Melanie was home yet. I'd already gone over there and knocked twice, once before my shower and once after, in case I missed her. But I still kept catching myself staring through the eyehole.

I'd called Tim and Chris thirty times each with no response. Where the hell did they go? Were they ok? Did they get knocked out too? I told them they wouldn't get hurt. And who the fuck was it anyway? I paced some more. Looked out the eyehole. Shook my head. Dabbed at the cut above my ear with a wet paper towel.

Had Alex come home and caught us there? If so, wouldn't he have come in the front door? His place wasn't like mine where it's more convenient to use the back. He would have come right through the front door and found me first, rummaging through his shit. And finding my money, I should add. So it wouldn't have been him. Plus if it was, I wouldn't have gotten off so easy. Not after what he did to Ian.

Someone else then? Who?

I didn't want to think about it anymore. My head was already hurting and hanging so low in defeat. I'd had the money back. In my hands. And lost it, again. I shook my head some more and looked out the eyehole. Melanie wasn't home yet.

I texted Ellie. Yes please, Ellie. Nothing like a beautiful girl to chase away the blues.

And she responded! Relatively quickly even!

"Just hangin out."

Maybe bringing it up the other night had worked. She was making more of an effort?

My head felt better instantly. I told her it would take me forty-five minutes to get there on the train and I'd bring a bottle of wine. She said she was out with a friend, but should be home by then. I said "great" and left the apartment immediately.

The liquor store on the corner was open. The night was warm and still young. People brushed by, coming together in a knot at Clark, then thinned out again along Diversey toward the bars on Halsted. The southbound train rolled in thunderously overhead just before I got to the station, as always. Fuck it. I was in a better mood, felt like splurging. I spun around and hailed a taxi. It had been a long day, to say the least. I was looking forward to the good part happening, and I sure as hell didn't want to wait another thirty minutes for the next train.

The cab driver barreled across town, through light traffic, with disproportionate rage, and got us to Wicker Park in fifteen minutes. I was twenty minutes earlier than I'd told Ellie I would be. As we turned onto North Ave., I texted her saying I might get there early, hoping she'd be home already.

Her building was only a few blocks from Ashland and we passed it before she responded. I told the cabbie I'd get out at Damen, figuring I'd get a beer or something.

There's a ton of bars around that area and people clog the narrow sidewalks as if waiting in line. In the perpetual knot of traffic near the five corners, my cab got stuck. I could have walked to the corner faster than the taxi could take me, but I wasn't in a hurry. I watched hot girls and corny dudes walk by while I waited for Ellie's text back. The breeze felt good coming through the open window. A car ahead of us in the line was blasting reggaeton and yelling sporadically.

I looked at my phone impatiently. I looked out at the upcoming bars and watched for girls who looked like Ellie. That girl really looked like her. Shit! It was her!

Ellie! Walking toward me on her way home, two cars up, coming right at me. I beamed. My eyes went wide with excitement. I started to throw a hand out, but froze.

Cold dread washed through me like death.

ALEX.

I snatched my arm back and ducked down, shitless. What the fuck? My heart squeezed tight like a fist. I crouched down onto the rubber floor mat, scared they'd seen me.

What the fuck was *she* doing with *him*? He was the fucking enemy. Didn't she know that? Maybe she didn't, but what the hell? She couldn't be with Alex.

Cautiously, I let my fingers find the windowsill and pulled myself up just enough for my eyes and nose to peek over the door. She was texting with her head down. Alex was walking close to her, leaning in, watching. He was close, comfortably close, intimately close.

My heartbeat was weak and in my throat. I let my eyes follow them, still crouched in the narrow space of the backseat. Why were they walking so close? Did he have his hand on her back? The bastard.

The taxi started moving and I lost them through the parked cars lining the street. No, his hand wasn't on her. Surely it was just my imagination running wild. They were friends, sure. They couldn't be hooking up. No. He'd introduced us for Christ's sake. Encouraged me even. It had to be some coincidence, had to be. But, man, Ellie sure seemed to be around a lot of dudes. Sean the other day, now this.

My phone buzzed. A message from Ellie. A message Alex watched her send. I sat up and read it, "Be home in fifteen."

I told the driver to stop around the corner and got out. Why Alex and why now? Of course they weren't *seeing* each other. That was ridiculous. It was a coincidence. Maybe she went to his show? He was just seeing her home. She didn't know what was happening. I'd purposely not told her about any of it.

I was being hysterical, running to conclusions. Wound up by nerves and physically beaten. I was imagining grandiose schemes. No. It was nothing. Coincidence.

And she didn't really lie. Of course it was only a five-minute walk to her house from there, but maybe she wanted extra time to freshen up before I got there, that's reasonable. A coincidence is all it was.

Luckily, there was a bar handy. I needed a drink.

Chapter 24

I don't know if it was the concussion, or the two double whiskeys, but I missed the step down coming out of the bar and stumbled three huge steps across the sidewalk, catching myself just before I fell into Damen. A girl squawked as I spun around, straightening myself as neatly as Charlie Chaplin. A wall of taxis lined the street waiting. The sidewalk was as crowded as it had been a half hour before. Young couples laughed and pushed each other, while somebody yelled at a bouncer that his friends were already inside.

Feeling suspicious and subversive, I crossed the street between two unmoving cars and walked along the sidewalk until Ellie's apartment windows came into sight above the drycleaner's. I knew something was going on with her. I just didn't know what. So, I stopped short and waited to see if any, and which, lights were burning inside. She was expecting me by now, so I knew Alex would be gone. But I still wanted and see if anybody was moving around in there.

Sitting over the couple of drinks I'd had, in the thirty minutes I'd been waiting, I decided to play dumb. I feel this tactic works best in pretty much all circumstances. If you don't know what to do? Play dumb. People like to think they are smarter than you. They like to think they can put something over on you and, if you allow them to believe it, will often give away more about themselves than if you confront them.

So, when Ellie buzzed me up, I swallowed my pride and acted as happy and relieved to see her as I had originally thought I would be. And, once I saw I had her to myself, it wasn't too hard.

"Jesus, Michael, did you get beat up again?" Her hands went immediately and lightly to my forehead.

"Ahh, you know," I said with a hint of drunkenness. "It's a tough world out there."

"Especially for you," she said, slowly and sweetly with touching tenderness. In fact, looking back on it, that was probably the nicest thing she had ever said to me. But then, I was kind of drunk and concussed, my judgment somewhat impaired. She led me gently to the couch by the hand. She sat close to me on the same couch cushion. Her lips hovered gently over my left eye as she moved to kiss my forehead. Her breath was warm and slightly sweet with the smell of whiskey. Mmm.

"Do you want a drink or something?" she asked, with her mouth open, paused in mid-kiss only inches from mine. "I still have some whiskey."

"Mmm, yeah," I whispered back. "In a minute," and pulled her in. I didn't know what had happened since the night before, what had changed in her, but I sure wasn't thinking about Alex anymore.

Aw, Ellie, there you are. Her lips were soft and full as they moved, perfectly in tune with mine, just the right amount of pressure, firm and occasionally aggressive, as if we'd been practicing it for years. Yet, her mouth was small, contained like the rest of her features except her eyes, which were too big and amazingly deep. I knew there was something heavenly in them, but couldn't hold her gaze long enough to find out what it was. My hand slid smoothly and fit exactly, as if by design, along her slender neck, my thumb gently following the line of her jaw, my fingers wrapping around under her hair. Her high cheekbones, slightly puffy cheeks; hints of the softness waiting in all the right places.

My hands went searching for bare skin. They found some, and encouraged, set out to find more. But before I got too far, she pushed back softly.

"Hold on," she said smiling. "Let's have a drink first. We don't have to hurry."

I ran my hand along her stomach. "I'm not in a hurry," I said. "But I don't want the fire to go out either."

"Oh, don't you worry," she purred, sliding away. "This fire will burn all night."

"Mmm. In that case, you better put some water in mine. I don't want to fall asleep on you, miss the main attraction, like last night."

"Ooh," she moaned, "a little sore about that are we? You were the one bleeding on everything. What was I to do?"

"Well, I'm all better today."

"Hmm. I hope so," she said, batting her eyes over her shoulder as she went to the kitchen to pour drinks.

I straightened my clothes and sat up. Man, I wanted her bad. And she was playing me good. Any complaint I was thinking of raising went completely out of my head.

She came back to the couch and sat down just as close. I sipped my drink and started to move my mouth to say something, but she stopped it with hers. With slight considerations for my facial wounds and brief pauses for gulps of booze, things went on, progressing as things of that nature do.

But something wasn't lining up quite right, not fitting together properly. The further we went, and the closer we got to moving into the bedroom, the more robotic it all started to feel. My mind was refusing to stay on task. It was like some kind of autopilot was trying to take over and I couldn't stop it. My mouth was going through kissing motions and my hands were automatically seeking and caressing skin. But it started to have an out-of-body-experience quality to it, like repetition and habit were taking over and I was stuck sitting behind my eyes looking out, as if they were windows in a big spaceship.

But I didn't want to be stuck behind glass. I wanted to be *in* my body feeling the warmth and caress. My brain was busy doing calculations, forcing me out. They say if you're trying to last longer in bed you should think about something else, something mundane like baseball, but I *wanted* to concentrate on what I was doing. I wanted to squeeze Ellie's boobs, feel the weight of them against my palms and enjoy it. But my damn brain wouldn't play along. It knew something wasn't right. And it was staging a coup. Movements between us were growing plastic-y, false.

Hell, maybe her brain was doing it too. Maybe that was why I couldn't concentrate. Maybe *my* brain could detect *her* brain in there humming away, scheming, and was retaliating with counterinsurgency. I mean, how could she be solely thinking about making out with me, when she had just been fraternizing with the enemy?

We stopped. We sat back simultaneously and wiped our lips, grinning. It was as if the boiling had moved from our loins, where it belonged, to our heads and forced us to stop before something blew. We both took a drink.

"So, how was your day?" I asked, sardonically, smiling.

"Oh, you know, pretty good." Ellie pulled her bangs forward and back to the side where they belonged, looking up at me demurely.

"Sorry to show up bleeding on your doorstep again so soon. I usually like to wait a month, or so, before I crawl to a girl and curl up crying in her lap."

"Yeah, well...." She put a hand to my head, closing the distance between us again. "Maybe it's easy to forget that someone might actually need you sometimes. Maybe it's kind of nice."

"Hope I didn't tear you away from anything important." I watched carefully. I wanted to skirt the issue and see what I came up with.

She drew her hand back and started touching the buttons on her shirt, which I had worked so hard to undo a minute ago. "Oh, not really, I just got a drink with my friend Selena."

Oh, ok, so it was going to be a cover-up. That's fine. A trigger switched back on in my head and I came down out of the driver's seat behind my eyes. Once I knew she was lying, it took the tender disappointment away and I could enjoy it in a more base, animalistic sort of way, if you know what I mean.

"I was ready to go anyway. You can't really get a word in with her. She just talks over you, no matter what you say."

Suddenly afraid she might start buttoning buttons, I reversed course.

"Yeah, you have to be careful of those people who try to barrel over you," I said, and leaned over her. "You never know what they'll talk you into." I put my hand under her shirt and my mouth on her neck. She squeaked and fell back under me.

Yes, my mind was conflicted. And yes, I felt betrayed. But the last time I was over here, I was stonewalled. And if I haven't mentioned it before, Ellie was beautiful with a body that made you want to kick a donkey. So after a few more minutes, we moved into the bedroom. I didn't get to find out why she was with Alex. I was sure I'd still be curious about it later and could probably bring it up then.

Chapter 25

Sleep had me down hard when something nudged my foot. I opened my eyes in a thick haze to Ellie coming back to bed, probably from the bathroom. She climbed in next to me and I made some half-hearted pawing motions at her, turning over. Sleep came back immediately and heavily; the best feeling in the world.

BANG, BANG, BANG woke me the second time. Like bombs going off and scenes of war. BANG, BANG, BANG right next to my head.

No, in the hall outside.

BANG, BANG, BANG. Not the police, louder even. At Ellie's door. Not a fist, something hard on steel.

Ellie was up, in a robe and out before I could even unclench my butt cheeks. I threw the covers back and sat up. The banging stopped. The bedroom door was torn open in a whoosh. Light from the living room came in like a flash. It was swallowed up quickly by three large shapes, bodies moving in like teeth chomping.

I lurched to get up. Something snatched my left foot and pulled hard. I was weightless for a second. That white light flashed behind my eyes with a click as my head hit the hardwood.

I grabbed at the door frame on the way by. There was too much force. They flipped me over. Duct tape wound around my hands and my feet.

A boot kicked my ribs when I bucked. Something hard hit my head. Again. My head again. I don't know where Ellie was. My eyes were too busy rolling back to look at anything. I think someone picked me up. But I don't know. I went back to sleep. It wasn't as good.

Chapter 26

Water kept trying to go up my nose. I blew out and blew out and it rushed back in. I was on the Slip-N-Slide in my grandma's back yard. My brothers were yelling behind me, cheering me on. I was going really fast, it was a good one. Except that the ground was rubbing too hard against my cheek. I tried to put my arm down, but they were both caught behind me. I couldn't get them loose. All of my weight was pressing on my chest and face. My left cheek was smashed, grinding against the ground. I wanted to open my eyes, but water would get in them.

And I must have gone off the end of the yellow, heavy plastic slide because I could feel grass on my face. It smelled like dirt. And somehow I was going backwards, the wrong way. And it wasn't my brother's yelling, the voices were too deep, grown. I rolled and tried to roll over, but the angle was wrong like my legs were in the air. I couldn't shift my weight. I started freaking out, wriggling my shoulders back and forth, the ground resisting.

There were only a few empty feet past the end of the Slip-N-Slide before you hit the rusty fence at the edge of the corn field. You had to be careful. I had to stop. When the grass got too wet you had to stop yourself, or you'd slide into the fence and catch your toes in it.

I rocked back and forth, trying to get my arms free to stop me. A stick ran under my chest, ripping across my shoulder. I groaned into the sloppy grass and forced my eyes open. My legs hit the ground with a shock and I stopped immediately. I tried to roll over again, but my feet were caught together too, tied. I made it half over onto my side when someone yelled.

"Goddamnit, Paul." I heard a hand smack. "Can't you hold him for five seconds? It's right there. *Right there.* Jesus!"

All I could see was shoes, but I knew exactly who it was. Alex. His voice twisted in a tight cool rage.

"Paul, you have one leg to hold. That's it. Five more fucking seconds."

"His legs all slippery. You try pulling him." Paul's voice was whiny by contrast, but still tightly pinched.

"Just fucking *pull* him." Alex said, the sound turning away.

I instantly remembered being pulled out of bed. The three figures that had darkened the bedroom door were obviously Alex, Paul, and Pratt. My legs jerked up again and my body weight shifted back onto my cheek. Cold wind licked at the wet hair on my legs, and arms, and back. Was I naked? No, I couldn't feel the grass on my balls. My briefs were yanked up hard in the front, in a reverse wedgy, grinding in as they pulled me by my feet.

I would have asked them to stop, but there was tape over my mouth. I sucked air in through my nose as best I could with the wet grass lapping me in the face. I bucked wildly like a calf bound and tied in a rodeo. Sliding unhappily along like a wet noodle, I bent and strained against the momentum pulling me backwards. I folded myself in half, driving the ground harder into my face. Something ripped. My legs hit the ground again.

"Fuck, Paul," Alex yelled. "Come *on*, *Jesus*." I heard smacking again.

"Stop fucking hitting me. What the fuck is wrong with you?"

"With me? You're the one can't hold him."

With my legs free, I flipped over and spun easily on the wet grass. Alex was in Paul's face while Pratt stood hulking alongside, waiting. There was another guy I couldn't recognize in a black hoody standing off on the fringe. I was up on my feet and running. I shook the water from my face, feet slipping in the dew-covered grass.

We were in the Lincoln Park next to the lake. The city in front of me. The darkness of lake behind me. Lights and car horns ahead on Lake Shore Drive.

I made it a good ten feet before I tripped over nothing and went face first into the dirt, my arms still tied. A rush of kicking feet and sharp knees fell on top of me almost instantly.

"You idiots are amazing," Alex snapped, behind hard breathing. I groaned against the tape on my mouth as a knee dug into the back of my neck.

"The fucking tape broke." Pratt said calmly, in a voice as deep as he was wide.

"Well, fucking grab him then," Alex said, quickly. "Get him down by the lake before somebody sees us."

As they pulled me up, I could see they had dragged me most of the way across the park while I was knocked out. I hadn't even begun to close the distance with my great, daring escape. Pratt pulled me to my feet. He and Paul grabbed my arms.

Once I was situated safely back on my feet, Alex turned around and punched me square in the face. My head snapped against my shoulder, blood dripping from my nose.

"That's for running away," he said, then marched on ahead like Napoleon having smacked someone with his glove. Evidently there was a dark side to him.

I let my head hang down while scrawny Paul and massive Pratt did all the work of moving me forward. The ground looked blurry. Even though it was so close, I couldn't seem to focus my eyes on it. The grass was cold and wet with dew. My bare feet slid along under me as they dragged me toward the large concrete ledges stepping down to the lake's edge.

The grass stopped at a low wall in front of the ledges. I jabbed my feet against it with sudden fury and shoved backwards, throwing my head into it in a last-ditch effort.

Paul lost his weak grip on my left arm, but Pratt held fast, snatching any momentum I'd hoped for like a bear catching a salmon. I grunted and strained at his hold. Alex turned again and threw a shot in at my ribs. I tensed with a jolt, then quit. They dragged my shins over the low wall making sure to scrape all the skin off on the way.

Paul stumbled, trying to keep up, as Pratt yanked and pulled me down the five oversized steps. The heels and tops of my bare feet scratched and scraped on the fresh concrete as I tried in vain to stop our forward progress. Alex stood at the edge overlooking the lake and black sky. The guy in the hoody was standing off to the side. It looked like he had his phone out, taking video. With a huge heavy hand, Pratt forced me to sit down obediently on the last step.

Alex turned to me, smiling manically. The suffused light on his face made him look greenish yellow against the darkness over the lake behind him. His teeth were grinding over each other inside his closed mouth, his jaw working in muted circles. He was buzzing, obviously jacked on something, coke probably. No, with Paul there, it would be pills.

"Well, Michael," he said, in a friendly tone. "Thanks for agreeing to meet me like this, though I know you were probably reluctant at first. But still, I'm glad you decided to come just the same. Now," he bent toward me. "I'm gonna take this tape off your mouth and ask you a question. Just one question and you're gonna answer it." His smiled dropped when he said, "And don't yell, or do anymore sissy shit, or I'll have Pratt put his fist down your throat." He straightened, putting the smile on again. "So answer me one question, and then we can all go home. Easy as that." He ripped the duct tape off my mouth in one motion I barely felt. He narrowed accusatory eyes at me and said, "Ok. Where's my money?"

I couldn't answer. I looked up at him, at Alex, and it occurred to me I might still be dreaming. You know how your friends take on weird roles in your dreams sometimes: your best friend is suddenly a cop and he's pointing his finger in your face asking you how much you've had to drink, and your mom is the bus driver and she's insisting you pay the fare or you'll go to jail, but you don't have your CTA card and she forgot to give you your lunch money that morning, and you're all in the desert, and you're really thirsty, and your high school girlfriend is *still* your girlfriend, and she needs money to pay the babysitter, and there's that dog chasing you.

Well, that all crossed my mind as I was forced to sit there looking up at Alex, my friend as of two days ago, looking up at him, sitting in my underwear, with blood running down my face, while two cronies held my arms, and some other dude recorded it, probably put it up on YouTube.

What was making him do all this? I was sick and confused. There must be something big behind this. Something really big, but I didn't know what it was. I just moved to this town a few months ago. I just wanted to get a job. Sell some weed to make ends meet.

I didn't answer him.

"Michael," Alex said again, bending down in front of me like a grownup in front of a kid, "Tell me where the money is."

"Wha..what are you talk...talking about?" I eventually got out, "You have it." It hurt to speak. It hurt to clear my throat too.

He took a breath, grinding his jaw around. "Alright. You got me. I admit it... I broke into your place. There. Now you know... But that was then, this is now. Where's my money?"

"Wa the fuck?" I said. "You've already got it," I coughed. "And..And it's *my* money."

"Hah," he boomed, "*Your* money? It's my money, bitch." He stepped beside me and laughed, then bit it off with a sharp jab into my rib cage. Every time he hit me, my whole body tensed, using up precious energy.

"Now, tell me where you put it."

"No." I croaked. "I'll get it back."

He slapped me open handed. On the recoil, Pratt yanked me to my feet. Without missing a beat, Alex planted his fist deep inside my gut, somewhere near my backbone.

All the air leapt out of me in a low complete grunt. I crumpled in half, knees banging on the hard concrete.

"That money's mine, Mike." Alex hissed next to my ear. "Now where is it?"

My breath was gone, far, far away. It was gone for a few moments. I had to reach deep, deep down for it, like bringing a dead soul back from the going into the light. I held onto with everything I had, rescued it to hurl back in Alex's face.

"Fuuuhhck youu," is what it said when it came out. It was sepulchral. "It's my money. And you have it."

Everything was silent. My body was rigid and quaking. The wind blew. Drool hung from my mouth and danced on it. Waves crashed against the concrete wall below us. Pratt and Paul pulled me to up my feet. Alex looked clear through me with hate.

"You're gonna tell me what you did with that money. That's my money and you took it."

At the nod of his head, Paul and Pratt jerked me closer to the edge.

"Wait," he said, clapping his hands together loudly. "I got an idea, spin him around." He laughed, pleased with himself. It was amazing how small he looked. "Watch this." And he pantsed me, yanked my underwear to the ground.

Now, there I was standing with my back to the lake, naked, in the middle of the night, wet with dew and freezing cold, while being repeatedly beaten. Alex wrestled the underwear from my feet and held them in front of me.

"Michael," he said, content smile broad across his face. "We're friends. I don't want to hurt you anymore. And," gesturing with my underwear in front of me, "it's a long walk home from here without any clothes on. You might even scare some people, or get arrested even, who knows. Now," he paused, "you tell me where the money is because I already know it's not at your place, and we'll take you back to get your clothes and stuff, and this will all be done with. You fuck off back to Iowa. We take the money."

"Alex," I said, naked and shivering. "I don't know what you want. You already stole that money from me *twice*. Stop asking me where it—it is."

Pratt's grip came off my right arm. It was replaced with a crack in the kidney. My knees buckled. I wanted to fall, but he held me up.

God I wished someone would come by. Where are all the people in this town? But we were ten feet down, by the water's edge. No one would be able to see us.

Paul let go of my left arm and, this time, Pratt spun me around to face the water, my dick pointing its shriveled head straight out toward Michigan. He pinched my elbows together and pushed me forward till my toes dangled over the edge.

"Michael," Alex said, close and loudly in my ear. "I will push you in that lake, with your hands tied behind your back, if you don't give me that money."

"Stop." I said, weakly. "What happened to Ellie?" I said it quietly over my shoulder, not wanting to know the answer. "Did you guys hurt her? Where is she? What did you guys do to her?"

"Ellie?" Alex said, and laughed some more. "Man, don't you know anything? Can't you see what's going on around you? You're asking me about Ellie?"

"Where is she? What are you saying?"

"Oh, man, you're great Mikey, you really are. Don't you know how the world works? Ellie doesn't give a shit about you. Nobody's looking out for you. You have to *take* what you want in this world. It isn't given to you. Ellie. You don't get Ellie. You don't get anything. You're in over your head Michael. There's nothing for you here. Go back to bumble fuck. You country fuck. There's no jobs, no working your way up anymore. You don't go to school and get a good job. It's fuck or be fucked...Shit, people don't even know they're fucking other people anymore. It's corporations and companies. They got it down to a science—"

At that, I stopped listening. It was dumb kind of stuff shitty people say to themselves in the mirror to justify their actions. The black choppy water loomed underneath me, kicking up to lick my toes. I didn't have the energy left to keep my head afloat. I knew I would sink down, straight down. I didn't know where the money was. Fuck him.

And I guess I missed a funny joke. They were all laughing when Alex repeated himself.

"Michael? You still listening to me? You better be. And you better start talking pretty quick." They all laughed again.

One of them smacked my bare ass. I heard it, but couldn't feel anything. Then Paul reached a hand around in front of me laughing. "Hey, Mike," he said. "Watch this." He curled his middle finger and flicked my balls.

I didn't laugh.

"Last chance, Mike," Alex said.

Fuck him.

"Ok, Pratt," Alex said. On command, Pratt pushed me out over the water, holding my arms, so that only my toes were on land. "Tell me where it is and we'll take you home."

Pratt leaned me further out. I was on tiptoes trying to push back, not to fall in. He held nothing but the duct tape tying my hands together, dangling me out over the churning water. My shoulders strained in their sockets. I could feel the muscles in my chest wanting to rip. Even if I'd wanted to, I wouldn't have been able to talk.

Snap!

The tape broke.

Falling.

Breath.

Smack.

Cold.

Dark.

Chapter 27

Two things happened to me when I fell, face forward in a flat head-dive, into the lake that night. First, I got really cold, deep-to-the-core cold. Second, and more significantly, I got convicted. I don't mean convicted like sent to jail, I mean convinced, but harder than that. I became convinced so hard it was something else, something that bound me, convicted me. I became instantly aware of what I had to do, saw clearly what had to happen.

Lying/sinking in the water with bruised face and ego, scratched-open feet, sore ribs and jaw, bleeding mouth and scraped knees, I found conviction. That was it. I was done taking punches, done beating around the bush, done being nice. My true opponents had unmistakably made themselves clear and I'd had enough.

The dark water was so unexpectedly cold that at first my body was frozen with shock. Electric impulses of that hard conviction flashed across my brain like emergency beacons on a life vest.

Suddenly, in a total muscle clinching spasm, I came to life. In a few powerful, determined strokes, I swam up through the ten feet of water. I broke the surface gasping air, invigorated.

I instinctively scanned the concrete shore for Alex and his flunkies, but nowhere. In those few moments, the water didn't feel as cold. As the shock receded and adrenaline took its place, I was getting used to it. It almost felt good against my battered face, and especially on my ribs. I floated on my back for a second, breathing in the crisp air, my shriveled penis barely bobbing in the short waves like a fat, baldheaded shipwreck victim.

Shit. No matter how newly determined, I was in some tough spot. And I had no idea how I was going to get home. Thank you Alex.

I doggy paddled to the wall and climbed the slimy yellow emergency ladder, my bare ass pointing out over the lake toward the coast of Michigan ninety miles away. The Chicago wind wrapped around me. Goose bumps the size of sand dunes covered me. But I emerged a new man, beaten and convicted. All I had to do was get home, naked, without getting arrested.

I climbed up onto the concrete ledge with mean memories of standing there minutes before, forcefully, with my hands bound. Two steps up, I could see the occasional jogger, a biker riding along the bike path. It was much too late at night for that kind of thing, but that's one of the beauties of living in the big city: living among crazy people.

Alex had conveniently, depending how you looked at it, dumped me in the lake not too far from my house. I was in Lincoln Park on the other side of the Lake Shore Drive near Belmont Harbor, which meant I had to cross under the highway. They must have parked on the curvy little road that runs along the park and dragged me under the pedestrian bridge by the end of Barry. I was only about a fifteen-minute walk from my apartment. The only problem was the obvious one (dangling.)

The attractive, concrete-stepped shoreline curved along all the way to Diversey. Because the big steps rose up ten feet to the meet the park, I followed it along the lower step, unseen in calm privacy, nervously twisting my head around to make sure I was alone.

The breeze dried my skin as I went, so I could spend less energy shivering and more shitting myself with nerves. Where the shore curved in at Diversey, I could hear people laughing before I could see them. I inched slowly around the last curve until they came into view; three kids drinking from paper bags, their feet hanging over the edge.

A: Creep quietly behind them, but still stay out of sight, down on the steps?

No way, I would have to get within eight feet of them. And if they caught me creeping up behind them naked in the park at this hour, it would be humiliating to say the least. They would yell and point and maybe even chase me around laughing, drawing all kinds of unwanted attention, even if there weren't very many people around. No way.

B: Go up above them into the park, out in plain sight of joggers and bikers and traffic? Damn. I had to go up.

To get my head level with the grass, I crept up the ledges to watch a jogger run slowly past, the line of skyscrapers providing a picturesque backdrop, lights flickering through leaves on trees. Lake Shore Drive runs closer to the water from here into downtown, but cars were going too fast to worry about. By the time a driver noticed I was nude, they'd be half a mile away. The bike path was amazingly close, maybe forty yards away, and that distance disappeared to nothing as it went over the bridge to Diversey Harbor and above the underpass to the park on the other side.

A lady approached from the south. A biker going much faster from the north. I watched the biker pass, waited for the lady. As soon as she passed, I jumped up and ran for the biggest tree in a group twenty feet away. The tree wasn't big enough to hide me completely, so I clasped my hands over my junk and didn't dally long.

The next cover was ten more yards and even skinnier trees. I shot a look behind me and one to where the kids were below me. I ran fast in that ridiculously upright way you have to run with one hand on your ass and one on your crotch; knees high, butt tucked in. The branchless trees offered zero cover.

I danced behind them looking one way and the next. A bike was coming too fast to hide from. The path went up over the bridge beside the highway, or down through the brightly lit underpass. I went down. The last thirty feet were in full-on brightness; my feet slapping, street lights radiating off the new, bright concrete. There was no hiding.

The path stopped at the harbor channel and cut sharply right under the road. It was a small path the width of the sidewalk, but sheltered. Once inside, I pressed myself against the wall panting.

Psheww, safe. My chest heaved with the effort and relief.

A shuffling sound grew in the narrow tunnel.

Shit, someone coming.

I shook my head, nowhere to go, but on.

The shuffling was slow and inevitable. I ran toward it.

An old man came slowly around the corner as I neared it. There was no place to go. He was coming toward me. I was naked.

But his head was down. I don't think he even saw me until I threw my hand up and pulled on an imaginary horn like a truck driver, yelling, "Hooo—Hoot!!" as I ran past. Just another crazy college kid out streaking.

I didn't look back. There was no one else on the path ahead of me. It was darker on the other side where tall trees blotted out most of the overhead light. Thank God!

I slowed to a jog and kept close to the trees between the harbor and the parking lot. At the far end near the road, there was a parking attendants shack with no one in it. I cut across the lighted lot at a sprint, arms pumping, junk flying all over the place. There was a thick row of bushes along the fence by the driving range. I jumped in behind them and sprawled in the darkness, wheezing.

So far, so good.

The next part was the hard part: two blocks through the city, a major four-lane street, three more blocks and an alley, then, getting inside. I breathed. My ribs hurt.

Diversey itself is too brightly lit. I had to go the long way around, in the shadows, down the smaller street behind it, Oakdale. The hospital office buildings on the left side of the road were closed and mostly dark, so it was relatively easy going up and around the corner.

But the corner of Sheridan and Oakdale couldn't have been any brighter in daylight.

There was a retirement village high rise on the right side of the street with a short row of scrawny bushes lining the sidewalk. I crawled in with them like a hairless dog, feeling like Ren from Ren and Stimpy, and hoped the incongruity of the scene would keep anyone from really noticing me. A bus rushed by so close I felt the wind on my butt hole.

I squeezed my eyes shut hoping I was invisible.

I waited for the light to change and went for it, care be damned, running full speed across the street. Across all four lanes, arms swinging, balls bouncing.

A taxi almost turned into me as I dashed across the intersection in front of him. He honked on reflex. I smacked my hand on the hood and yelled, "Watch out," just to keep up appearances.

Half a block up, I stopped. Heart racing, I crouched between two parked cars like a kitchen rat being chased by a cleaver. But I was still too exposed. There was no resting. I kept to a squat and ran along the edges of the parked cars, doing my best to stay in the shadows.

Further up at the next major street, a few drunk people crossed back and forth, but no one was coming toward me. A few car lengths away, Pine Grove lay blessedly dark, thanks to the wonderful, beautiful street light that was burned out. I'd never been so excited to see a darkened street, alone, late at night in a big city. I worked my way beside the cars, then flashed across the street as a car pulled up to the stop sign. I ducked as far down as I could behind a Mercedes. The car turned slowly toward me, its headlights burning on my naked ankles. Please go on, please.

The car inched slowly on, looking for parking. It stopped immediately next to the Mercedes I was crouched behind, its headlights lighting the street ahead of me. I froze.

The engine turned off, but the lights stayed on. Damn. Tightly tucked down in my crouch, I duck-walked slowly back along the Mercedes separating me from my potential unintentional flasher victim. Fuck. The cars were parked too closely. I couldn't slip in between them.

I heard the car door open and more light flooded the area around me; a strip of grass, green and yellow, throwing stick-like shadows. A woman's voice said, "No, I just came from the airport. I'll call you back in a minute. I have to take my bags in."

Shit. Run? Or wait and hope she doesn't see me?

Impossible. I was a six-foot tall naked guy crouched two feet away in the semi-dark.

Shit.

I stood up tall with dignity and poise. The woman, arms full of bags, audibly caught her breath as I emerged, approaching. With all the grace of a gentleman, I raised my wrist to peer at an imaginary watch, then tipped my imaginary hat in her direction and said, "Good evening, miss. Rather warm out tonight, don't you think?" And broke into a sprint.

With my alley in sight and most of the danger behind me, I sprinted at full speed, bare feet slapping painfully on pavement, dying for it to be over. I careened around the corner flailing wildly out of control into the haven of the alley. And there was Paul!

He was smoking a cigarette, standing in the light behind the bar next door to my place. There was no way I could stop on the glass-studded alleyway. Momentum carried me on.

I veered left with my eyes locked onto him. He wasn't looking my way.

I'm not sure how, but in two giant leaps I scaled the seven-foot wooden fence behind the house next to me and landed safely in my neighbor's back yard. So many nights I'd spent fondly gazing out my window over the alley at this wonderful back yard, but I never could have imagined how consoling it would be to land safely therein, safe on the other side of the fence from that crazy pillhead Paul.

Yes, I *had* gained conviction, but part of that was being prepared. And I hadn't even made it home yet! My wounds were still fresh and I was still naked. Naked!

Motion detector porch lights came on immediately. I was, quite literally, bathed in white light. Scanning quickly, I dashed for a long shadow stretched out behind a low plastic lawn chair. I pulled my legs in from the light and calmly proceeded to hyperventilate.

Paul was standing guard at my place. They were waiting for me to come back, to pick me up again. I was naked and trapped.

Melanie! Beautiful, life-saving Melanie!

I had to get Melanie's attention. I hoped she wasn't sleeping.

After a couple of minutes, the automatic porch light went off. I got up, moving in exaggerated slow motion, the way we used to practice as kids, so the detector wouldn't flare up. I peeked over the fence on tiptoes, my forehead just high enough to sneak a peek without Paul seeing me. He was still smoking and looking at his phone. Thank God for smartphones and attention deficit disorder, the perfect combination.

Melanie's window was lighted. I crouched back down on my haunches and waited patiently for a stroke of genius to hit. I really wished I had my phone, but it was at Ellie's with my pants and clothes and keys and everything else. Somehow, I needed to attract Melanie's attention without attracting Paul's. But given Paul's attention span, plus the pills he was always on, I figured it wouldn't be too long before he would be distracted on his own, by something.

Three minutes later, while I was enjoying the cool tickle of the breeze on my balls in my neighbor's nice, spacious back yard, the back door of the bar slammed open, the noise banging and reverberating out across the alley. Adrenaline and shock jerked me to my feet causing the motion detecting light in the back yard to come on again. Damn.

Startled and naked in the light, I stutter-stepped one way, then the other, trying to decide which way to go. I hurriedly, yet carefully, looked over the top of the fence. Clatter and noise burst out of the bar ahead of a drunken college guy flailing before two big dudes in skin-tight shirts. Paul jumped back out of the way with his hands up, laughing.

I shot a look back at the house in time to see the kitchen light go on. Someone coming!

On the other side of the fence, shouting was happening. I looked over again. The light above the back door burned brightest on the wide shoulders of the two bouncers. They were pointing and yelling things at the college kid as he tried to pick himself up, drunkenly, off the ground. The light faded near Paul, who was standing out of the way with his back to me.

Taking advantage of the loudness and confusion, I climbed over the fence using the inside braces. Landing flat on aching feet, I scurried across the alley and squatted under Melanie's window between two parked cars like a homeless guy taking a shit.

I listened to the yelling going on fifteen feet away and took a second to catch my breath, making sure I was tucked safely out of sight in the shadows between the cars. My poor feet were scratched, poked and probably bleeding. Broken glass and tiny rocks were everywhere. I tried not to think of the diseases I was contracting. I tried not to think of all the bums I had seen sleeping back here and getting drunk and who knew what else.

The next trick was still the same trick: getting inside, naked, with no keys.

I was directly under Melanie's window, so that was something. A couple of girls followed the noise and bouncers out of the bar. While the bouncers were still busy prodding the drunk kid, Paul started his ADHD talking machine up and began firing away at the girls, paying as little attention to what was coming out of his mouth as to what either of the them said in response. But if I could hear him talking, he was distracted.

I tossed little pebbles up at Melanie's window. I couldn't exactly stand up and wave my arms and I was too far under her window for her to see me. So I came up with little choreographed dance number to fit the scenario: 1. Peek to make sure Paul wasn't looking. 2. Throw a little rock. 3. Wave my hand to catch Melanie's attention if she happened to look out. 4. Repeat.

After several attempts, I started throwing two rocks at a time and harder.

It worked! Above me, Melanie's voice boomed, "Who's there? Who's doing that?"

The volume made me cringe. I pinched my eyes and secretly looked out at Paul. Thankfully and magically, he hadn't heard. I waved my hand rapidly and shushed in three short bursts, "Pshh, pshh, psh." I quickly leaned out far enough for her big eyes, slanted with suspicion, to see my tortured face. I sliced my hand across my throat repeatedly, telling her to cut it out.

She got the message. "What are you doing?" She whispered, still too loudly. "Why are you out there?"

I cringed again, tightening the muscles in my neck.

"Let me in," I whispered back quickly, and pointed toward Paul.

"What?" she said. "What's going on out there?"

"Shh."

"Why? ...What?"

"SHH!"

"Ok, ok—"

"Let me in."

"Okay-ee," she said, with a kind of snotty impatience. "I'm coming."

Paul was still distracted, but looking over his shoulder as the uglier of the girls was talking. I squeezed in front of the cars and hung close to the building (no pun intended) trying to keep out of the light as much as possible. Melanie came down the metal stairs on tiptoes and popped the back gate. I went for it in a flash and was up the stairs behind her before the gate clanged loudly home.

Chapter 28

"Your place, your place," I said quickly in her ear, nudging her from behind. She was closing the door behind me before she turned and realized I was totally naked.

"Oh," I heard her breath catch. "Oh. Well. Ok."

Exhausted and safe, I marched straight in ahead of her and fell heavily and thankfully onto the futon couch.

"Michael," Melanie said, with anxious concern. "What are you doing? And why are you naked?"

I felt a tingle in my balls as she stood over me looking down. I was so relieved to be inside. I'd forgotten my manners completely and sprawled out openly on the couch.

"Oops, shit," I said, and covered myself with a pillow. "Sorry."

She was dressed in pajamas: striped cotton pants, that same t-shirt with the neck cut out hanging off her shoulder, hard nipples, hair hastily piled on top of her head and falling.

"Michael, what the hell's going on? Look at you." Her hands went up in a what's-wrong-with-you gesture, motioning with astonishment to all the far corners of the Earth. Her boobs juggling loosely. "Where are you clothes? What's going on outside? Why were you hiding?"

"Wait, wait," I said, throwing a hand up, blocking her questioning. "I just...give me a second.... I ran all the way here from the lake."

"The lake? Now? What were you doing out there? With who?"

"Wasn't my choice." I was really worn out. Now that I was safe, I didn't feel like talking about it.

Melanie slapped my knee. My head perked up. "Michael, what the fuck is going on? You can't just show up at my house naked in the middle of the night and not tell me what's going on. Why were you in the lake?"

"They threw me in. They wanted my money. But I don't have it."

"Who?"

"Alex!" Why was she bothering me with this? Exhausted, my voice slowly tapered. "And Paul, the fucking pillhead, and that big kid, Pratt, and somebody else. I don't know. They kidnapped me. Threw me in the lake." The last sentence was down to a bored whisper.

She sat down close to me and put a tender hand on my leg. Another tinge ran through my balls, swirled around my belly.

"What does that mean? Michael, you're not making sense." She took a long breath, patted my knee, then said comfortingly, "All right, Ok. I think there's some things you're not telling me. You need to start from the beginning. But first." She stood, taking her hand with her. "Let me get you some clothes." From the closet, she threw me a pair of sweat pants and a t-shirt. "They're Phil's. They might be a little big."

With as little effort as possible, I pulled myself upright and hung the t-shirt over my head. I looped the leg holes of the sweat pants around my feet. Without getting up and in one motion, I bucked the pillow off my lap and yanked the pants up to my waist.

"He doesn't leave any shoes here, sorry. Here's some socks though."

"It's ok, thanks." Who cared. My energy was gone.

She sat beside me again, pulling one leg under her. "Ok, now let's have it from the beginning. *Who* are you talking about? What the *hell* have you been doing?"

I slowly pulled the night's events in around me like a warm blanket, looking at them as one cohesive material, searching for the right place to start. The last few days had been such a mess of fucked up circumstances and screwed up goings-on that it was hard to find the correct place to start. I couldn't remember what Melanie already knew. Who she knew. What I'd told her.

The last time I saw her was...the Ian mangling. I dropped her car off in the morning, then....

Tim and Chris! They disappeared. That was tonight! So much had happened, I'd forgotten.

"Melanie!" I bolted straight. "Let me use your phone!"

She tilted her head at me confused. "What? Where's your phone?"

My eyebrows lifted. "Really?"

"Oh, right." She sank back.

"Come on, where is it?"

"It's over there, on the bar. But who are you gonna call?"

"Tim and Chris," I said, standing up. Across the room, I looked down at the phone, took it in my hand and stared at the blank screen. I didn't know their number. And without my phone, I couldn't call anyone who might. I put the phone down.

"Let me use your car."

"What? Now? No, it's the middle of the night."

"Yes, now. Come on. I've got to see if they're all right. Don't you understand? This is important. I need those guys, *some*body, on my side."

"I don't know what you're talking about. And *I'm* on your side." She didn't get up, but she leaned forward on straight arms like she might. "You won't even tell me what's going on. And now you want to use my car? No way. It's the middle of the fucking night. You're all beat up. You came here naked, Michael."

I reached down, grabbed her hand and pulled her to her feet. I flicked the light switch off by the door and led Melanie through the dark to the large window faintly illuminated by light coming in over the alley. With my face close to the blinds, I twisted the plastic stick just enough for thin slices of night to appear, just enough for us to see out. Her body pressed against my back. I pointed quietly at Paul, smoking another cigarette, standing in the half-light behind the bar. The bouncers and bumbling girls were gone, about time for the place to close.

I slid around behind her so she could see better. Standing close with my mouth by her ear I said, "See that guy out there?"

"Who? The skinny guy?"

"Yeah, right there."

"*He's* the one threw you in the lake?" She said quietly, but obviously unimpressed.

I backed up a step. "Well, not just him. There was four of them. The other guys were a lot bigger. Him? He flicked me in the balls."

"Ouch."

"Yeah, you wouldn't think it would hurt that bad, but it does."

She turned to face me, her eyes tilted up, close and whispering. "So, what now? You want to go out there and beat him up or something? Or you want me to call the police?"

"No. Not right now. Maybe later. I need help first. Which is why I need to borrow your car."

"Right now, really?"

"Yes. Now. I need to make sure my friends are all right. And I don't have a phone, thanks to these assholes, so I have to go over there."

"I don't know Micha—"

"Melanie." I took her hand in the dark again. Her face was in shadow, her back to the light slanting in through the window. "Let me borrow your car for like thirty minutes. I'll be back before you go to sleep, I promise."

"I was already asleep before you showed up."

"No you weren't."

"Almost."

"Your lights were still on."

She shrugged, looked down. "Even if these guys are home, you think they'll be up at 3 o'clock in the morning?"

"Yeah. And if they're not I'll wake them up."

Melanie's car was one of the ones I had hidden next to behind her apartment. We stayed there looking out the window for a couple more minutes, watching Paul smoke to make sure he didn't move.

Satisfied, I left Melanie in the dark to watch me slip outside.

The metal stairs were cold on my bare feet. I moved silently down. Paul played with his phone. I held the door knob on the gate, closing it carefully until it latched without a sound. Melanie watched me squeeze past the car next to hers and unlocked her Toyota. As quickly as I could, I opened the door, swung myself in, closed and locked it. Shielding my face from the interior light, I started the car. The hole in the tail pipe gargled exhaust. I didn't want to look. I knew Paul *had* to look. I barely missed the fence as I backed out.

A hand slapped loudly on the glass next to my face. Paul's mouth was open, yelling. He waved his hands rigorously.

I flipped him off hard, my middle finger shaking, and tried to peel out.

Chapter 29

As I drove up Lake Shore Drive in the late night wind with the radio off, a slow rage was growing in my guts. That brief clash with Paul the Pillhead had touched off a sour shame that pissed me off. All of the pain and agony I had endured in the past few days was flowing together, infusing a boiling mass of molten hate-lava in my stomach. I had been hurt and humiliated, beaten, kidnapped, stripped, thrown into the lake. I was done with it. It was time for it to end. I would do it alone if I had to.

I drummed my fist against the top of the steering wheel. I hit the dashboard with the heel of my hand. The sun-rotted vinyl made a cracking sound like corn chips. Oops.

I couldn't do it alone, who was I kidding. I had just been alone with four guys and gotten the shit kicked out of me. I couldn't do it alone, I needed help. But at least I now knew *who* was responsible, that was something. But it wasn't doing much to cool the rage in my stomach, or the burning behind my eyes.

The streets near Lincoln Square were empty, all the families shut up happily inside, and all of the parking spots full. I parked Melanie's Toyota next to a fire hydrant outside Tim and Chris's apartment.

There was a light burning in the upstairs window, but I still had to lean on the buzzer for a full minute before someone let me in.

"Dude, what the fuck, Mike?" Chris said, as I got to the top of the stairs. "What are you doing here?" His right eye was swollen and pink; the new stamp of my friendship.

"Can we talk?" I said, brushing past him through the half-open door.

"We don't want to talk," he said weakly, closing the door behind us.

Tim was at the dinner table, computer open in front of him. "Great," he said, as I walked in. "Just who I was hoping to see." Both of his eyes were black. He must have fought back harder.

"What happened to you guys?" I said, not meaning the obvious. "Where were you?"

Tim looked at Chris. "You hear this guy?" he said, with a thumb pointed at me.

"Uhh," Chris said, sounding like a sixth grader, "you can't tell?" He made a circling motion at his face. "Try a guess. Come on, just one." Being a smartass didn't look good on him, he was too small. It came off bratty.

I ignored it, feeling defensive. "Ok, what?" I said, shittier than I meant to. "The cops came and beat you up? I told you not to smoke that joint."

"Are you kidding, you fucking asshole?" Tim cut in, jumping to his feet. His outstretched finger swishing at me, pointing all over, wildly like Zorro. "You got us into this. You're the one responsible for all these black eyes, you dick. Don't tell us it's our fault."

"Ok, ok, ok." I said, patting the air all around. "I'm sorry I said that. We're getting off on the wrong foot here. I need to talk to you guys, let's calm down a second. I'm sorry I said that. Look at me." I pointed to different parts of my face exaggeratingly. "And you can't even see my broken ribs." I raised a shoeless foot. "They dragged me out of bed, threw me in the lake."

Tim and Chris looked at my feet and back and forth between each other. They visibly calmed down, especially Tim, shaking out his hands, pacing in a tight circle. They each sighed and stood quietly looking away from me.

"I need your help," I said, pleadingly.

"No way," Chris said, waving both hands.

"No way," Tim echoed. "You've had our help. No more."

"What do you take us for," Chris said, challengingly. "Tough guys? Look at us." He pointed at Tim. "He's an actor. We weigh two hundred pounds between us."

"I'm not asking you to fight anybody."

"Yes, you are," Tim said, pointedly. "You might not think so, but you are."

I couldn't argue with that. "But really," I said calmly. "What happened to you guys tonight?"

"Don't you know? They obviously got you too."

"Yeah, but I didn't see them then. Not at Alex's when you guys disappeared."

"Well, you know it was those guys Gino and Sean, right?" Tim said.

"Yeah. Wait. What was those guys?"

"What do you mean? It was them. Didn't they get you too?"

"What was them?" I was confused.

"That's what we're talking about," Chris said. "We were outside like you said. You went in Alex's apartment. We were about half way through the joint when Tim heard something. We turn around and Bam! Gino hit me. That guy Sean hit Tim."

"I fell, got up and he hit me again," Tim said. "Told us to 'Get the fuck out.'"

"Sean and Gino? Why? Why would they be there?"

"I don't know," Tim said. "You tell us. You're the fighter."

"What happened to you?" Chris asked. "Isn't that how you got your face?"

It was a weird way to put it, but I knew what he meant. "Yeah, but it wasn't Sean and Gino. It was Alex."

"Wait," Chris said with wide eyes. "What? Alex was home?"

"No, he wasn't home. This was later."

"What?"

I waved my hand around some more. "Ok, look. I found the money. It was Alex all right, the money was in a cabinet in his kitchen, but nobody was there. I got the money. I came back out. You guys weren't there. I made it around to the alley and somebody hit me with a board....I was knocked out flat."

"You didn't see who?" Tim said.

Chris was nodding his head. "Sean picked up a board when they chased us off."

"But why?" I said, rhetorically. "What have they got to do with this?"

"Why?" Tim said. "For the money, asshole. It's what you just said."

"But them too?" I asked no one. "Is everybody in on this?"

"I don't fucking know," Tim said. "But I know who's not. We're not! Not anymore."

I turned slowly in a broad circle. Sean and Gino too? It's me against the whole goddamn world. Who are these people? Who did I get mixed up with?

Tim and Chris looked at each other, then at me.

I turned to them. "You guys have to help me," I said.

"No." They said it in unison, flat.

"Come on, you guys are the only friends I got."

"No way, man." Tim said. "There's no way."

"We tried to help you once," Chris said. "That's it. Look at us."

"I don't have anybody else," I said, pleadingly. "Come on, I'll give you free weed, money even."

"No way, Michael," Tim said. "It's not gonna happen."

I stood there looking hopelessly between them. I couldn't do this alone. But I had to go after these guys. I had to get my money back. And I *had* to get that weed back. It was bad enough with Alex and the idiots, now Sean and Gino too? Who knew what else I was up against?

"Guys," I tried desperately. "You *have* to help me. What am I gonna do?"

"We're done, Michael," Tim said. "You have to go. We're not helping." He turned around, crossing his arms over his chest. I looked at Chris. He turned around too. They stood side by side with their backs to me.

"Seriously, guys, come on." I pulled on Chris's small shoulder. He pulled away.

I watched their backs and the boiling started in my stomach again. I couldn't believe they were *actually* turning their backs on me. I always thought that was just a figure of speech, but Tim and Chris both literally, physically, turned their backs on me. I couldn't believe it. They were supposed to be my friends. Or at least, sort of. They were customers, people I knew, my fellow man. You don't turn your back on your fellow man! Not when he needs you! Where I came from people didn't turn their...whatever. Fuck you guys.

I turned on my heels and marched out the door. I'd find a way. I'd find a goddamn way.

I drove home mumbling to myself over the rumbling of Melanie's shitty car. Mumbling about people being weak, never being there when you need them, only looking out for themselves, getting to be your friend just so they can steal from you, or use you to get what they want, using girls against you. Girls. Fuck girls. They aren't any better, lying to you, using you, sleeping with you while some other fuck breaks into your place, everybody screwing you all the time, they all fuck you and fuck you, that's all anybody wants anymore is to fuck you, even the ones who are supposed to be your friends, shit, especially them, they fuck you, friends, bullshit, there's no friends, they only want to be your friend to.... Wait.

Friends. That's it!

I slammed on the breaks. I wasn't alone. I did have friends! They just didn't live in Chicago. But that didn't mean I didn't have friends! Hah!

I drummed drum rolls on the steering wheel. Hah. Why didn't I think of this sooner? I was an idiot. I had all kinds of friends. I even had some pretty good friends, friends that wouldn't turn their backs on you, or run from a fight. Some that might even go looking for a fight. Hah. I had one in particular who loved a good fight. One I knew I could count on for something just like this. I drummed on the wheel. I drummed on the dash, careful not to crack it any more than it already was.

The ride home was different from then on, my face lit up and grinning in the green dash light. Everything was going to be different. It was going to be ok.

 I knew what I was going to do. For the first time, I saw the way out.

When I pulled into the alley, Paul wasn't there; another sign of things changing.

I didn't make it back before Melanie fell asleep, but she let me in anyway.

She did her best to listen to the good news. But she couldn't keep her eyes open.

Before I went to sleep, I used her phone to call B. I didn't have his number, of course, so I called the bar where we both used to work, knowing he'd be there. He was drunk and belligerent. I had to promise him five hundred dollars for one night's work to convince him to come, not because he wouldn't come otherwise, but because he was drunk and wouldn't listen to me otherwise. There's only one way to get a drunk man to listen to you and that's to talk about money. Or women maybe, but I didn't have any of that to offer.

I told him the train left Lafayette, Indiana, at eight o'clock in the morning, his time. Three hours from now. If he was on it, I'd give him five hundred dollars.

He told me to fuck myself.

Then, asked who it was again.

I told him. "Five hundred dollars. Train. Chicago. Eight a.m."

He'd be on it.

Chapter 30

I woke up accidentally spooning Melanie, or maybe not accidentally. Where Ellie was the small, fragile kind of girl you slept with your arm around to protect her from danger; holding the arm curved-out slightly, never letting the full weight of it crush her delicate waist, Melanie was the nuzzle-in-close, throw-your-leg-over-and-sleep-hard-til-noon type of girl. Which is probably why I woke up so contentedly, heavily, and yelled, "Fuck!"

It was eleven o'clock. B's train got in in half an hour. Like a high school kid in an eighties movie, like Revenge of the Nerds, or some Corey Haim movie, I ripped the covers back fully dressed. Not because I was clever and planned it that way, but because the only clothes I had to put on, I was already wearing: somebody else's baggy sweat pants and huge t-shirt. All of my stuff was still at Ellie's house. Ellie, the asshole. Ellie, the betrayer. As soon as she opened the door for Alex, I knew I'd been had. I'd made a grave mistake letting my little head do the thinking. I should have cut and run the minute I saw them together. Ellie, the conniving, beautiful asshole.

I couldn't think, or say her name without "asshole" attaching itself to it like a hair clinging to a staticy shirt; Ellie's the shirt, the asshole part of her is the hair, all twisted and curled in on itself, repulsive.

Melanie moaned at my voice and rolled over lazily. I whispered to her gently, "I'm gonna take your car, ok?" I said it rhetorically, almost too quiet for her to even hear.

Her breath went back to the completely heavy rhythm of a person sleeping.

"Thanks," I added politely. "Be back soon."

The car keys were with others on the bar. I twisted them off the key ring and pulled the door silently open and shut behind me.

The metal stairs were cold in the morning, as they had been at night, under my bare feet. I really needed to get some shoes. I walked flat-footed across the glass- and gravel-flecked pavement. The sun was high and bright overhead. A warm wind blew dust down the alley.

I had the windows down and the R&B channel up as I veered onto Lake Shore heading downtown. It was a beautiful, late summer day. Despite being late, I *felt* like a bright summer day.

I smiled around my lumpy, busted lip and swollen black eye at the glare-hazed city. For the first time in days, there was direction in my life. I knew what I was doing. On the left, the beach was crowded all the way up to Fullerton, getting worse closer North Avenue.

I loved this part of the drive; coming down the little dip toward downtown, the wall of high-rises on the right growing into skyscrapers, the lake glistening all over just opposite. It's like the training sequences in Mike Tyson's Punch Out, coach riding his bike behind you as you jog past the endless row of buildings.

Man, I used to dream of living in the city when I was a kid, playing Nintendo in the basement, house surrounded by cornfields. And now here it was stretched out all around me. The city of Chicago, the place of legends and urban myths, of gang shootings and corruption. There were no cornfields for miles, and no grain silos, no deer running across the road. The city, where worlds meet, people from everywhere.

It was nice driving downtown. I didn't get to do it enough.

It stopped being as fun once I got into downtown itself; buildings blotting out the sun, and cab drivers, people running across the street without looking, bicyclists darting in front of you, then flipping you off. And it was always so damned confusing. Where to turn, remembering which street went to Union Station. I took a roundabout way, but I found it. And only fifteen minutes late.

I guess B's train was early, because I saw him as soon as I turned the corner, sticking out like Buddha in a crowd of bankers. I fought my way to the curb in a heap of taxis climbing up each other's backs. B was standing close to the crowded doors talking to a girl much too pretty for him. He was holding a green plastic Sprite bottle and smiling at the girl, working his magic. I honked, but the horn in Melanie's Toyota was swallowed up by the din of buses and taxis and jackhammers. I yelled his full name, Brandon Josiah Partridge, to much better effect. His ears perked like a pit bull's. He hated his name. He gave me the finger and a very-funny head shake, then waved a one-handed hold-on.

A pile of honking stacked up behind me. I didn't look in the rear view mirror. I tapped fingers on top of the steering wheel and stared at my old friend B.

He was dressed like an emissary from the Nation of Indiana come to the big city to represent his people. His khaki cargo shorts were huge and baggy and hung halfway down his calf. The double XL camouflaged t-shirt came straight out of the hunting section at Walmart and was customized with the sleeves cut off, thick, independent wads of black hair glued to his triceps like arm toupes. He wore a once-neon-yellow Miller High Life baseball hat, gone greasy on both sides of the curved bill where he touched it, and big tan work boots that were caked with dried mud. They were the clothes of someone who worked for a living, or of someone who worked real hard for a couple of days, then spent three days getting drunk, too busy chatting up fat girls to change clothes, or give a shit.

But he was charming either way, and he was my friend.

I saw him hold a matching finger up to the girl, asking her to hold on. He crossed the sea of taxis to lean in the passenger's side window.

"Hey, man, give me twenty bucks."

"What? I don't have twenty dollars."

"Whaddaya mean you don't have it?" The smell of liquor on his breath made my eyes sting. "Just give me a ten then."

"I don't have that either, man. I don't have any money."

"You said you were gonna give me five hundred bucks."

"*Afterwards.* I didn't say now."

"Well, hell, what am I supposed to do then?"

"What are you talking about? Come on. Get in the car."

"I can't now," he grunted. "My bag's over there by her."

"What? You left your bag over there? Who is that girl?" I looked closer at his eyes. "Are you still drunk?"

He glanced around blankly for a second. Honking ensued all around us. B smiled and waved "be right there" to the girl.

"Damn," B muttered, shaking his big head, and trotted back to the girl. He picked up his duffel bag at her feet, then said something to her, moving his hands a lot. He gave her a quick gesture like "ah-hah," like he had an idea, then trotted back to the car. This time he dropped his bag onto the seat through the window and leaned in like before. But he didn't say anything.

"B," I said. "What the hell are you doing? Come on, lets go."

"Ok, ok. Just trying to sell it a bit." Carefully and ever so slightly, he pulled the door open a sliver, then yanked it open and jumped in.

"Alright," B said out of one corner of his mouth, while smiling at the girl out of the other side. "Go."

B waved to the girl. Her smile twisted a bit, lost its luster. Her eyebrows crinkled in confusion. Her mouth formed some words, but they were drowned out by sounds of the city as I pulled away.

We stopped at the next light. I looked at B. His head drooped exhaustedly.

"Well?" I said. "What was all that about?"

"What?" he said, like nothing had happened. "Oh. Forget it."

I drove on to the next light. "You know that girl back there? She was pretty hot."

"Yeah, she was, wasn't she? Too bad you screwed me. I coulda called her."

"I what? How was any of that my fault?"

"Cause, you're supposed to have money for me. I borrowed a twenty from her and told her my buddy's pickin' me up. He'd have money."

"You stole money from some girl that's too hot for you and it's my fault?"

"Too hot for me...That's why I got her number?"

"Probably 'cause you owe her money. She gave you her number so she could get it back."

"You know what," he said, the words running together, making them sound like a city in Alaska: Junoaat. "It don't matter. More importantly, what does matter is, is why don't you have any money?" He turned in his seat to face me. "There better be money in this, Mike."

"Jesus, man, you just got here. How 'bout a hand shake? A 'how-you-been?'"

I had to concentrate on the streets for the next minute. All of the one-ways were backward now, giving me trouble.

"Aw, man, I know you been fine. You finally in the Big City like you always been talkin about." He gestured around with his big square hands. "Or maybe not," he said more slowly. "which must be why you called me in the middle of the night." I felt him looking at me. "What happened to your face? ...And what's up with the sweat pants? I thought city folks had fashion."

"I've only been gone a few months."

"Well it didn't take you long, huh?"

I gave him a dead look. "Just hold on a second and let me concentrate. I'll explain in a minute."

We finally crossed Michigan Ave. and went along the park back to Lake Shore Drive. There was some more difficulty driving, but my mind wasn't on it. I was busy trying to figure out a way to tell B how I'd gotten myself into trouble without sounding like a complete boob. Nothing was coming to mind.

He sat quietly looking out the window, his head bobbing intermittently, keeping himself awake. There was more honking.

The sun glinted brightly off the cars passing us. White sailboats floated on the brilliant blue water of Lake Michigan. I relaxed a bit once we were settled into the throng of traffic speeding north. The rest of the drive was easier.

"Look at us," B said, sitting up. "Just like old times, driving around. Where's the joint? Tell me you at least brought a joint."

"Yeah," I said, reluctantly. "About that..."

"Jesus, Mike. What the hell've you been doing up here? I thought you were selling drugs. What kind of drug dealer doesn't have any drugs? No wonder you're having it rough."

"I'm not a drug dealer. I'm just selling weed. It's not drugs."

"The police might think so."

"Yeah, well you're not the police. And you know what I mean."

"Well, then you better tell me what's happening, 'cause I'm not too sure what I'm doing here. No weed, no money, I bet no women either."

"Would you just hold on for a second? Give me a chance to explain."

I drove, moving from the far left lane to the far right, anticipating the exit. I could feel B's eyes on me and my busted head.

"What been going up here, Mike? Seriously. And where are your shoes? You getting weird on me Mike? Join a cult or something? Did you bring me up here to recruit me? Save Mother Earth or some shit?"

I smiled and chuckled noiselessly through my nose.

"You know I love the earth, Michael, but I'm not walking around the streets of Chicago without any shoes on. Besides, I'm more of a 'Love thy bounty' kind of guy, you know what I mean. I like to eat and drink and appreciate God's gifts."

"Would you stop?" I said, still smiling and shaking my head at him. Then, the smile drooped on one side, got a little embarrassed. "I was gonna ask you. You wouldn't have an extra pair of shoes in that bag would you?"

"Mike, I gotta say, this is starting out some weird trip. Not exactly what I was thinking, you know? You have to give me *some*thing to boost my confidence. I mean, I didn't barely sleep at all and I was drinking right up til then. So come on, somethin'."

My voice got soft and I stared forward more intently, not looking at him. "Alright. Look, man. I called you 'cause I kind of need some help. Some shit is going on and, well, I need a friend, you know, someone I know I can trust."

Our turnoff was coming up, so I had to talk and drive. "I'll tell you the whole story as soon as we get somewhere, but let me put it into some quick perspective." I cut off an SUV swerving in front of traffic, coming out of the beach parking lot. "We can't go back to my place right now, that's one thing. And I don't have a phone, that's another. I don't have any shoes on either, but that's part of the story. Hopefully you can give me some, or we can stop at Walgreen's, or someplace, for some flip-flops until we can get mine back. But what's most important is, just know, I didn't call you for no reason. I called you first 'cause I need your kind of help."

B let all of that hang thick as body odor in the air. I got us off Lake Shore Drive and up Cannon Drive closer to my building. Melanie wouldn't be home anymore, but I wanted to leave the car just in case. Two blocks away I stopped and pulled against the curb.

"This where you live?" B said, bending down to look up through the windshield, searching for the nearest building.

I was looking up the street in front of me. "No, it's up there." I pointed ahead. "I'm not trying to be dramatic, but somebody might be waiting for me. I want to see."

"Like *what* do you mean? Who?" He looked where I pointed, not knowing what he was looking for.

"Not sure," I said. "Could be one of a few different people. I'm just making sure."

As I started moving again, B said, "Alright, Mike, you got my attention. You're gonna have to tell me what's going on pretty soon."

"I know. I will."

I turned into the alley slower than usual and kept my eyes trained for Paul, or Sean, or anybody moving suspiciously. It took me a full minute to seesaw back and forth and wiggle Melanie's little car into her parking space behind the building.

B dug around in his bag for a second and pulled out a chewed up pair of rubber soles with some strands of fabric hanging off of them.

"Here," he said, shoving them at me.

"What's this?"

"Beach sandals, what do you think? I'm comin' to the lake, I'm bringin' my beach gear. Got swim trunks too."

"And I'm supposed to wear these things? Do they even stay on?"

"It's that or nothing. Which do you want?"

"All right, I guess. Thanks." I said, and tried to put them on. The sandals were the type with one thick Velcro strap going over the top like you see guys wear in locker rooms, or with socks. The strap on the left foot was almost torn completely off and it slid sideways under my foot when I walked. But it was better than walking on glass.

It was several hours till dark and I had plenty to talk about. Melanie wasn't home. My keys were at Ellie's. So, B bought us a couple of tallboys and pre-made sandwiches from 7-Eleven. We walked to the lake to eat and look out.

I told him about the last time I was at the lake. And how I'd gotten there. And about Ellie. And about how she'd sold me out to Alex and his flunkies. I told him about Ian, Tim and Chris. I told him how my money was stolen and how I stole it back. And how it was stolen again.

Next, I told him my plan. And he understood why I'd called him. We toasted PBRs. I admitted I didn't know all of the facts, yet, and I didn't really have much of a plan.

He knew what I meant. We'd figure it out.

He smiled, looking eager and almost excited.

Chapter 31

We wasted the daylight hours talking, wandering, slowly drinking a beer an hour so that no buzz ever set in. We worked our way around the neighborhood until dark finally came on and we could go to work. The slow beer pace kept my courage up and listening to B talk about all the melodrama continually going on back home emboldened my drive to never live there again.

Melanie still wasn't home and I couldn't see any reason why B and I should take the train all over town when I had the keys to a perfectly good car, or at least functional car, in my pocket. Without Melanie there to argue the point, I had to assume she wouldn't mind if I used it for a little while longer. Plus, if we were going to accomplish everything I had in mind, we were going to need a car.

So, off we went.

We both decided I needed my phone and clothes and wallet and shoes back in order to do this thing right. But when I pulled to the curb across the street from Ellie's, I said to B, "Looks like she's not home. No lights on."

"You don't know that, maybe she's watching TV or somethin'."

"No, we'd see flashes in the dark. I guess we're gonna have to wait, try again later." Or maybe I was getting cold feet.

"Let's go up anyway, give her a try. She might be in the bathroom."

I looked up at the dark windows. "I don't think so, man. Have you ever known a girl to be at home in the dark and not turn any lights on?"

"I don't know. You never know."

"No, *you* never know, because you've never been alone at night with any girl."

"Fuck you." He slapped my arm and moved to get out. "I'm goin' up there, see what's up."

"Girls turn lights on." I said as he pulled on the door handle. "If she was home, in the bathroom or not, there would be a whole string of lights on." He shrugged and went anyway.

I sat back and watched him cross the street to ring her doorbell. I looked up at Ellie's darkened apartment, her empty bedroom window. There was a tightness in my gut, like dread or regret. I shifted in my seat. I felt a pulling. It was like there was a string tied from my heart to my stomach like a soup can telephone, when something happened on one end, I felt it telegraphed to the other. Or maybe it was gas. I couldn't get rid of it.

I had been fooled by Ellie. I had been taken *with* her first, then *by* her. She was the girl I wanted, the kind I'd hoped to meet by moving up here. She was beautiful and had good taste, which showed in the way she wore her hair, her clothes, the things she said. She liked to do things and go places. Too many girls back home just didn't want to do anything. They were content to watch other people's lives go by on TV. They were boring. And there weren't enough of them. But Ellie, now that was it. The thought of her made my heart go warm. But the truth was hard in my bruised ribs. It went cold in my stomach. Ellie was a lie.

I wondered how many things she'd lied about. I wonder if she ever liked being with me. The sex was good. Well, actually it wasn't *that* great. She was sexy, and when we had sex she was naked and *that* was pretty good. But the actual sex part, the in and out, wasn't that great. I'd been with less interesting girls who paid more attention, and were warmer and more fun. Is it too much to ask that a girl be fun and sexy and interesting?

Anyway, that's what I saw when I looked up at her dark apartment. And I couldn't help thinking of Alex too. The two of them together. He was the guy ultimately responsible for all this shit. But he didn't have my money, or my weed. He had initiated the break-in and stole my stuff, but someone else had stepped in, taken control. My guess was my fair lady here had something to do with it. She was in the middle of the circle. I had personally broken into Alex's apartment and taken my money back. Then outside, someone *else* had taken it from me. Again. I never got the chance to see who it was, of course, because I was too busy admiring the fine wood grain pattern of a high quality two-by-four.

But Alex wouldn't have dragged me out of Ellie's if he had the money. No, someone else had taken the money the second time. Apparently Sean and Gino. And hadn't I coincidentally run into Sean at Ellie's a couple of nights before?

Someone had told them where the money was and it probably wasn't Alex, seeing how it was his place and all. They may not have known I was going there to break in, though. Hell, they could have been planning to break in themselves, until I did them the favor, then rolled over nice as a puppy and handed it to them.

But that was only part of it. Somebody *else* still had my weed. And I needed that just as much as the money. They were a package, my package, and I wasn't settling for half. I knew it wasn't at Alex's either. But I knew who his little helpers were and I was willing to bet they'd know where it was.

I looked up at Ellie's. She probably knew where the weed was too. But she wasn't home yet. I thought about her. Pictured her in the small blue silk robe that ended just below her ass. The scar on her stomach where her sister had stabbed her with scissors when she was a kid. But all of that was over now. I wouldn't see her naked again.

And I was sorry I would never get to sleep in that comfortable-ass bed of hers either. That thing was amazing. Until that time I was pulled out of it onto my head.

My fingers found the lump on the back of my head. It was still there. Hard now.

B came back to the car. "You're right, not home," he said, getting in.

I didn't look at him. I was looking far up the road now, at something that wasn't there.

"B," I said, somewhat gravely into the distance. "Are you ready for this? Really?"

He got a mad, questioning look on his face. "What are you talkin' about? We been talkin' about this all day. Shit."

"I know." I shook my head, small and serious. "But, I mean, like, *for real*. We have to end this. I can't go back. Not without the money I owe. And I don't want to. These fucking assholes broke into my apartment and stole my shit. I'm life-and-death serious about this. I'm getting it back."

B shook his head listening. I went on. "I didn't come to this city to be taken advantage of. I came here to make a new life. I *refuse* to give up. It's simply *not* an option. And to be honest, I feel kind of stupid about it, feel kind of embarrassed about it all. And *that* pisses me off even more. I feel like some small-town dope who got roped in by some pretty girl and her fucking pimp."

B smiled a little bit to one side.

"I'm *pissed*," I said with a sharp, bouncing nod. "And I'm serious about that five hundred bucks. It's not a lot, but its something. So I'm just saying. Are you ready to help me? Show 'em what a couple of small town country kids can do?"

"Ha-*hah*," B said and hit his palm with his fist. "Yes sir, some Big City ass kickin.' That's what I came up here for." He had a big-toothed grin on his face. He slapped the dashboard. It crunched like Doritos. I stomped on the gas pedal and the rusty silver Toyota purred gently away from the curb.

Chapter 32

I turned off of Ashland at Chicago and easily found a parking spot a block up. It was just after nine o'clock, so I didn't pay the meter. The last lingering hint of sunset was gone now, given over to darkness; the city light glowing orange off low clouds. There was a medium amount of people on the wide sidewalks, some in groups. A lady and two kids went into the dollar store. B and I rounded the corner on to Ashland and the people disappeared, one guy a few blocks ahead. The short row of businesses ended at the alley, where I stopped and pulled B in behind Paul and Pratt's coach house.

We stood beside a line of trash cans, all of them overflowing, and an old mattress with a giant 'X' spray painted on it in black paint, meaning bed bugs. We backed away from it. I leaned in close to B and whispered.

"Ok," I said, "you go around that way." I pointed down the Ashland side, past the billboard. "And I'll go around this way," motioning toward the small, dark gap between buildings. With our heads huddled together, I drew on my palm with a finger like kids planning a touch-football play. "The front door is like six feet up. There's a concrete staircase leading up to it. There's space underneath. We'll meet there. It's closer to your side, so stay low and wait for me."

"What if they see me?" B said, nodding along.

"Why would they see you?" I flashed him a suspicious look, but I could see he genuinely meant it.

"They could be out smokin', or somethin'."

"They won't be. And if they are you'll hear 'em. But don't let them see you. Just go along and look for any open windows. Try to listen to see where they are and what they're doing. We'll meet under the stairs and figure a way in. Ok?" I gave him a commander's strong reassuring nod, then added, "The front window is a big bay window, and someone could see under the stairs if they were close enough, so be careful." Then I gave the nod again and moved off toward the dark.

The small, black corridor between the coach house and the building next door smelled like piss and trash and wet concrete. It was just over a shoulder's width wide so that two people couldn't pass each other in it without touching. And it was dark. It was the kind of dark, narrow, creepy, city space where rats mutate and transform into super villains, then go on slime-tinged rampages.

I regretted my decision immediately. I was the one calling the shots, I should have sent B this way. I wanted out. I wanted to run to the light on the other side, but I needed to listen at the windows. I wanted to shuffle my feet, so I wouldn't trip in the dark, but was afraid of what I might touch.

I kept my hands out and stepped slowly, one foot, then the other, looking up at a lighted window at about where the kitchen should be. I tried to focus and listen, but something dripped on me. Hopefully it was just water from the roof, but I didn't want to look up, get it in my eye. I shivered and moved.

The next little darkened window must be the bathroom. The air got thicker with moisture halfway down the corridor. It was charged with wetness and pee, and I took extra care not to touch the damp walls. Flashes of light hit against a longer, skinny window slightly ahead of me. The couch sat under that window, I knew from painful experience, facing the huge TV. Machine gun sounds and mumbled cursing came from it. Someone was watching a movie, or playing video games.

My foot touched something squishy. I froze. My throat closed and my mouth went dry. A million possibilities ran through my mind. I looked down at my bare foot in B's shitty sandal, but it was too black to see. It squished again. It wasn't a something-dead-and-rotting kind of squishy. It was more like a wet blanket squish. I moved a foot over and tried again.

Squish. My face screwed up into itself. I patted the squish under my foot searching for a way around. Squish, squishy. Then it moved.

A shutter ran up my spine. My flesh went cold.

It moaned.

I scrambled automatically and slipped on the squish. Both feet slipped. I lost my sandals. Barefoot. It *was* a wet blanket. Or the ground was covered in thick moss, thick moaning moss. I ran in place, slipping on the squishy. I reluctantly grabbed at the slimy brick walls. No good. My feet went out from under me.

I landed on someone. The smell hit me instantly, erupted under me like a dust cloud. A bum.

A writhing groan lashed out at me, "HRR-grr-Grr."

Bucking began under the wet blanket and me. I scrambled trying to stand, yet not touch anything.

"MHrr-HRR-grr-th-fuckk."

The ground moved beneath me. I screamed as it rose up with me like a golem. "Aahhh," came out of me raspily and thin like a screech.

I made for the patch of lightness in front of the coach house, bisecting the corridor. I got a foothold and lunged. The bum rose up everywhere around me. I lurched. My foot caught in the blanket, sending me careening forward on uncontrolled momentum, continually tripping, unable to catch my balance.

With outstretched hands, I ran clamoringly head first into a big, metal Weber grill, in front of another Weber grill, next to a little charcoal grill. Ashes poofed. Metal rang and banged and bent under me.

B ran to me as I stopped rolling. Even he screamed, "Uhhh," as the dirty, wet homeless guy dragged himself out of the darkness, clothed grotesquely in the stinking muddy blanket. "Ga-hett ooutta here. Da-hammit," the guy barreled.

Lights came on overhead. Pratt slammed through the door to the top of the stairs, huge and hulking in his own right.

"What the fuck?" he said. Then recognized me. "You."

He bounded down the stairs in three steps. B jerked. Pratt sailed down toward him. With amazing agility, B spun on his left foot like a discus thrower and caught Pratt's hand as he hit the bottom stair. Using his momentum against him, B spun and whipped Pratt forward like a pro wrestler throwing a guy against the ropes. Except the wall didn't give. There was a sick, mushy splat sound as Pratt's head slammed full force into the brick wall.

Paul ran out next. It was crazy how fast he reacted. Like the springy little rat he is, he jumped over the stair rail and landed, six feet down, nimbly on the concrete near me. I clamored some more to my feet. B continued after Pratt. Paul waited a millisecond too long deciding who to hit. I scooped up a domed grill lid and let him have it on the side of the mouth. B picked Pratt up by the back of the pants and drove him head first into the concrete stairs. It was ugly. Pratt took a blunt stair to the top of the head. He crumpled, wriggling, awkwardly twisted on his stomach. Paul reeled dazedly from my blow and took my place in amongst the toppled grills. Hopefully one of them was his, because whoever's they were, they were going to be pissed.

I breathed a lot, shaken. "Let's get 'em inside," I yelled to B. "Quick before somebody comes running out."

The homeless guy had disappeared back into his crawlspace. I shook the grill lid threateningly at Paul and kicked him up the stairs. He was quiet and mad and bleeding at the mouth. B had to manhandle Pratt to get him up. He was too beat to fight back, his head bleeding. B wrestled him up the stairs alone, while I pushed and nudged Paul.

Inside, I found duct tape on the floor beside the coffee table. I had a funny suspicion it was the same duct tape that had tied me up on my trip to the lake. So, appropriately enough, I suggested to B we put it to the same use. Paul and Pratt disagreed, simultaneously murmuring things like, "Fuck you," "I'll kill you," "Assholes," and some other stuff I couldn't make out, until I kicked Paul in the ribs and B plunked Pratt's head against the hard wood.

Man it was nice to have a partner. Well worth the money I'd had to promise to get him up here.

Speaking of money, we turned their apartment upside down looking for the money and my weed. Paul had a cubbyhole in his room built under the stairs where a sharp angle of ceiling led to the apartment above. It was a makeshift storage space lined with shelves and filled with clothes and shoes and hats. And a good-sized metal safe box with a loop in it for a lock. He didn't have a lock on it. He should have locked it. There was almost two pounds of weed inside. My weed. There were four bottles of prescription pills in it too, and a little baggy tied in a knot with white powder.

It was pretty obvious Paul was the storekeeper, while Pratt was the security. B turned up nothing in Pratt's room, but dirty sweat socks. And a decent pair of Nike high tops which were much more comfortable than B's old sandals, even if a size too big for me.

In Paul's room, I'd found pills, coke, my own weed and a little something extra I was happy to take along: Cash, just over five thousand dollars worth.

So that certainly confirmed what I already knew; Alex and these clowns broke into my place together. Alex took the money. Paul and Pratt got the weed. It looked like most of the weed was still there, thankfully, so the extra money must have come from somewhere else, which probably had something to do with the other stuff in the box.

I shoved the envelope of money down into the waist of my sweat pants and pulled the drawstring tight. This time I wasn't going to lose it. I took the metal lockbox into the living room. Paul immediately started squirming and bucking with his hands tied tight behind him. We ignored the moans straining against the silver tape wound round his head over his mouth.

"They're coming with us," I told B, motioning with my hand.

"Coming with us? What do you mean?"

"I'll pull the car around to the alley. We'll take them out the back. Put 'em in the trunk." Paul moaned about that too.

"Yeah sure, just plop 'em in the trunk," B said. He looked down at Pratt's bulk, gave him a little kick in the side. "Sure. No big deal."

Neither one of them wanted to go easily. It took both of us to carry each one. B bounced Paul's head on the floor until he stopped struggling. Pratt we dropped several times. I started to understand why Paul had had so much trouble carrying me, it's not as easy as it sounds, carrying someone that doesn't want to be carried.

The back door led to a crude back porch used as a storage shed with rough wooden stairs leading out to the alley. We ended up pulling Pratt down the stairs by his legs, letting his head bang off of each step until he finally went limp at the bottom. The trunk of Melanie's Toyota, surprisingly, held them both comfortably with room to spare.

Chapter 33

"Hah!" B said and slapped his fist against his palm. "That shit was awesome. I didn't even think about it. I just did it. The way I whipped that guy against the brick."

"Pratt. The little guy is Paul."

"Whoever. Shit was awesome."

"I know. I can't believe it worked out. I can't believe we actually did it. And it worked! I got the weed back! I didn't think I was ever gonna see that shit again."

"Fuck yeah."

We were off to a banging start. B drummed on the dashboard, dust puffed up in the passing street light coming in windshield. I smiled at myself as I drove, squeezing the wheel hard in waves of disbelief. A success! I couldn't believe I'd scored a success. I smiled, but we still had a ways to go.

I narrowed my eyes, forcing myself to concentrate on the next task at hand. It made my eye twitch. The next part was going to be tough and more emotional. But who cares? I don't. And we were off to a banging start. I was done with playtime and dream girls.

As soon as Ellie's building came into sight, we could see lights on in her apartment. It was real this time. It was going to happen.

A thudding noise started up behind us in the trunk. B looked at me with a knowing look. We'd been waiting for it.

I turned down an alley and found a relatively dark spot behind a garage. B stretched out two long lines of duct tape and spun the end making it into a tight, sticky length of cord. I popped the trunk. Paul was bucking around, kicking his feet against the side wall. B smacked him.

We had arranged them head to foot facing each other like a yin yang symbol; hands taped tightly behind backs, feet taped together. Working quickly, we yanked Paul out onto the ground. He bucked. B kicked him while I looped the cord around his wrists and ankles linking them together, so he couldn't kick without yanking his own arms out. We threw Paul back in with his head in front of Pratt's feet. If Pratt kicked he would only hit Paul and I hoped he did.

I drove around the block and parked under a dark tree. B and I got out into the late night quiet. Cars crisscrossed the ends of the block sporadically. We crossed the street to stand in the shadows, looking up at the back of Ellie's building. After what she had done last night, I knew she wasn't going to simply buzz me up as if nothing had happened. So I had been thinking of the best way to get in ever since.

I clapped a hand on B's back and pointed up at Ellie's back window, sighting down my arm.

"See the top window on the far right?" I said. He nodded silently. "That's her place." Then I pointed down the alley. "There's a metal gate that's locked. They don't lock the back door on account of the gate. So that's it. Over the gate, up the stairs. The last door you come to, all the way up on the far right. That's hers. There's no way you can miss it."

"Sounds easy enough," B said.

"I don't know what the lock is like. But I don't think you'll have any trouble."

B clutched his gut in both hands and jiggled it. "I got two hundred fifty pounds of locksmith right here. I think it'll do the trick."

"Alright," I said, patting his back. "Now, when I go around the corner, you wait for one full minute, ok? Let me see if she'll talk to me."

"Sure, man, I got it. Easy as pie."

"And listen. Don't hurt her, or do anything too crazy."

"Thought you hated her."

"Well, yeah. But that doesn't mean I want her to get hurt."

"Sure, man, I wouldn't do any of that. What do you take me for?"

I clapped him on the back again and went to the corner. B was still there waiting at the end of the alley. I held up one finger. He waved in acknowledgement. I went around the closed coffee shop to the front door and laid that finger on Ellie's buzzer.

It took her a full thirty seconds to answer. I was worried B would get there too early, before I got a chance to talk. Then it occurred to me there might be someone else in there with her. Alex even. I hadn't thought of that. How could I be so stupid? She could have a whole crew of dudes up in that apartment with her. Lord knows she wouldn't have any trouble finding them. Wherever she went there was a man there. She had a way of getting guys to go along with her. I'd fallen for it myself and look where it had gotten me. B could walk in on a shit storm. Damnit.

But it was too late for that, the ball was already rolling. And it would be too convenient, too easy if Alex was there anyway.

The buzzer box finally cackled. "Yeah?' she said, sweetly. "Who is it?"

"It's me, Ellie, Michael."

"Oooh," she said, almost with pleasure. "What's up?"

"I need to get my stuff back. Let me up?"

"I don't think so, Mike." She said with a sharp giggle, the idea amusingly preposterous.

"Come on, Ellie, I just need my stuff." I kept my voice plaintive. "I need my phone and keys. You know I do. Let's talk about this. I'm not even mad at you. Let's just talk, huh?"

"I'm sorry, Mike," she said softly, almost like she meant it. "I don't think I can let you in...I'll send your stuff tomorrow. I'll get a messenger. Or have Alex run it by." Ouch. Before she let go of the button, I heard a crash in the background. The box went dead.

What seemed like minutes passed. I took a step back to look up at the windows. I pushed the button a couple times. I stepped back again, looking around. What was going on in there, B? Guys waiting? Guns? Murdering?

Then, the box came back to life with a series of clicks. "—amn it. How's it—," it said between blips. The door buzzed for a second. I pushed exactly as it stopped. "Damn it, come on, B," I said to myself, looking up and down the street. It buzzed again and I pushed through.

Ellie's door was ajar when I got, breathlessly, to the top of the ridiculously long staircase. I pushed it open and found B standing in the center of the room with his hands on his hips, the thick roll of duct tape around his meaty wrist like a watch or super hero bracelet. There was glass on the floor and picture frames lying broken on the ground. The coffee table was pushed askew and a broken mug, broken plates on the kitchen floor.

Ellie and another girl, her friend Selena, were sitting obediently on the couch, not happy. Ellie had her left hand up covering half of her face. Selena was glaring up at B through snarled teeth, huffing and puffing exhaustedly, her face red. She didn't even see me. There was death in her eyes.

"What's going on B?" I said casually. "Took you long enough."

A low growling noise came out of Selena.

"This crazy girl jumped on my back, tried to stab me with them scissors." He flicked his finger at the pair of scissors with orange plastic handles thrown under the coffee table.

"I'll kill you," she screeched and lunged. B's big hand met her half way up. He smacked her quick, sitting her right back down.

"Damnit, B." I hit his arm immediately with a back handed slap. "Don't fucking hit her, man. What's wrong with you? I just said that outside."

"Wrong with me? Girl's crazy. She tried to stab me with them scissors. Didn't I just tell you that?"

"Still, man. What the fuck?"

I looked at Ellie. She didn't look back. Her curly hair was ruffled, pushed haphazardly up and off to the side. A bobby pin had come loose and clung to a random strand like a bird feeder dangling from a tree branch. Bangs fell across her face, unruly; one bent curl hooked around, framing the right eye perfectly. She wore tight, high-waisted black jeans and a flowing shear black tank-top you could see through. The top did little to hide the black lace bra and the perfect little boobs it supported, but it wasn't really meant to.

"Hey, Ellie," I said, slowly, leeringly, full of sarcastic swagger. "How's it going? I see you met my friend B. B," I passed my hand between them, "Ellie."

"Fuck you. And fuck him." She cut me short, the cocky humor had gone out of her voice.

"Ok," I said, putting my hands out. "Just trying to be social."

I turned and went into her bedroom. My clothes were kicked thoughtlessly under the bed, my phone, wallet and keys in a pile on the dresser. Wasting no time, I shook out my clothes, stripped off the baggy sweat pants, got back into my jeans, sans underwear, and put my belongings back in my pockets where they belonged. My phone was dead, of course, but at least I had it.

I rejoined B in the center of the living room feeling far less ridiculous than I had all day. I looked down at Ellie again. My head shook unconsciously with disappointment. I couldn't help it. I had really liked that girl. I gritted my teeth. I worked a hand over my mouth thinking how to start.

"All right," I said, looking away. "Now, there are a lot of things I'd like to ask you, Ellie, but I don't want to be here all night, and honestly, I don't really care that much anymore. So I'm gonna stick to the most obvious question and keep it at that...." Then I said, dejectedly, like it was dumb I even had to bother. "Where's my money? I know you know where it is. Hell, it might even be here for all I know, but you're going to have to tell me. You have to."

She lowered her chin, looking up at me with only her eyes. "*I* don't know," she said, kind of snotty, obviously.

"You know, Ellie. I know you do. And I'm doing my best not to be mad at you. I mean I sort of hate you right now, but I'm sure you can understand that. So let's be civil, huh? I don't really want to be here anymore, or be around you. I had to come here to get my stuff back and now I want to go. But I have to have that money, and you seem to be the one person who's in the middle of it, touching all the parts. I keep thinking one person took it, then somebody else. And I keep being wrong. But *you* know. And we," I pointed to B, "aren't leaving till you tell me where it is, or who has it."

She turned her bored look to Selena and rolled her eyes. In a guttural monotone, she said, "Fuck you, Mike. You're an idiot. I'm done with you."

B stepped forward, raising his hand instinctually. I caught his arm. "Damn it, man."

"What?"

I glared at him, then back to her.

"Ellie. I know Alex broke into my place. And I'm willing to bet it was no coincidence that I happened to be sleeping in your bed that night. Of course, you had me completely whipped. I'll admit it. I like how you held out on me until the time was right. That was genius. And you did a good job of acting all surprised and caring and nurturing along the way. You did. Looking back on it, it was impressive. But I saw you with Alex the other night. And I know you are in on it. But then, I saw you with Sean too. And somebody else tells me Sean and Gino have the money now. So... I'm asking you nicely. Where is my money?"

She looked at her nails.

"Tell me, where it is."

"No."

I clapped my hands loudly. "Damn it," I yelled. "You're going to tell me."

She looked at Selena and laughed. "Hey, easy, Mike, don't get all tough guy on me."

My fist tightened. My teeth grinded.

"You know what," Ellie said. "You've scared me straight. You win. I'll tell you. That guy Zeke has your money. You know the graffiti artist guy with big glasses. Or wait," she clicked fingernails against her teeth. "No, you know, I think it was Tyrone. You know him, tattoos? Funny haircut?"

She thought she was being funny.

I looked at B. He rubbed his hands together and shrugged a question. I turned and kicked the coffee table. It sailed into the wall with a loud bang and a snap, the corner punching a hole in the drywall.

How to get a stubborn girl to answer your questions? I wasn't going to hit her. I wouldn't. And I wouldn't let B. I was smarter than that. But she didn't have to know that. I spun back around. I shoved a dagger-like finger in her face.

"Who's got my money!?" I yelled.

Ellie was unimpressed. She looked at me like I was stupid. "Anybody. Everybody. I don't care."

I looked at B again. Hmph.

"I don't know why you're doing this to me—"

"'Cause you a fucking hillbilly," Selena blurted out. "What are you from Idaho or some shit?" The girls started laughing.

I said softly, "Indiana actually."

They laughed even harder. "Even worse, you country bumpkin."

B hauled off and smacked Selena before I could stop him. She went for him. She jumped straight into his midsection with both fists. B caught his arms around her and they went rolling off together into the glass on the floor.

Ellie made a move of her own. She used the distraction to lurch past me. But I saw it and caught her shoulders, shoving her back before she could get any momentum going. Selena yelped across the room. B snatched her up with her arms behind her back and threw her to the sofa again.

"We have to do something with her, B. She's gonna keep getting in our way." I looked around for ideas.

B rushed toward her suddenly. Selena tried to fend him off. There were some smacking sounds but he caught her wrists and twisted her over. Ellie pulled her feet up under her on the edge of couch, trying to get out of the way. B put his knee in Selena's back, pulled a length of tape from the roll on his wrist and bound her hands behind her in one move like a rodeo cowboy roping a steer.

Ellie pushed away as far as the couch would let her. B flipped Selena over and slapped a new piece of tape on her mouth, shutting her up. The tape concaved. She sucked air desperately through her nose. Her cheeks puffed out. In and out with a wheezing sound. Her eyes were wild, tearing at B. He stood up beside me again, letting out huge breaths.

"That girl's something else," he said, winded. "She's kinda cute too." A small cut began bleeding on his arm.

"Knock it off with the goddamn hitting," I said. "Please."

"What, Mike? She called us bumpkins."

I shook it off. We both turned back on Ellie, her eyes darting between us, not so much scared as calculating.

"Ok, Ellie. Tell me where the money is. I don't want to hurt you."

Selena wheezed around the tape loudly. Ellie glanced at her, then back at me.

"Go to hell!"

Damnit.

"This is fucking stupid, Mike," B said. "How many people could have it? Let's just go beat it out of somebody else. Somebody we can actually beat on."

"Why would we go running all over town beating people up," I said to him. "When the one person who knows for sure is sitting right here?"

"Well she ain't talkin' and you ain't makin' her. That's why."

I swung around looking for something else to kick. There was a way to get her to talk. I know she knew where it was and I had to make her talk. I thought of the lake. I thought of me being in the opposite situation with Alex standing over me. I hadn't known where the money was. But Ellie did. And Alex had a tool I wasn't going to use: violence.

There must be a way. I paced around the room.

"You're an idiot, Michael," Ellie said savagely. "You aren't cut out for this. You're a sucker. You aren't up to it. You're weak. A weak little country fucking bumpkin."

B looked at me, asking with his hands. I ignored her. I paced around the kitchen. There *must* be a way to get her to talk. I looked for some means of coercion. Ice? Could ice be used as torture? I paced. Indian burn? That hurts pretty bad and isn't directly violent.

"You really are just a hillbilly." She made her voice low with a country accent, "You comes up to the Big City to get yourself a *big* time job." She laughed. B shook his head patiently waiting for me to stop being an idiot.

She went on. "You come up here trying to sell weed. But you don't even know anybody. And you're so small town you'd trust anybody. Shit, you even showed Alex exactly where you kept the shit. You showed him where you put the money."

B couldn't help himself there, he said, "Wait, he knew where the money was? And it took you how long to figure out who took it?"

I shook my head. "It wasn't like that," I said. "We were friends. I was selling to him like three times a week. I trusted him."

"Yeah," Ellie said. "And I was your 'girlfriend.'" She made air quotes.

"Mike, what are we doing here?" B said.

Ellie chuckled, proud of herself. I rushed the couch and grabbed her by the chin. "Tell me who has the money."

"Fuck you," she said between her teeth and kicked at me with her foot, but missed. Selena tried to kick me too, but couldn't reach from the weird angle.

I pushed Ellie's face and turned away in frustration.

Then I saw it.

It came to me there, glimmering in the light, obvious. I spun around.

"B. Tape her feet," I said, pointing at Selena. I went into Ellie's bedroom and came out with a desk chair. I slammed it down in the middle of the room as if it alone concluded my argument. I nodded to B. We closed in on Ellie. She screamed and squirmed. Selena floundered. We got Ellie into the chair. B held her down tight while I taped her feet to the chair and her arms behind her. I put tape on her mouth and she was secure, unable to move.

"Now we're getting someplace," B said. "What's next? Waterboarding? Whatever that is."

"No," I went to the far side of the room. I came back wielding the shiny pair of metal scissors like a deranged mad scientist.

Ellie's eyes went huge. Veins stood out on her slender neck, contorting the beautiful lines with bumpy typography. A high squeal rung in her throat, couldn't escape her mouth.

Selena groaned and bucked so hard, she fell off the couch onto the floor. I pointed at her and told B, "Put her in the bathroom, something."

"Should I put her in the shower?" he said.

"I don't care." He deftly scooped her up in one arm and carried her off like a proud caveman. He closed the door on her moaning and came back quickly to see what I was going to do.

I leveled the scissors at Ellie, pointed the tip toward her struggling eye.

"Now, Ellie," I said calmly. "Tell me who has the money. I'm not messing around."

I nodded at B to take the tape off her mouth. She screamed. Loud. He clamped it off with his heavy hand. She played that game where you try to bite the hand over your mouth, but B moved around behind her, readjusting his hold so she couldn't.

I asked again, "Ellie, one more time, where is the money?"

B took his hand off. She didn't scream, but sucked in breath. She said, "Don't."

"Hold her head," I told B.

I ran my left hand through her hair. I picked a beautiful lock of wonderfully curly hair and snapped it off with the scissors, close to the scalp. Ellie went quiet immediately and buck wild in her chair. Slowly, I brought the shock of hair in front of her face. Her arms strained, shaking with rigidity, to touch the spot it had come from. B shook his head chuckling.

"Who has it?" I raised the scissors again.

B let her speak. "What are you doing? What are you gonna do?" she said frantically.

I clipped the end off a piece from the other side and let it fall in front of her. She strained her neck. B held her head. Tears welled up in her eyes.

I picked out another strand and held it in my fingers, working the scissors in the air, making that nice scissoring sound of sharp metal bird chirps. The tears fell. I brought the scissors closer to the curly strand. Her defiance melted. Her head went slack in B's grip. I clipped.

"Tell me, Ellie, before it gets bad..."

"Stop, stop..." Her whole body shook with sobs. Aw, vanity. "You're right," she mumbled down into her lap. "Alex put me up to it. He needed it."

"Ok," I said, "keep going." I kept the scissors in close, reflecting the overhead light.

"I loved him." Real tears came then. "The fucking prick. He took me with him to Vegas. He lost his tuition money."

What?

"Wait, what?" The scissors drooped in my hand. Vegas? Fucking Las Vegas? How lame can you get? I said, astonished, "Are you saying he did this to pay his college tuition? Because he lost it in Las Vegas?"

"Fucking rich kids," B said under his breath.

"His dad put money in his account to pay the bill," she said. The tears stopped. "But it was only half. His dad was going to make him get a job. Make Alex work to pay the rest." I couldn't believe it. "He thought he'd win some more in Vegas."

"You're kidding me," I said. "Right?"

B was looking as confused and amazed as I was. He sat back wringing out his hands. Ellie shook tear drops from the end of her nose. Started crying again.

"So why me? What's this got to do with me?" I said, still shaking my head, amazed.

"He wanted to use what was left of the money to buy a bunch of weed. Sell it at school. Make the money that way."

"And?"

"Something went wrong the first time." The Ian debacle. "Then you came around."

"So he sent you after me? His own girlfriend? Why would he take you on vacation to Las Vegas, or wherever, then pimp you out? And why would you do it?"

"You don't know him, the fucking bastard. I love him."

"But then I guess you got mad, huh?"

She dripped tears into her lap. "Yeah, well, he isn't exactly a romantic. It wasn't the first time he asked me to do some shit I didn't want to do." The tears stopped. "It was the last."

"Why didn't he just ask his dad for more? It seems a lot easier."

"Fucking rich kids," B said again, still shaking his head.

"Are you kidding? He wouldn't even tell his dad he changed his major. I think the only thing he's scared of at all is his dad."

None of this did much for my self-esteem. A kid that didn't feel like working.

"So, he stole my money, because he lost his dad's?"

"He told me he was going to invest in more weed, or something else, I don't know. Do it right this time."

I thought about the deal he and Ian had, then about the pills I'd found in Paul's closet. I wondered what Alex's thoughts were on pharmaceuticals.

It was time for me to pace again. I kept the scissors in my hand as I walked in a circle, letting the spoiled brat thing take hold. She had done a nice job of selling me on Alex. She would give him up willingly because he had used her. But back to the matter at hand.

Alex didn't have my money. Someone else had stolen it the second time and Ellie had something to do with it. She knew all about it. And she was hurt.

I turned back to her, sympathy gone, scissors ready.

"Boo hoo hoo," I said meanly. She had laughed in my face, now it was my turn. "Now tell me who has my money. You fucked me over more than once and fed me to the wolves. That was a very nice story, informative and very touching. But I'm not as simple-minded as you might think. You're too self-involved to see it. I liked you. I liked the lie you sold me. I thought you liked me. But that's done. You're a beautiful girl. But fuck that. I couldn't give less of a shit."

She met my rant with defiant anger. She strained against the chair. "Let me up, you stupid fuck!" she screamed. I grabbed a chunk of hair and snipped.

"Tell me who has it!"

B wasn't ready. Her head whipped crazily. She almost poked herself in the eye as I went in with the scissors. B scrambled to hold her steady as I chopped. Hair cascaded all around like strands of confetti. I'd cut one short, one long.

"Sto-hop. Puh-lease, sto-hop." She finally shook again with sobs. "Gino," she gasped, beaten. "Gino has it. I told him...I told him...." She couldn't get it out, but I knew what she was getting at. I'd been roped in by her myself. Maybe she'd tried Sean first. But Gino accepted.

"Get some more tape, B." I said, satisfied. "She's coming with us too."

"Ok. What about the cute girl in the tub?"

"No."

Chapter 34

Getting Ellie in the car was much easier. We tried not putting tape over her mouth, but she seemed to have a lot of negative things to say about us, and loudly, so I had to tape it shut after all. B was behind the wheel taking simple directions from me as I played with Ellie's phone.

There's a guilty pleasure in reading someone else's text messages. Especially when that person has screwed you over and is forced to sit quietly and watch while you discover exactly how many strings of lies she had going and who all was involved. She had sent and received a string of messages over the past several days. The tone suggested former intimacy worn thin by mistrust, yet comfortable. After quickly reading a few of the texts, I mimicked her tone easily when I texted Alex. I continued the thread naturally enough saying, 'Need to talk. Coming over'.

Some muffled thumping sounds came from the trunk when we stopped at a red light, forcing us to turn up the radio to drown them out. The night air was warm coming through the open windows. It blew Ellie's hair across her face. If she wasn't such an asshole I would have brushed out of the way for her. But screw that, I hope it tickled like crazy and drove her nuts.

Alex responded to Ellie's message by saying, 'Home in thirty'.

So that was that. We would simply show up on Alex's doorstep and he'd buzz us in. He'd be expecting Ellie. He'd get me and B.

The extra thirty minutes gave us plenty of time to make a much-needed stop. There was one very obviously important detail I had to sew up before the night was over and it just happened to be on the way.

I used Ellie's phone to let them know she was coming. B turned down Belmont toward Lakeview, then south on Clark as I directed him. Ellie's eyes started flicking back and forth, suddenly very interested in where we were as we got closer to Sean and Gino's building.

Their street was serenely quiet as it usually is in the evening; a guy looked at his phone while his dog pooped on a patch of grass, a few people walked past the end of the block carrying plastic grocery bags.

"Alright, B," I said, before getting out. "When you see me in that window," I leaned over and pointed up at the top window on the left. "Open Ellie's door and make her lean out. Ok?"

"Why? Whose place is this?" he said, looking mildly confused, but not too concerned.

Ellie was watching me intently. I pointed at her. "She knows." They both watched me walk to the double glass doors and push the buzzer; Ellie's eyes smudged with mascara above the silver duct tape.

Gino wasn't really surprised when he opened the door to their apartment and found me standing there instead of Ellie. He gave me an inevitable smile and small shrug. We talked some things over with Sean in the living room. I took them both to the window and pointed out. We all watched as B made a quick, discreet display of Ellie bound in duct tape. The prettier a girl is the more exaggerated and dramatic they look tied up. Or maybe they make every situation more dramatic and fantastic, and it only seems more jarring when it's not something nice and pleasant.

Gino and Sean and I had never had any problems before. The only ill feeling between us was over my getting hit in the head with a board, but I was in a place, now, to be more understanding. I couldn't really hold Gino too much at fault, he was manipulated by that little thing a lot of men want. And it's a powerful thing. Also a little greed too, but who isn't?

I came back to the car carrying an over-stuffed manila envelope with masking tape across one end and a green rubber band. We all knew what was in it. B shook his head in disbelief.

"Now, how did you—?"

Ellie sank heavily back into the seat, more defeated than ever; her blown hair still out of whack.

I gave B directions to Alex's apartment in Uptown. He had a little fight with a cab, but he held his ground, looking like he enjoyed it. My mind was stuck on what was next. There was light in Alex's windows. I texted him with Ellie's phone. I took a deep breath and fist bumped B.

I didn't feel very good about leaving Ellie alone in the car. What if she climbed over the front seat and honked the horn with her chin? Or put the car in neutral, causing is to roll down the street, or bump into other cars, making their alarms go off. No, that wouldn't be any good. There wasn't any room for her in the trunk and we couldn't exactly bring her with us. A tied-up a girl is a bit conspicuous. And Alex might get suspicious.

Ah hah, I snapped my fingers. B got out and I went around to her side. I pulled the seatbelt as tight as I could over her lap with hands tucked in behind her. She couldn't move around, or push the button to get out. I felt better: tied-up girl safely immobile, doors locked, no audible sounds coming from the trunk.

B and I went up to ring the bell. Ellie was expected.

The buzzer clicked. We were ready. We were ready to run up the half flight of stairs silently like assassins, except instead of ninja masks, we wore high tops and ugly camouflage. Alex lazily pulled the door open in his cool, self-assured way. He couldn't even be bothered to look out. He just stared at his phone, waiting, expecting Ellie to saunter up.

We rushed him, taking the steps in twos. His eyes saw us before it registered in his brain. I batted his phone away with my left and drove my right fist hard into his nose. But I missed. He reacted just fast enough to turn his head. I punched him in the soft side of his neck. His right foot kicked out automatically, hitting me square in the left shin. Oww! I bent over. B was there, coming in as I fell back. He punched Alex in the nose, and actually did. Alex's head snapped back. He tried in vain to keep his footing, but collapsed onto the wall behind him, slid down, his feet straight out, blocking the open door.

B quickly stepped over him, around me. He pulled Alex deeper into the apartment by his shirt neck. I limped upright, shut the door and followed. Alex clutched at his bleeding nose with his right hand and tried to push himself up with his left elbow. B kicked the arm out from under him. I rushed in and stood over him pointing my finger down into his bloody face. His eyes were pinched together with shocked terror.

"Fuck you," I yelled, maturely. I wanted to have a grand triumphant moment and shout morally superior things in his face. I wanted to cut him down, cause him to rethink everything he had ever done wrong to anyone in his life. Shame him for picking on people. But there wasn't anything to say. After all I had been through with this asshole, after all the chasing and running and running down and getting beaten up, all I wanted to do was punch him. But B already did that. Perfectly. I stood looking down at him, knowing I had him beat and I didn't know what else to do.

"Fuck you. Why'd you have to do it?" I yelled, spit raining down. He made an effort to sit up. B stomped on his shoulder. I went on with the finger pointing.

"Tell me." I demanded. "Did you really do it 'cause you're afraid to tell your daddy?"

"Fuck you, bumpkin," he said through bloody teeth. Bumpkin? Where did these people get that word? Who says that anymore? Had he and Ellie come up with that word together? So cute. I slapped him.

"You're afraid of your dad." I smacked him again. "You're afraid of your daddy." I sort of laughed. But it made me mad. "You stole from me and almost ruined my life because you're too afraid to tell you father you're a spoiled, greedy, lazy prick and you lost his money. You ran Ian out of town because you thought he screwed you over. You looked for the easiest way out and you just lost. But that shit happens. There's no guarantees. Hell, you tried to prove *that* to *me*." I guess I did have a few things to say. "You don't get what you want all the time. Didn't you tell me that? You can't bully people to get your way. And you can't take other people's shit." I smacked him again.

But I could see in the hopeless, whiney-little-kid, hurt expression in his eyes that he wasn't hearing me. I was never going to convince him of anything. He was much more worried about how his broken nose was going to look. I kicked him in the ribs and turned away.

I heard the hollow shwawk-cawk-cuk of duct tape. B pulled Alex's arms behind him and ran the tape around his wrists. He tried to buck us off and flip over, but I caught hold of a chunk of hair and bounced his head off the floor. Blood was still leaking from his nose. We had to wipe his mouth with his shirt to get the tape to stick over it. We thought it would be easier and more discreet to walk him out to the car, so we didn't tie his feet.

There was some confusion at Alex's front door, who was going to open it. I told B to go first. He thought I was going to open the door. Alex struggled continually and the three of us bounced off each other in the narrow alcove. B finally managed to pull the door open and Alex kicked it back shut with a clap. I punched him in the kidney closest to me. B pulled him hard to the right. With momentum going their way, I reached out and got the door open. Alex reared back into me shoving me against the now open door. It slammed against the wall. The door knob punched a hole behind it. We all ricocheted off. B's feet got tied up and he fell, bringing us all down with him.

A strange man's voice came from the hallway, high pitched with concern. "Hey, you guys all right?"

Alex moaned and groaned for help against the tape.

We were all laying in a pile, our heads just out of sight. All of our feet kicking at each other in the open doorway. I left B to deal with Alex and struggled to my feet. "Oh, hey," I said, plugging up the door with my whole body. "Our friend just passed out. We were trying to get him inside." The guy was very tall and skinny with a long neck. He was careening it around me, trying to look inside.

"You think he's ok? Is he drunk, or what?" His voice went up and curved like his neck.

"No, no," I said, stepping further out in the hall to prevent him from seeing. "We think maybe he's sick, or something. Maybe a..a seizure or something."

I don't know why I said that. It only made him more concerned. And his face showed it. I hoped B was containing Alex, but I couldn't look. I had to rely on the guy's curious expressions to guide me as I improvised.

"I'm sure he'll be all right though. We're just trying to get him inside. His legs are like jelly."

"Well, maybe I should call an ambulance. That doesn't look too good."

What doesn't? "Oh, um, yeah. Why don't you do it? Better be on the safe side."

The guys arching eyes finally pulled down as he brought out his phone.

"Shit," he said. "No service in here. I'll step back inside."

"Yeah, uh, good. That would be a great help. He was kind of flopping around a little. Maybe it's worse than we thought."

He went across the hall into his apartment. The door shut slowly behind him on its own. I spun back. B had Alex pressed against the wall inside, controlling him by forcing his bound wrists up between his shoulder blades. Alex's legs trembled with pain. His eyes were closed, forced into the wall; his cheek smushed flat.

"All right, let's go. Now." I yelled softly at B, grabbing Alex's left arm and pulling. We wrestled him out into the hall as the neighbor's door came open. I got behind Alex, hiding the tape that tied him and pushing him forward. B guided him down toward the front doors.

"Don't you want to wait for the ambulance?" The skinny guy's high voice yelled out from above us. "They're on the way."

"No. I think we're gonna take him," I said, keeping the grunting out of my voice. "Be faster that way."

"But they say you're supposed to wait—" Thankfully he didn't try to follow.

We taped Alex's feet before we shoved him in back with Ellie. I drove. B watched the two of them bounce off each other as we went fast around turns.

Alex didn't feel like working his way through college. He didn't want his dad to know he'd gambled and lost the chunk of tuition money he'd been given. What a prick. I went to school on loans and B couldn't afford to go at all. My loan payments were late. Rent was due. And I couldn't get a real job.

Fuck Alex and his dad who paid his way. I was doing it myself. All I wanted to do was sell a little weed to get by until I could land that dream job. Or, shit, even a bartending job. I just wanted to move to the city, put my hat in the ring. Assholes. A whole car full of assholes.

I went too fast around another corner, the tires squealed. Alex smashed against Ellie. B laughed.

Chapter 35

If someone had asked me a month ago how things were going, I would have said everything was looking up and up. I was making friends, making some money, sending out my resume, hoping to land that big job. And in less than a week it had all come apart.

I slept with a beautiful girl and my circle of friends was reduced to a run-out-of-town would-be drug dealer, two black-eyed geeks too afraid to leave their house and a car full of bound and gagged assholes.

And trick with these assholes was, they all had my number and each of them knew where I lived. Chicago is a big enough town to avoid people in, but not when they know where you live, and especially not when they know you have something they want.

So the trick *now* was to put some distance between them and me, to give myself some breathing room until I could figure out my next move. Basically, I needed to get rid of these assholes. And I had a good idea of how to do it.

The first stop was Melanie's. She was absolutely frantic when she opened the door.

"Where the hell have you been? I've been going out of my mind. I've called you like a billion times. Don't you have your phone? Have you checked your messages? Jesus, Michael I could murder you! You took my car, like yesterday. Did you even sleep here? I don't know. I wake up, look for my car? It's gone. I was supposed to pick Phil up from school like three hours ago. Three hours ago! Why didn't you call me? I've been waiting here all night. All night, yeah. You shoulda called. Or something! But no, you just leave me here all day, sick. I've been pulling my hair out." All of that in one breath.

I had come here to tell her something. I needed her to stop and listen. But she kept going.

"Everything that's been going on with you is crazy. You're running around naked in the middle of the night. You're calling me at all times. Getting beat up. Getting your friends beat up. Scaring me to death—" She kept on going, but like anybody else, when faced with someone berating you, I tuned out. I watched her face become flush. I looked out the window past her. I looked at the floor beside her. I started to get worried about B being alone with all of those guys. What if Alex and Ellie coordinated an attack and surprised him, got away. I watched Melanie's chest heave and lips move, words streaming out. I watched her boobs quake as her body shook with the effort. She was bordering on hysterical.

I grabbed both of her arms to stop the quivering. I felt her pillowy soft skin. Her lips were a rapid blur. I stuck my tongue in her mouth to shut it up. Hot breath and garbled words kept bubbling out. I wrapped my arms around her, leaning her back. That helped.

I could have stopped. I'd stopped her talking and that was the point, but I didn't want to. It felt good, reassuring. I was excited and nervous. Her tongue fought back, deep and anxious. There was a battle going on in there and both sides were winning.

I finally pulled back. She immediately said, "What the fuck, Michael?"

I said, "Your car's been stolen. You have to call the police."

Her eyebrows danced around on her face for a second. Then she said, "What? What did you say? My what?"

"Your car. Some guy just stole it. Call the police. I just saw him. He took off toward Clark."

"My—"

"Call now! I'm going after him." I was already turning away. "It'll be fine. You've got insurance." I bolted for the door, picking up the ever-so-important, precious metal lockbox where I'd dropped it on my way in.

Back across the hall, I unlocked my apartment, with my keys, for the first time in two days. The air was seemed stuffy. I opened the lockbox, took out a few things, threw the money in and stashed it back in my old hiding place in the emptied closet. As soon as Melanie reported the car stolen, the cops would come looking. Time was crucial.

I grabbed some rolling papers from my desk. I picked up this massive old dictionary I'd gotten free from the library once, cradled the heavy-ass thing under my arm and jammed the rest of the stuff into my pockets. Quickly as I could, I locked my door and bounded down the back steps to Melanie's car waiting out of sight down the alley.

"What the hell is this thing?" B said when I dropped the dictionary in his lap.

"It's a dictionary, but I wouldn't expect you to know that."

"Nice one."

I slammed the car into drive and peeled out. Or I would have if the car wasn't so weighted down. There was so much weight in the back, the hood pointed slightly up to the sky. I mashed on the gas pedal, *trying* to peel out, but it was like slamming a door with a pressure hinge. We drove slowly away, the engine roaring.

I knew exactly where I was going. I had the perfect spot in mind. Negotiating the one-ways through the neighborhood, I brought the car to a stop just shy of the intersection at Broadway and Oakdale. An over-hanging tree blocked out most of the light from the street lamp above, leaving us in relative shadow. But we wouldn't need it for long. We had to act quickly.

Carefully looking all around, I climbed out of the car, only a few blocks from home, into the warm breeze and relative quiet. No signs of life. B got out with me. I pulled open the back door on Alex's side.

I looked in at him and said, "Change of plans. You're going in the trunk."

He shook his head, mumbling something. I cut the tape at his ankles and yanked him out. B helped me get him back by the trunk. Ellie tried to twist her head around to see out the window behind her, but couldn't. B held Alex in place against the car. I went to the passenger's side and grabbed the dictionary off the floor.

I moved fast, keeping the book low as I ran around the car. The dictionary was huge, five inches thick, like the ones they keep open on little stands at the library, the paper edges painted gold like the leaves of a bible. I wound the old thing up over my head like an axe swinging and brought it down hard against the back of Alex's skull. He dropped in a pile at B's feet.

"Jesus," B said, jumping back. "You could have warned me."

"Shh, I didn't want them to hear."

"Shit," he said looking at Alex. "I wondered why you brought that thing."

"Well, man," I said, still holding the book in both hands, "we had to do it somehow. I figured this way they wouldn't die or anything."

"They?"

I didn't want to do it. It made me kind of sick to think about it, but if she wasn't unconscious, it wouldn't work. She'd try to run, or talk her way out of it, or something. It had to be done.

I put the book down so we could pull Alex onto the grass beside the car. B opened Ellie's door. She tried to wiggle out of reach like an earthworm squirming from the fish hook. He undid the belt and pulled her out easily by himself. When she saw Alex on the ground she really freaked. She bucked and wriggled and twisted and went limp, then bucked some more. B wrestled her up against the trunk holding her still with his body weight.

I came in from behind with the book high over my head. I didn't want to hurt her. But I had to knock her out. I swung down hard. But lost my nerve and pulled back at the last second. The book glanced off the back of her head, hitting her squarely on the shoulder. She dropped to her knees. B let her fall onto the grass. Groaning behind the duct tape over her mouth, she tried to look up. Too soft. Shit. Quick. Up on tip-toes, I brought the musty old book down hard with a sickening wooden thunk. She ricocheted off B's thighs with a shudder and slumped at his feet.

It was awful.

We debated pulling Paul and Pratt out of the trunk and plunking them in the backseat unconscious as well, but decided against it when we heard sirens somewhere in the distance.

Time was running out. I ripped the tape off of Ellie's limp hands and scooped her up in my arms like a discarded bride. B leaned in the driver's side to start the car. It took some delicate balancing work to get the passenger's side door open with my arms full, but I didn't have time to mess around. I leaned against the window, pulled the latch with my finger tips, then shifted our weight back catching the door at the bottom with my toe. It took two tries, but I got it. I arranged Ellie neatly on the seat as if she had been riding shotgun the whole way and pulled the tape from her sexy lying mouth.

In the meantime, B pulled Alex up by his armpits and slung him into the driver's seat and ripped the tape from his hands and mouth also. They looked like a nice young couple passed out in the parking lot on their way home from a concert.

I dug all the toys I had brought with me out of my pocket. From the box I'd found in Paul's room, I put the bag of coke and a rolled up dollar bill in the glove box. I stuffed some pills in Alex's pocket and scattered a couple at Ellie's feet. From my own personal stash, I staged a little joint rolling session on Alex's lap like he'd been trying to roll one up and drive at the same time. I shook some weed out on the dashboard and crumpled up a couple of papers to throw into the mix. Looking in the window it looked like they were having themselves a pretty good time.

The sound of sirens got louder. B jogged up to the intersection to make sure the coast was still clear. I put the car in neutral and turned the wheel slightly, aiming it across the intersection. There was a glass fronted dry cleaning store on the opposite corner with a mannequin wearing a wedding dress yellowed from the sun. A neon sign shaped like a shirt glowed in the window next to it. The store was closed, but the shirt was still lit, making a good target.

The sirens grew closer. The Toyota's engine revved when I dropped the old dictionary on the gas pedal beside Alex's foot.

B gave me the thumbs up, nobody coming, and then motioned for me to hurry. I looked back to make sure no cars were coming from behind and we both crossed our fingers. The sound of the police sirens was echoing down the deserted, narrow corridor of Broadway. I had a giddy, fluttering nervousness in my stomach. Alex's dad didn't want to pay for tuition? Let's see how he felt about this. My hands were shaking. From this distance, no one should really get hurt. I didn't think.

Standing inside the driver's side door, I slammed the gear shift into drive. The engine squealed and the car took off out of my hands, the driver's door still open. It shot away from me straight at the intersection. It looked like it might miss everything and steer clear through. I leaned my body trying to make it turn right as if it were a bowling ball steering for the gutter. Going, going. Too straight. Then, it hit a huge pot hole on the right. The car bounced, the tires hooked perfectly. They gained speed. The car kept going, faster, on target, on target.

They crashed up the curb, smashing directly into the cleaner's. A thundering shower of broken glass exploded as the car jammed to a stop halfway in, the yellow mannequin bride lying broken in half across the Toyota's hood.

Almost immediately, flashing blue lights swarmed the area. I ran to where B was watching at the corner. We stared at each other in shocked amazement, our eyes big as tractor tires. Out of curiosity and dismay at our accomplishment, we trotted over to the scene like concerned citizens drawn to a fire. The cops immediately held us back while others surrounded the vehicle, guns drawn.

Suddenly, maybe it was the guns, or the intensity of so many police officers, but I wanted to get away. No one was hurt, that was my only concern. I pulled B's arm, slowly backing away as more police rushed onto the scene.

I couldn't believe it had worked. Part of me wanted to stay to see what happened when the cops found Paul and Pratt in the trunk, see what they would think. That would've been something to see. But we thought better of it. I could just imagine one of them pointing us out, yelling to the cops. We walked faster, getting farther away, turning back now and then to watch the scene from the growing distance. My heart eventually calmed down, but I still wished we could've stayed to see what happened.

There was an all-night greasy spoon down the street. I offered to buy B some country fried steak. Or maybe a beer.

Chapter 36

"How'd you get that kid to give you the money?" B asked, cutting a piece of gravy-soaked fried steak. "From the looks of it everybody you know's been fightin' over it. He just up and hands it to you?"

"Well," I said sympathetically, "I had a pretty good idea of what had happened. Ellie probably sat down too close to him one night, rubbed her boobs against his arms, breathed on his neck a little bit. She's good at that. I'd've probably fallen for it again if you weren't there."

"That's why you called me."

"Exactly. She was busy tying everybody up in the middle, manipulating all three sides together and planning on sneaking out the back when the time was right. Apparently, she told Gino I beat up Ian and lied about my place being broken into in order to divert attention while I stole everybody's money. Sean had tried to warn him about her, tried to warn Gino, but none of it worked. He told him it was too good to be true. But it's hard to say no when a girl has her hooks into you."

"And her hands hooked around your penis."

"Especially a girl like Ellie."

B nodded, chewing on a bite so big his lips wouldn't close around it.

"And get this. She said she was going to rat Alex and those guys out for selling drugs. She said she'd split the money with Gino, who offered a cut to Sean if he helped get the money from Alex's." I chewed. "I did them the favor of breaking in myself. But I guess Sean thought I would, which is why they followed me up there."

"But how come you're ok with these guys? Seemed like you were ready to burn the whole town down to me."

"Yeah, you're right, I was. But I couldn't really blame those guys. They were just looking out for themselves, and maybe Gino's libido. I don't think they really meant me any personal harm. Those other guys though, they attacked me, personally. Willingly. I can't go in for that kind of shit. And I don't know, maybe I just needed to narrow the fight."

"Yeah," B said, washing down biscuit with orange juice. "It was kind of fun though."

"Shit, for you. You weren't here for the hard part, the getting-your-ass-kicked part."

"Wouldn't a happened to me," B said.

"That's 'cause you never had a girl like Ellie."

"Hah," B grunted and looked up at me from under his eyebrows. "You owe me five hundred bucks."

"Yeah, yeah," I said. I had it and more. I'd been through hell. But with a little help, I came out slightly better off than I was before. Of course, I had no more clients to sell to, or friends left in town, but that'd sort itself out.

Maybe I'd take the train back with B and settle up what I owed, or give the rest back while I still had it. I could use the extra couple thousand I'd taken from Paul to get me by until I found a job. And a cheaper place to live. And, what with all of the break-ins I'd been having, I shouldn't have any trouble getting out of my lease.

THANKS TO

Thank you Savanna. Only we know how much you've helped me and in how many ways.

Thanks to Lester Jacobson for lending his valuable services as editor, giving this first book much needed legitimacy.

Thanks to Heather Seksinsky for making this thing look good.

Thanks to everyone in my family for letting me search for my way.

Thanks to all of the friends I've known over the years in Indiana, Chicago, and New York who have contributed to the writing of this book in ways they may never know.

Thanks to the friends and coworkers who were the first readers.

And thanks to Dianne Fox for some last minute suggestions.

ABOUT THE AUTHOR

Daron Pearce grew up in a patch of woods surrounded by corn fields outside of Galveston, Indiana. He has a degree in Creative Writing from Purdue University. After years of travelling the world, living life and bartending, he has now turned to writing for real. This is his first book and introduction to the series.

www.daronpearce.com